Corfu

A NOVEL

Robert Dessaix

Scribner

First published 2001 in Picador by Pan Macmillan Australia Pty Ltd
First published in Great Britain by Scribner, 2002
This edition published by Scribner, 2003
An imprint of Simon & Schuster UK Ltd
A Viacom Company

1 3 5 7 9 10 8 6 4 2

Simon & Schuster UK Ltd
Africa House
64–78 Kingsway
London WC2B 6AH

Simon & Schuster Australia
Sydney

www.simonsays.co.uk

A CIP catalogue record for this book is available from the British Library

ISBN 0-7432-2039-0

Printed and bound in Great Britain by
Cox & Wyman Ltd, Reading. Berkshire

For information about Kester Berwick's life I am deeply indebted to Patricia Manessi Green of Benitses, Corfu, as well as to Graeme Dixon, Reg Evans, Saskia Handley, John Slavin and, above all, Christopher Coote, who was exceptionally generous both in his willingness to talk to me about his friendship with Kester Berwick and in granting me access to Berwick's diaries and papers.

I am grateful to Peter Timms and Clara Mason for the many refinements to my text which they suggested, and to Helen Nickas for her generous help with correct Greek usage. To Judith Lukin-Amundsen I would like to express my heartfelt thanks for the knowledge and understanding she brought to the editing process. Her discerning comments and exacting criticisms were invaluable.

Quotations from *The Odyssey* are from the translation by Robert Fagles (Viking Penguin, 1996); quotations from Sappho's poetry (except for the poem 'Gone is the moon') are from *The Love Songs of Sappho* by Paul Roche (Prometheus Books, 1998); quotations from *Daphnis and Chloe* are from Paul Turner's translation (Penguin Books, 1989); Cavafy's poems are from *C.P. Cavafy: Collected Poems*, translated by Edmund Keeley and Philip Sherrard (The Hogarth Press, 1984), used by permission of The Random House Group Limited.

ALTHOUGH THIS NOVEL WAS INSPIRED BY THE LIFE
OF THE AUSTRALIAN WRITER AND
ACTOR KESTER BERWICK, THE NARRATOR
IS AS FICTIONAL AS THE CHARACTERS
HE ENCOUNTERS.

— KESTER BERWICK —

Born Frank Perkins in Adelaide, South Australia, 1903

Founded the Ab-Intra Theatre Company, Adelaide, 1930

Studied at Dartington Hall, Devon, England, with Michael
Chekhov, 1936–7

War years spent teaching in Australia

Teaching in London, 1955–60

Settled in Methymna (Molyvos), Lesbos, 1960

Moved to Gastouri, Corfu, 1969

Published the novel *Head of Orpheus Singing*
(Angus & Robertson, London), 1973

Died Corfu, 1992

— PART ONE —

... seventeen days I sailed, making headway well;
on the eighteenth, shadowy mountains slowly loomed ...
your land! My heart leapt up, unlucky as I am,
doomed to be comrade still to many hardships.
Many pains the god of earthquakes piled upon me,
loosing the winds against me, blocking passage through,
heaving up a terrific sea, beyond belief – nor did the whitecaps
let me cling to my craft, for all my desperate groaning.
No, the squalls shattered her stem to stern, but I,
I swam hard, I plowed my way through those dark gulfs
till at last the wind and current bore me to your shores.
But here, had I tried to land, the breakers would have hurled me,
smashed me against the jagged cliffs of that grim coast,
so I pulled away, swam back till I reached a river ...
So, fighting for life, I flung myself ashore
and the godsent, bracing night came on at once.

The Odyssey, Book Seven

*(Odysseus, a notorious if spellbinding liar, recounts his
arrival on the island of Corfu on his way home from Troy.)*

1

It was just on two. The train had arrived, thank God.

I'd had no warning dream about this moment, that was the extraordinary thing. There'd been none of those ragged, foggy patches lying low in the mind. On the contrary, I'd pictured it a thousand times in brightly coloured detail, each time with a small bolt of pure excitement. Even now there was no sign that anything had changed, none at all.

But no sooner had the train shuddered to a halt at Roma Termini, and his chunky black boot touched the platform, than I knew I'd made an appalling mistake. Some distance away behind a clutch of Polish nuns, I reeled. The second black boot touched the platform and a kind of anguish engulfed me, shot through with screeching wheels and muffled cries of joy.

There was William, entirely William, casually dapper in that unfussy way of his, demurely cocky as he always was, peering about in the yellow light, his suitcase at his feet, waiting to be rescued.

I caught his eye, smiled, and walked quickly across the platform – to hug him and to tell him the first lies.

2

If Kester had a favourite time of the year on Corfu, it was the week before Easter. It didn't seem to matter when Easter fell, early or late, or whether it was damp and chilly or shockingly sunny all of a sudden, something inside Kester always woke up that week, exactly like the tortoises struggling up from under the ground all over the hillside behind his house. A bit gnarled, a bit stiff in the joints and liable to lurch off in odd directions, but at the same time, in a sedate sort of way, delirious.

This Easter awakening was one of the first things I ever learnt about Kester Berwick. Inconsequential, you might say, but at that moment, when I was as fragile as a moth's wing, picturing the lurching tortoises buoyed me up.

The voice over the telephone that first morning in Corfu was not exactly faint, yet by no means robust. Certainly not youthful, but hardly quavering, either. It was sprightly.

'Easter's one thing I can't abide,' it said firmly. 'The crowds, the priests, all that jiggery-pokery – not to mention the pot-throwing – I try not to leave the house.' No accent you could put a name to, just a carefulness with the vowels. 'But the week before Easter is always a miracle – I have to *wade* through the wildflowers, you know, when I walk down the hill, I almost float up into the air on the scent.'

It was an odd thing for a man to say to a complete stranger, but I was actually looking at a vase of asphodels as I listened, so felt instantly drawn in. And then he mentioned the tortoises, 'doddering about' in the sunshine behind his house.

It was Palm Sunday, I remember, and he'd rung me from the Hotel Cavalieri in town where I'd come to rest after fleeing Rome (and William) several days before. I felt more like someone's shadow than a man. It actually startled me whenever someone spoke to me – a waitress, a child on the staircase, anyone – had they really noticed I was there? A few days earlier on the deck of the ferry, squinting into the sheets of spring rain and seeing Corfu Town, glowing like a painting, all umbers and pinks in a patch of sun to the south, I'd thought instantly: I'll stay here, I'll cast anchor here and ride out whatever comes until I'm myself again. (An inane thought, really – who did I imagine I was, if not myself?)

A day or two later, while I was leafing through the gossipy local newspaper with its advertisements for bouzouki lessons and coffee mornings at the Anglican church ('all denominations welcome'), Kester's tiny notice had caught my eye. *House in Gastouri for rent for 2 mths*, it said. *Occupant travelling. Reasonable rent.* Not, on the face of it, very revealing. Not even a telephone number to call. But I liked *Occupant travelling*, and I liked the idea of *Gastouri*, too, wherever it was. It rang a little bell. So I left a message at the newspaper for the travelling occupant to ring me at the hotel. Which he did, on Palm Sunday, just as the bells of St Spiridon died away, leaving everyone slightly stunned, as if abruptly purged of something.

It was a strange, disembodied sort of conversation we had that morning. Who Kester Berwick might be, what sort of house it was, where he was going – I learnt nothing about any of that. He just asked if I was newly arrived, made a few remarks about Easter and then said: 'Actually, I'm just about to set off – I've left it all rather late, I suppose – but you could come up and look over the place this afternoon, if you'd like to. I'll have gone, but Agape will show you around.'

And so after lunch I took a taxi up to Gastouri in the sweet-smelling hills behind the town with the curious feeling that I was the last piece this Mr Berwick had needed for some jigsaw puzzle he'd been working on. Missing until the last moment under a chair, perhaps, but I'd turned up eventually and been slotted into place. I'm not sure why I felt that – it was nothing he actually said.

3

Stuck awkwardly amongst straggly olive-trees on the high side of the road winding up from the village to the crest above the sea, the house had not a skerrick of charm. To tell the truth, it almost looked like a child's drawing of a house: a square, white block, with two shuttered windows upstairs and a door and one window downstairs. Some scruffy greenery drooped from the window-boxes. No sign of life. It was not at all what I'd had in mind. I stood and stared up at it glumly.

The silence at that time of the afternoon was so deep it was almost like a dinning in the ears. The odd whine of a motor-scooter somewhere down in the village only made the quiet more intense.

Spiralling down inside, I nevertheless climbed up the damp stone steps to the narrow terrace outside the front door and stood for a while taking in the afternoon. Purple honesty sprinkled the cobbles. Of course, at that time everything still reached my eyes through a William-coloured haze. A thousand times a day I saw those chunky black boots of his touch the platform at Roma Termini and felt my soul turn to lead. Over and over again I heard myself say 'I'm so

happy to see you' as my lips brushed the cheekbones
I'd once – indeed, just minutes before – thought
more beautiful than beaten gold. Well, certainly
striking.

Even now the gaudy mauve judas-trees across the
road amongst the cypresses swam towards me
through memories of what had happened when we
left the station – in the taxi, in the cramped, yellow
hotel room with its unforgiveably purple bedspread
filling half the room.

But all of a sudden around the corner came Agape.
Who else could it have been? No ancient Greek
crone, Agape. Grey-haired, a trifle hunched, a little
pear-shaped, but nimble and sharply alive, possibly
to things I couldn't see.

'Hérete,' she said with a smile, inspecting me in
careful detail and drawing a large key dramatically
out of her cardigan pocket. Chatting amiably to me
in Greek, she rattled the key in the lock, pushed
open the weathered wooden door and stood aside to
let me go in, nodding encouragingly.

At first it gave me a prickly, uncomfortable feeling, to be honest, prowling through someone else's
house like that. But Agape seemed perfectly at
home, opening doors, peering into cupboards and
flinging the shutters wide. She was wearing a deep-
blue dress, so can't have been a widow. Who was
she exactly? A neighbour? Surely not Kester
Berwick's mother-in-law? She made the odd comment in Greek, laughing softly once or twice and

not minding at all, it seemed, that none of her comments would be understood.

Although sparsely furnished, the house felt curiously far from empty. The downstairs kitchen felt talked in, the wobbly table sat around, and the cool silence in the two upstairs rooms strangely inhabited. It was a comfortable, intimate sort of silence, the sort of silence you can sit back and let creep over you at the end of a long evening with a friend. Was it the books crammed into the home-made bookshelves that gave me that feeling? E.M. Forster, *Peer Gynt*, Annie Besant, Clive James, *The Odyssey* and several old *Time* magazines – rather a queer assortment, actually. Was it the framed photographs dotted about the house? The amateur canvases high on the walls? The faint smell of dog? Whether the life lived in these rooms was small or big, though, was hard to tell – there just weren't enough clues.

From the upstairs window the view was actually more Italian than Greek: cypresses spearing the sky as far as the eye could see, pink and cream houses curving away to the left down the slope towards the jumbled village, while up on the brow of the hill that hid us from the sea, partly concealed by the huge holm-oaks in the gully between us, I could just make out a large, white palace of some kind.

Still, turning back from the window to meet Agape's eye, I wasn't sure I wanted to live in a stranger's house, eating off his plates, squeezing my clothes into his wardrobe, sleeping between his sheets.

But I took it, of course. It was less a decision than a matter of hearing myself saying, '*Ne*, yes, I'll take it.' Agape nodded peaceably and smiled. She'd never doubted it, apparently. She led me outside and banged the door shut.

'Thank you,' I said. '*Efharistó.*'

'*Bitte schön,*' she said, rather unaccountably at the time.

Walking up to the bus-stop outside the white palace, I had the strong, sudden feeling that the silence of Gastouri was almost certainly deceptive.

4

I should never have been in Greece at all, that's the point. I was actually on my way home. Greece, as we know, is full of foreigners who were once on their way home from somewhere and got stranded there. They wash up on the beach while floating idly past, disappointed by something or other – the lack of a new beginning, perhaps, wherever they've just been. They get snared amongst the driftwood and then can't move on. Swapping coffee-stained novels from home and complaining about the sloppiness of everything, they stay on, growing sourer, even about home. I wondered as I looked about me on my first morning in Mr Berwick's house if he was one of those castaways.

As I saw it at the time, *I* hadn't washed up anywhere. I wasn't entangled in any driftwood. I was just sorting myself out in picturesque surroundings. I'd hardly got in the door before I was unpacking briskly and wiping down benches.

So this was it. With the last shirt hung in the cupboard and my toothbrush stuck in a jar, the longed-for moment had now arrived: I'd finally cast anchor. Life was a smooth, wax tablet again, waiting to be written on. It was deeply unsettling.

I stared at the greasy sink for a moment and went upstairs.

Dear William, I wrote (first things first), seated at Kester's rickety table, gazing out of the window towards the palace (if that's what it was). On the bookcase to my right stood a framed photograph, unmistakeably of Krishnamurti, youthful, lost-looking, achingly handsome. I'd never had much time for Krishnamurti and so laid the photograph face-down on its shelf. I considered the *Dear* for a moment, but, really, in English one has so few options.

> This is a terribly difficult letter to write, but write it I must. At the very least I owe you an explanation.
>   When you suggested we meet up in Italy and then set out for home together, I agreed without a moment's hesitation. And I meant it. I didn't say 'yes' lightly.

No, I didn't. I'd first seen William some eighteen months before the Roman fiasco, on a nose-pinchingly cold November evening in an Indian take-away in North London. A few of us had popped up to the Shalimar on the Holloway Road to pick up some curries and chapatis – it was our first

read-through of *The Cherry Orchard*, and all of a sudden between Acts II and III we'd felt tired and
overexcited, needing the distraction of food. William,
who was designing, hadn't been there earlier. He must
have arrived at Clive's house just after we'd set off and
been sent on to join us at the Shalimar. In he came,
breezy but with a hint of shyness, in a floppy knitted
top and black jeans, to join the gang. How flattering
floppiness is to the slim. Late twenties, cropped black
hair, a sculpted look – but by a rough hand. I didn't
realize I'd particularly noticed him – after all, everyone that first evening was new and intriguing (except
Leila, whom I'd known for years – she was playing
Ranyevskaya, a part she scarcely had to act) – until I
saw Leila huddled with him by the door, warmly
cocooned with him, ignoring the rest of us.

Astonishingly, a tingle of *jealousy* started up at the
back of my throat. I watched Leila's slender fingers
straying across this young man's shoulder-blades, her
fingernails flashing mauve in the neon light. Taken
by surprise, I put the whole thing down at first to the
overpowering smell of curry and Leila's cigarillo.

As we walked back to Clive's terrace, William
stayed glued to Leila, I remember, with Gareth, who
was Welsh and eager to be noticed, nudging at them
like a silly puppy despite his years. At this early stage,
of course, we were all still sniffing each other out, so
it wasn't quite clear who Gareth hoped to be noticed
by. Anyone, probably. He was playing Leila's nin-
compoop of a brother, Gayev.

That first night we couldn't get the *comedy* of *The Cherry Orchard* to shine through at all. Cooped up in Clive's living-room, with its distressing wallpaper and too few chairs, we found the play unsettling, tragic, heart-breaking, pathetic, trivial, even silly, but not comic. Yet Chekhov had called his play 'funny, very funny', and at the top of page one in black and white it said quite unambiguously:

THE CHERRY ORCHARD
A comedy in four acts

This would eat away at us for days. To start with Leila tried camping it up, which was disastrous, while Gareth simply opted for playing the ninny, which was embarrassing. We couldn't strike the right note. Clive, who'd had a smash hit with *The Seagull* the previous summer, just kept saying: 'Look, it's all *there*, the comedy is all *there* in the lines, there's no need to work at it. This is a *soufflé*, not a suet pudding. Just find the *truth* of it.' I hate it when directors mention truth.

But I ask you: a blowsy, hare-brained aristocrat, Ranyevskaya, comes home to her estate in some God-forsaken corner of Russia from Paris, penniless, ruined, emotionally ragged; she cries a lot, remembers things, blubs some more, throws a party and loses her estate, along with her precious cherry orchard, to a hard-headed businessman who starts chopping the trees down before she even has time to catch the train back to Paris. Is this funny? While she mooches about sniffling into sodden handkerchiefs, her children and various other hangers-on walk in and out droning on about money, love, radiant futures, pickled cucumbers and all sorts of other Russian nonsense. Is this comic? Ludicrous, perhaps, or even pathetic, but hardly comic.

Yet Clive did have a point. It's maddening to have to admit it, but there *was* something in Chekhov's straggly, often preposterous lines which was disarmingly 'true' – and not only about turn-of-the-century Russia, either, but of everyone in that North London flat. And when we hit on it, it made us want to laugh.

For the rest of that evening William, as designer, just sat on the floor by the window in the shadows, halflit by the tasselled standard lamp, listening. I knew he was there, I was aware of the rough-cut hair and watching eyes, but didn't know if *I* was being watched, as it were, or if his eyes were on Chekhov.

When we started to break up, something quite unexpected happened. Only two of us were left to walk up the road to the Underground – William and me. The others had all quickly melted into the fog or jumped into their cars and driven off. Even Leila, who just called out 'Bye, darlings!' as she jumped into her car and chugged off. Offering a lift on the first night could lead to awkwardnesses later on. I admit I felt a little prickle of pleasure.

'Feel like a coffee?' he said suddenly, as we ambled up the hill.

'Why not?' I said, although I didn't want a coffee at all. The tingle at the back of my throat again. It was disconcerting, completely unforeseen. Well, almost completely. Certainly, from time to time since my divorce I'd caught myself *looking* – I may have been invisible, but I could still see. On trains, say, or on escalators or in cafés, I admit I'd sometimes found my eyes flicking across calves and t-shirted chests, or resting briefly on the backs of necks and strong, bluish jawlines – but my throat had never once gone dry. And I'd hardly been aware of any impulse to reach out and touch.

'It's so scungy around here this time of night – let's go back to my place.' *Scungy.* No Englishman would say that. Unexpectedly, I thought of Adelaide.

'OK. Let's grab a taxi.'

⁓

Nothing *happened* in William's flat that night, needless to say: we just drank coffee and skipped across the surface of things – Chekhov, William's guitar lessons, and Adelaide, as a matter of fact, which was where his parents turned out to be living and where he'd first started dabbling in the theatre ('ages ago' – four years before). He hated Adelaide, he said, although I sensed he missed it. We weren't really talking about Chekhov, guitars or Adelaide, obviously, or only in order to mark out a space for something else to happen in. But nothing did. Except the toppling.

By midnight the slow toppling had begun and it was already too late to regain my balance. The mauve fingernails on the shoulder-blades, the whiff of coriander, the expectant glances, the glow of the tasselled lamp, *scungy* – trifles, pinpricks – had already clustered into an instant *after which it was already too late.* It's only in retrospect, of course, that I can say that.

'When you were reading,' he said, after a longish pause well past midnight, 'you were kind of transparent. It was great!'

I was shocked. What had he seen through *to*, exactly? Gathering up my script and coat, I leapt to my feet and made to go. He didn't move. So, not knowing what to do next, I bent over him and kissed his forehead. It may have been a mistake, but, after all, I *am* an actor.

'See you Tuesday,' he said. 'It's been fun.' And sat cross-legged on the couch while I let myself out.

Not a taxi in sight. I set off home on foot.

Transparent. It wasn't a word I'd thought much about, to be honest. Sometimes when you meet somebody – over dinner, in a foyer, even at a bus-stop – you have the immediate feeling that you are seeing *straight through* something to a life being lived right at that very instant – the real one. Straight through what, I'm not sure – speech, gestures, clothes, looks . . . although those words don't quite cover it. And at such moments you're apt suddenly to feel translucent yourself – uncovered, not quite there, while at the same time more solidly alive and yourself than you usually are.

What I can't work out is whether this feeling of transparency strikes you *because* of all the things in the way – the timbre of the voice, the cocking of the head, the lamplight on the hair, the angle of the knees – or *despite* them. Or is it the same thing?

When I eventually got back to the Holloway Road and was passing the Shalimar, now closed, the blue neon sign hit me with an almost blinding brilliance, and I realized, as the lingering smell of curried lamb pinched my nostrils, that I was experiencing a blue transparent moment right then and there in the empty street. It passed, of course.

See you Tuesday. Sitting at Kester's desk in Gastouri this afternoon a year and a half later I could still hear those four syllables as clearly as if William had just spoken them, standing behind my chair. So banal and said with such nonchalance, almost jauntily, yet brimming over with every meaning ever dreamt of. Or else no meaning at all.

On the Tuesday we read through Act III. Such a painful act – the stupid party Ranyevskaya throws while her estate is being auctioned off, while she's losing everything she loves and ruining everybody. It's painful for everyone, it's an orgy of humiliation and despair. And terribly funny, according to Clive, an expert in all things Russian.

'Remember, it's vaudeville with feeling,' he said to us as we were about to begin. Then, quite pleased with his little *bon mot*, he said it again.

Act III was particularly crushing for me. I was playing Peter Trofimov, the risible, moth-eaten, bespectacled, eternal student and former tutor of Ranyevskaya's drowned son. It hardly mattered that I was rather older than Trofimov, who seems to have been just under thirty – after all, everyone keeps telling me how old and ugly I've become since Ranyevskaya went away to Paris. 'Why have you lost all your looks, Peter? Why have you got so old? You were just a boy when I went away . . .' Leila loved saying that to me, I'm convinced, although she had a stab at fond pity.

It's in Act III that I mock Ranyevskaya's dreary foster-daughter Varya, the would-be nun. 'If only we had some money,' she bleats, 'even just a little, I'd give everything up and go away. I'd go into a monastery.' Piffle! She's avid for money and all it can buy – and for sex, needless to say, although 'love' or 'marriage to a good man' would be how she'd put it. And so I mock her. Just one or two barbed words.

Like all righteous people, I am merciless. Her mother – almost *spongy* from all her illicit loves – tries to protect her from me.

RANYEVSKAYA: Don't tease her, Peter, you can see how distressed she is already.

TROFIMOV: She's got a one-track mind, she's too pushy by half, always poking her nose in where it's not wanted. We've had no peace from her all summer, Anya and I. She's afraid we might start an affair. What business is it of hers? Anyway, I haven't given her the slightest cause to think such a thing. That kind of vulgarity is foreign to me. Anya and I are above love.

RANYEVSKAYA: Yes, well, I must be below it.

Absolutely. She's drowning in love, raddled with it, mostly for men who mistreat her. And for her daughters and servants and old furniture and the cherry orchard and Russia, of course . . . all the things she's throwing away as the orchestra plays on.

RANYEVSKAYA: The reason you can resolve all life's important questions, Peter, dear, is that you haven't yet had to *suffer through* a single one of them . . . I was born here, after all, my mother and father lived here, and my grandfather . . . I love this house, I can't even imagine life without my cherry orchard, and if it has to be sold, then I might as well be sold along with it. *(She embraces Trofimov and kisses him on the forehead.)* And my son drowned here . . . *(Cries.)* Have some pity on me, Peter, my good, kind Peter.

TROFIMOV: You have my wholehearted sympathy, Lyubov Andreyevna, you know that.

However, when I call her Parisian lover a no-good nothing of a man, no better than a petty thief (she's squandered everything on him), something inside her hardens and she hits me right between the eyes:

RANYEVSKAYA: It's time you became a man, Peter, at your age it's time you understood people who love people. And it's time you loved someone yourself . . . time you fell in love. *(Angrily.)* Yes, it is! You're not *pure*, you're just a prude, just a ridiculous crank, you're unnatural . . . 'I'm above love'! You're not above love, you're just a nitwit. Fancy not having a lover at your age!

TROFIMOV: *(In horror.)* This is horrible! What is she saying? *(Leaves the room, clutching his head.)* This is horrible! I can't take this, I'm leaving . . . *(Leaves, but immediately comes back in.)* It's all over between us! *(Goes out.)*

RANYEVSKAYA: *(Calling after him.)* Peter, wait! What a funny man you are, Peter, I was joking! Peter!

Someone can be heard rapidly going down a staircase and then noisily falling down the stairs. Anya and Varya scream, but then straight away start laughing.

I was sweating profusely by the time we finished *that* little scene, I might say. Over by the window on his beanbag in the corner, those knees tucked up under his bluish, unshaven chin, William was laughing along with the two hysterical sisters. Then one or two of the others seemed to catch the mood and joined in. Alex, the snub-nosed young woman with the red hair playing Anya, had a coughing fit and had to be given a drink of water.

'Very good!' said Clive, in his usual businesslike way. 'Very good! Almost believable.'

But it was unfair, that laughter. If Trofimov was a high-minded prig, clothing his shyness and lack of experience in grand phrases about being above sordid, everyday feelings, then Ranyevskaya and her daughters were just as uncomprehending, just as pitiless towards my failure to be a man.

Soon afterwards we called it a night. This time, when William turned to me, whipping his scarf across one shoulder, to see if I was ready to set off for the station, I said I thought I'd walk home. 'I need to clear my head,' I said.

'See you Thursday, then,' he said with a friendly grin, unfazed. But on the Thursday the beanbag by the window stayed empty.

5

On the subject of Greek driftwood, by the way, and getting entangled in it, Sisi was a classic case. Having a terrible weakness for palaces, by which I really mean *palazzi*, not castles, *châteaux* or anything English, I strolled up the hill the next morning to cast an eye over the strange white building, so out of place in this higgledy-piggledy village, which, from my window, I could see on the crest above the sea. I was hoping for a tonic.

It was built, as it turns out, by that stupendously miserable creature Elisabeth, Empress of Austria – Sisi, as everyone called her with a mixture of affection, pity and disdain. Hopelessly adrift on dreams of Homer, Sisi called her palace the Achilleon.

Sisi was in love with loveliness – her own mostly, to be frank, which was the talk of Europe, but also Corfu's orange-scented beauty, aglow with drifts of golden broom when she first saw it as a young woman. But she had little eye for beauty of more cultivated kinds. In 1887, at the age of fifty, she took a perfectly nice old Venetian villa, perched idyllically on the edge of an escarpment with views across the town and the glittering straits to Albania, and turned it into this lumpish little *Schloss* with classical pretensions. 'At last I've come home,' she said, and in a sense she had.

It was the perfect place for an unhappy empress to wait for death, gracefully, amidst olives and myrtles, and that's why she had it built – God knows, she didn't want to die in Vienna surrounded by all those lunatics her family swarmed with, her nagging mother-in-law and her sour Hungarian ladies-in-waiting. In the event, however, even dying proved boring and she moved disconsolately on. Out strolling on the quay in Geneva one afternoon some years later, she was knifed to death by an Italian anarchist. Just a tiny puncture with a stiletto – she hardly bled a drop.

As you wander through the Achilleon's coldly vulgar rooms, you can picture the amber-eyed empress mooching about absently, vaporously, a volume of Heine in one hand (Heine's ghost came to her in the night), a fine lace shawl across her shoulders, one of her emerald-studded belts around her tiny waist, wondering if she'd really come to rest at last after a lifetime of wandering, looking for . . . what, exactly? Tranquillity? Solitude? Certainly not love – Sisi craved adoration, not love. I'm tempted to suggest insignificance.

In this white palace it was, a hundred years ago, as age crept up on her, that she bathed in warm seawater poured from gilded taps, here she lay in wet sheets impregnated with seaweed to slim her waist, here she spent hours of a morning dressing her famous auburn hair, here she lay on her leopard-skin couch to be oiled and pummelled by her masseuse . . . all in vain. 'As fresh and unspoilt as a green, half-opened almond', she had been when she'd first met Franz Joseph in the Austrian mountains. Or so her smitten husband-to-be wrote of her. Well, in Vienna's desiccating air she'd dried and cracked in no time at all, and by the time she took up residence here in the Achilleon it was too late for unguents and deep massages. She'd become that worst, that most unqueenly of things – spry for her age. And her only companion was an over-scented local hunchback, her tutor in Greek, Christomanos. Together this unregal pair would tramp at a furious pace up and down the hills through the olive-groves, discussing Homer and the futility of everything. The peasants round about called her 'the locomotive'.

But I must say, after staring at her palace from my window for several weeks, that I've grown rather fond of Sisi. This was her fairy palace, this was how she madly imagined that Alcinous, King of the Phaeacians, had lived here on this island three thousand years before. I like the craziness of those dreams. Yet what does Homer actually say about Alcinous' 'resplendent halls', his 'famous house' which once (if ever it existed) soared, high-roofed, amongst orchards of pears and pomegranates, teeming vineyards, rippling springs and groves of figs and olives, somewhere down near the present Hilton? As

Odysseus crossed the palace's bronze threshold,
Homer says, he saw:

Walls plated in bronze, crowned with a circling frieze
glazed as blue as lapis, ran to left and right
from outer gates to the deepest court recess
and solid golden doors enclosed the palace.
Up from the bronze threshold silver doorposts rose
with silver lintel above, and golden handle hooks.
And dogs of gold and silver were stationed either side,
forged by the god of fire with all his cunning craft
to keep watch on generous King Alcinous' palace,
his immortal guard-dogs, ageless, all their days.
Inside to left and right, in a long unbroken row
from farthest outer gate to the inmost chamber,
thrones stood backed against the wall, each draped
with a finely spun brocade, women's handsome work.
Here the Phaeacian lords would sit enthroned,
dining, drinking — the feast flowed on forever.

Yet what did I see? A few bronze nymphs with electric torches, illuminated bowls of glass fruit and
dozens of bad paintings scattered about a suburban
mansion with fake pillars tacked onto it. The casino
on the second floor was a stroke of genius.

Yet . . . what can I say? The woman who dreamt all
this up, the woman who fled Vienna's brilliant court
and her extraordinary family of emperors, dukes,
archduchesses and queens spread across the world
from Mexico to Budapest, in order to be nobody, to

come to rest and just be herself, this woman set off sparks inside me. Her moonstruck life was a stupendous failure, and failure on that scale is fascinating.

How often, I wonder, did she think back to her childhood, before her fateful meeting with Franz Joseph, to the silly snowball fights in the streets of Munich, the sleigh-rides through the Bavarian forests with her brothers and sisters, the times she and her father, Duke Maximilian, would dress up as strolling players to strum the zither and sing bawdy songs at village weddings? Nobodies – fabulously wealthy *royal* nobodies, certainly, but for an hour or two, for an afternoon, of absolutely no significance.

Marrying His Imperial Majesty, Emperor of Austria and King of Jerusalem, Margrave of Moravia and King of Bohemia, had been an appalling mistake.

Just before she built her fairy palace in Gastouri, her son Rudolf killed himself together with his mistress in his hunting lodge at Mayerling. Or someone poisoned them both. Or one of them. No one knows. Sisi lost her faith in everything apart from her slimming cures after that, and her melancholy shrouds that house as if it were a mortuary temple. That's why, I think as I write this, only one thing in the whole palace has any life in it: the sculpture of the dying Achilles, out in the garden amongst the palms and cypresses. Vitality in every stretched muscle, every contorted limb and vein and fold of marble flesh.

Why Achilles? Because he was the dead son she'd

have liked to be the mother of? A demigod with utter contempt for both gods and men? For his stone beauty?

I made a mental note to browse through *The Iliad* again one day to look for other clues. It was sure to be somewhere on Kester's shelves. Such a tedious book, unfortunately, the sort I can't help dozing off over. Perhaps it needs to be read aloud by someone manly from the BBC. *The Odyssey*, on the other hand, is as engrossing, as exciting, as voluptuously pleasurable a book as any I've read. I wonder which of them Sisi loved most?

After my encounter with Sisi I couldn't go back to my letter. I couldn't find the voice. I just sat at the desk by the window for a while and gazed back up the hill at the white palace. Eventually, to distract myself, I eased the desk drawer out an inch or two and peered inside. I wondered briefly, I remember, whether it was immoral to rifle through someone's drawers uninvited, but decided it was neither moral nor immoral *of itself* and pulled it all the way out. It smelt delicious – papery, powdery, ancient glue and lavender. I was going to enjoy this drawer.

Poking around amongst letters in English and German and old envelopes with exotic stamps, I unearthed yellowing notebooks, small diaries, several manuscripts, newspaper clippings (some fifty years

old) and, scattered amongst them, photographs –
uninteresting at first: a dark-haired young man on
the doorstep of a weatherboard house somewhere far
away and long ago, a different young man on a
motor-bike (perhaps even before the war), another
young man seated on a low wall with his arm around
a young woman, a gentle-faced elderly woman at a
piano . . . There were several more recent colour
shots, too, of a smooth-faced, serenely smiling older
man, white-haired, in the company of some frisky-
looking foreign sailors (here in a crowded taverna,
there shirtless in the Greek sun). And here he was
again, leaning back against a whitewashed wall, here
dining with friends *al fresco* . . . and here overcoated,
rather more austere, caught standing awkwardly in
an archway.

And then, just when I was on the point of taking
out one of the letters and perusing it (just for fun), I
came upon another snap, hidden inside an envelope
with an English stamp. It showed two men sitting
naked on a rock in shallow water, with a panoramic
view behind them stretching over the sea to snow-
capped mountains (possibly Albania), yachts in the
distance, brilliant sunshine. One was my older man
(coyly posed), his nose and thin smile unmistakable.
The other (less coy, but hardly brazen), relaxed but
alert, without a shadow of doubt and to my great
astonishment, was William.

6

Good Friday morning in Gastouri (Great Friday as they call it) – the sky so blue you'd have thought someone had slapped the paint on with a thick, cobalt-laden brush – and I was just sitting in the downstairs kitchen, thinking how dingy it was and wondering for the umpteenth time who this Kester Berwick was whose house I'd landed up in – when there came a rapping on the door. Sharpish.

'Anybody home?' A throaty, woman's voice.

One always thinks of Jehovah's Witnesses at such moments, but standing in the doorway was a smartly dressed woman in her late fifties, greying hair beautifully coiffed, with just a hint of gold jewellery – nothing to focus on. No witness to Jehovah, this one.

'Why, hullo!' she said, smiling. 'Kester still in bed?'

'No, Kester's gone away, actually. I'm just renting the place for a couple of months.'

'Really? How extraordinary! He didn't say anything to me. Where's he gone? And where's Terpsi?' She pushed passed me into the gloom of the kitchen. A whiff of something quite expensive.

'Terpsi?'

'The dog. I bring over the contraceptives for her

every fortnight. How very odd. I do hope he hasn't had her put down.' She cast an eye around the dim, high-ceilinged room. 'You've had quite a little clean-up in here I see. It's usually a shambles.'

I started to mumble something, but this woman with well-rounded vowels and stylish shoes was already off on another tack.

'I'm Greta, by the way, and you are . . . ?'

Marvellous eyes, they'd seen a lot. I explained a little about being on my way home, about being an actor (just for effect), and finding the advertisement in the local newspaper.

'Well, you must come to lunch on Sunday,' she said, moving back towards the door. 'It's an event, you know, here on Corfu, Easter Sunday lunch. Lamb on the spit and so forth. I'll pick you up at twelve.'

This was too sudden. I wanted to keep my wax tablet blank for a while. But before I could demur, she was half-way down the steps to the road.

'Going down to see the procession today?' she called up to me. 'You really should. And the pot-throwing, of course, tomorrow morning.'

'Well, I'm not really religious, you see.'

'Religious?' She looked nonplussed. 'Religion has nothing to do with it, it's Greek Easter, a completely heathen affair. Why don't you pop in the car and I'll drop you off.'

'Well . . .'

'Come on, it's a hoot, don't be so stuffy.'

Was I stuffy? Would she know?

But Greta was already in the car, heaving books and cardigans, and presumably contraceptive pills, onto the back seat. Two minutes later, without my even shaving, we were hurtling up past the palace, over the rise and down towards the sea – not at all wine-dark that morning, by the way, nor is it ever, in my experience, and I can't imagine what Homer was thinking of.

When we got to that tangle of streets on the outskirts of Corfu Town, just in from the sweep of Garitsa Bay – not far from where Odysseus, as a matter of fact, was supposedly found in a wood by the virgin princess Nausicaa and her band of white-armed, braided maidens . . . somewhere there near the airport, where she first came upon him, a god come down from the blue, his curls 'like thick hyacinth clusters' wet from the surf and streaming in the wind, and called to him to follow her in her painted wagon to the city 'ringed by walls and strong high towers', past the trim, black ships hauled up on slipways beside the road, through groves and orchards to the palace of her father, the Phaeacian king . . . or perhaps not, no one can be sure, it may have happened at Kassiopi further to the north, and, besides, that was all part of Sisi's fantasy, rather than mine – at any rate, somewhere there, just near the end of the airport runway, I said to Greta as we roared past the hideous jumble of hypermarkets, petrol pumps and garish nightclubs: 'Tell me, who exactly *is* this Kester Berwick?'

'*Berrick*,' she said, 'he says *Berrick*. Nobody, really, just an Australian. Wrote a book once. Dear man.' But her mind was elsewhere. Beside the road a swarthy man was hosing down racks of melons, oranges and paintbox-yellow bananas. We swerved into the spray, came to a jolting halt, and Greta was out of the car, scooping up an armful of them.

'Just the thing for Sunday,' she said, getting back into the car and we shot out into the traffic again. 'By the way, you're not a vegetarian, I hope? It's all flesh and entrails on Easter Sunday, you know, bits of dead sheep everywhere. That's the trouble with Kester – won't touch meat, a dead loss on Easter Sunday, I've given up inviting him. It's the Buddhism thing, I expect – or is he a Mormon? I get them all mixed up. Something bloodless, anyway. You're not one, are you?'

But by now we were snarled in an enormous, seething traffic-jam on the road beside the bay and Greta decided to toss me out to find my own way into town. I sauntered off with the crowds towards the city on the hill, my eyes on the fabulous Venetian citadel towering up out of the sea on a rocky outcrop to my right. And atop its walls, proclaiming the death and resurrection of Jesus to the infidels in Albania across the straits, stood the most brazenly monstrous cross in Christendom.

There's nothing Greek about Corfu Town. In fact, that's probably why many foreigners find it so appealing. It's a Venetian town, a maze of narrow, cobbled streets clustered between two massive Venetian fortresses. After all, the Venetians were here for over four hundred years. Along the clifftop, between the Old Fort, jutting out into the sea with the cross on top, and the colonnaded elegance of the old town itself, lies a stretch of parkland, ablaze with purplish judas-trees at Eastertime, where the Corfiotes like to stroll about in noisy groups and occasionally to play cricket.

The festivities weren't due to begin for several hours – at the hour of the crucifixion, to be precise, and indeed there were violently black storm-clouds already piling up above Albania across the water just to put us in the mood. So I did what people do in strange places with time on their hands: I sat at a table under the arches facing the park (more Paris than Venice, actually, this stretch of cafés, built by the French to remind them of the rue de Rivoli), ordered a coffee and began to write a postcard. This was where, in the Durrells' day before the Second World War, everyone gathered (everyone well-dressed, that is, all those with money in their pockets) to scandalize each other with bits of juicy gossip. Perhaps they still do at quieter times, but that day the tables were jammed with overdressed Athenians, not to mention the hordes of Danes and towering Dutchmen.

A brilliant invention, the postcard. Pithy, genuinely meant, but not sentimental. An offering – no one is *obliged* to send a postcard – which elicits nothing in return, except a brief remembrance. Good will in a dozen casual words. Perfect for my purposes, as it happened. I'd determined to spare both myself and William the strain of a sensitively worded explanation and send him a cool but friendly postcard instead.

The image on the reverse side is always vital. No one at home gives a fig about where you are or what you've seen – that goes without saying. Nobody could care less what the beach at Paleokastritsa looks like or the Monkey Forest at Ubud. No, the image on the reverse side, barely glanced at by the friend at home, is a style statement, nothing more, although crucial to the exercise. That's why for William on this occasion I chose an amusing shot of the Dying Achilles in Sisi's garden: '*Achille mourant*, rear view'. Cascading mane of marble hair, painfully contorted shoulder-blades and amazingly life-like buttocks – solid, fleshy, workaday haunches, nothing gym-trim about them, right buttock tapering magnificently into heroic thigh and balletically extended leg. (He's dying sitting upright, helmet on and spear in hand.)

Greetings from Corfu, I began. Was that perhaps *too* cool? Of course, I was *feeling* cool after chancing on that photograph in Kester's drawer, but had little right to be – if anyone had behaved badly, it was me, in Rome. But then, it's very hard to forgive someone we've wronged, isn't it?

Our paths actually hardly crossed, William's and mine, during the rest of the rehearsals of *The Cherry Orchard*. He came along a few times, watched from the sidelines, chatted with snub-nosed Alex and Leila a bit, and then went away and designed. When he did come – always in that blue floppy knitted top and black jeans – I felt naked and longed for him to vanish again so I could be reclothed. Strange, isn't it? Because another part of me craved nakedness, craved almost to be flayed. Apart from anything else, that's when I gave my best performance.

In the event, if I say so myself, our *Cherry Orchard* was quite a triumph. There's something about Chekhov's plays the English-speaking public everywhere just loves, although I can't quite put my finger on what it is. If I could, I think I'd be more at home in the world.

Be that as it may, we had a full house every night for the whole pre-Christmas season. They laughed, they wept. Leila, understandably, was very smug indeed about her crits – 'unbearably tragic performance' (the *Metro*), 'a touchingly comic *tour de force*' (*Ham and High*, the local rag), 'stunning stage presence' (*Time Out*). I'm not sure I was ever specifically mentioned anywhere, but the supporting cast was certainly praised in general terms in the more prominent reviews. And the design got rave notices as well, at least in one or two of the newspapers – well, in *Time Out*, anyway. William went for realism in the end, but in a minimalist vein because of the tight budget. Clive felt it was symbolic of the stripping back of emotion.

The party after the final performance on Christmas Eve was a bit of an ordeal. In the first place, I'm hopeless at parties, I have no small talk and they always make me wonder if I should get married again, possibly to someone in the room. And, in the second place, this was to be the last time I'd see William, and something – just a sentence or two, but something – had to be said in parting. One has one's dignity.

Most of the evening I spent slumped in the old beanbag beside the window, swapping inanities with whoever ended up squatting beside me. On a little map in my mind, though, regardless of who I was talking to at the time, I was tracking the movements of the spiky-haired Australian in the blue jumper. He was like a tiny blue blip on a screen inside my head. While Gareth was wittering on about fly-fishing in Wales, for instance, my mind was on the blue blip edging towards the Leila shape, swathed in the smoke from her cigarillo, in the top left-hand corner. When Clive's wife Rosemary pinned me to the beanbag and started reading out to me her daughter's poems, it was the little blue blip huddled with red-haired Alex I was really focused on, not the daughter's dactyls.

Suddenly, just before midnight, it jerked off the screen.

'Rosemary, must just dash off to the loo,' I said,

heaving myself up past her generous bosom and heading for the door. The moment had come.

William was in the hallway wrapping his scarf around his neck.

'Oh, are you going, William?' I said, trying to look as if I were actually on my way to the bathroom.

'Yeah, I'm off,' he said, adjusting the scarf over his Adam's apple. A slender neck, quite long, at odds somehow with the strong line of his jaw. 'Meeting a few friends for . . . Christmas drinks.' He was lying, of course, but it didn't matter.

I'd worked out what I'd say while Clive's wife was reading the poems. I knew my lines. In my head was a short dialogue, suave but sincere, friendly but detached, in which I'd make it clear that I valued our momentary intimacy, and liked him tremendously (as a person), but . . . I thought he'd perhaps misinterpreted my inclinations, as it were. I wouldn't put it quite like that, naturally, but that's what would be delicately implied. The whole thing would take less than a minute.

'Look, I'm sorry we didn't get to –' I began.

'William!' It was bloody Gareth, lumbering into the hallway with bits of Black Forest cake all down his jumper. 'Are you off, dear boy? Let me give you a lift. Got to get going myself – having the nieces and nephews over for drinkies in the morning.'

A couple of handshakes, his hand on my shoulder – did it stay there just a nanosecond too long? – and they were out the door. I stood there staring after them for half a minute. Behind me in the stuffy living-room Clive was shouting boisterously over Nina Simone ('That old warhorse! How in God's name does *he* keep getting work?') . . . someone else was trying to sing along . . . '*My baby just cares for me* . . .' Leila laughed smokily, somebody dropped a glass . . . I stepped out into the drizzle, clicking the door shut behind me.

It was time for the crucifixion. Just as the first sheets of rain swept over the crowded streets, and the violet-black sky turned to streaky grey, the procession set off. Jesus had been nailed to his cross in far-away Jerusalem and Corfu was plunged into festive mourning.

It was the big, fat tubas I liked best. As the bands slowly goose-stepped past, all decked out in brilliant reds and blues, the deeply mournful lowing of the tubas filled the squares and stony laneways, drowning out the trumpets, horns and drums, the flutes and clarinets. Jesus was dying, but the crowd seemed delighted with the cacophony of clashing dirges. They smiled and waved at their smirking children and spouses as they marched by, peering around umbrellas to cross themselves as lurid, tasselled pictures of saints, or possibly Jesus, were paraded past. Priests appeared in small contingents from time to time as well, a smugly plaintive expression on their bearded faces, and as they swayed past in their sumptuous purple, rose and mulberry robes the throng would quieten.

It was an utterly untransforming experience. You could have been in Bournemouth on a wet bank holiday weekend.

7

Holy Saint Spiridon, pray to God for us!

Many centuries ago (almost seventeen, in fact, before Constantine founded Constantinople) some Cypriot peasants returning from their fields were trudging past a church as evening fell and heard the chanting of a choir – exalting, kindling in them an awe they'd never felt before – and, peering through the windows of the church, they saw a vast congregation gathered in the candle-lit gloom for vespers. Drawn to join it by the overwhelming beauty of the singing, they entered the church to find . . . *no one there*, except for the bishop, Spiridon, the deacon and their handful of assistants. They were transformed by what they'd seen, of course, these peasants, and they believed and were taken up into the bosom of the church.

Born the son of a simple shepherd, like one or two patriarchs before him, Spiridon specialized in startling transformations of this kind. He cast out demons and healed the sick from an early age – a word from Spiridon was like a lightning bolt, scouring out evil. He converted sceptics and divined where lost valuables were hidden. When a man lay dying of hunger by the roadside, Spiridon seized a snake from amongst the stones and, turning it into a chain of gold pieces, he gave it to the starving man who rose and ran to the town to buy food for himself and his family. An even greater miracle, some might say, occurred when the shepherd's lad convinced a venerable philosopher at Nicaea of the reality of the Trinity.

Some fourteen centuries later, in 1716, when the Turks were besieging Corfu, the saint appeared in the night skies with flaming sword and routed the unbelievers. The Turks, for their part, reported nothing more than a stiff south-westerly squall blowing up at just the wrong, or right, moment, but then, in their unbelief, they would. Still, I can understand the Corfiotes' ecstasy at their deliverance: in this part of the world, when a city fell to them, the Turks had a nasty habit of sending back salted barrels of heads and lopped ears to the Sultan in Constantinople – Turkish, apparently, for 'all's well, wish you were here'.

Miraculously, just a few yards from where I'd stood that Good Friday afternoon, St Spiridon the Wonderworker of Trimythounta is still to be seen in remarkable health. After many posthumous adventures it was in Corfu that his body finally came to rest and it can now be viewed in a tiny candle-lit room beside the iconostasis in the church named after him near the main square. In fact, you can still line up there with thousands of others in the incense-laden gloom to kiss his miraculous feet. For reasons no one can clarify, not even Gerald Durrell, although Spiridon never steps from his silvered casket, his dainty embroidered slippers wear out each year and have to be replaced. Every August tiny pieces of worn silk cut from his old slippers are given to the faithful, talismans against disaster and disease. And several times a year he's paraded upright through the streets of Corfu Town. The day before Easter is one of those days.

So, next morning, back I went in the bus to the park in front of the Old Fort to see what I might see. More bands in the patchy drizzle, white-gloved, some wearing splendid red-plumed helmets this time, and altogether more showily solemn than the day before. Resurrection is in the air, though, and everyone's beginning to feel quite keyed up.

The sun comes out to dazzle us, red and gold icons glitter, gilt Venetian lanterns sway on tall, encrusted poles, flowers are scattered on the gleaming roadway, two long lines of black-capped priests appear, their silken robes afire in the sunlight, deep purple, gold, sky-blue and ivory . . . and then the saint floats by, a minute lolling head in a canopied casket, and all the Dutch and English tourists follow it in their viewfinders, flashes flash, women cross themselves, murmuring softly, and it's all over.

Nothing, again I feel nothing. Most of those around me seem *enlivened* by something they've glimpsed, but I don't. Even the Durrells, both the brothers, who dog your footsteps everywhere you go in Corfu, reminding you of what's been lost – and not just woollen-vested sailors, either, with their moustaches curling back around their ears, or kilted Albanians, or ginger-beer stalls, or wetlands teeming with wildfowl – even the Durrells, who seem to have believed in nothing except their own enchanted, brightly coloured lives – and certainly not in silk-slippered mummies and their tricks – even they appear to have been touched by *something*.

Vaguely hoodwinked, that's how I felt, the way you often feel at Christmas, when you come to the end of the day and nothing much has changed.

For a while I just stood around in the park, as you can in a place where you don't belong, waiting for the pots to be thrown. The locals milled around me, the older men in suits, their wives dressed up as if for some distant cousin's wedding, all looking comforted, at ease again, happily resigned to buying silly gewgaws, ice-creams or balloons. A man carrying a gigantic, gaudy banner of St Spiridon came lumbering along towards me, headed for the carpark – time to stow the stage-props away for another year. Suddenly a gust of wind lifted the banner, he stumbled against me and I found myself smack up against his glowering Spiridon. For just a second or two we were eyeball to eyeball. I stepped back and Spiridon soared away above me, sky-borne, unforgiving.

On the dot of eleven o'clock they threw their pots. Small, doll-like torsos appeared in windows all along

the esplanade, hundreds of them, clutching pots –
huge amphorae, tiny bowls, clay vessels of every
shape and size. The clock struck eleven and they
tossed them into the street below. The crowd
cheered. It had taken less than ten seconds.

Why they tossed them I never discovered. I doubt
they knew themselves. To taunt Judas, according to
Greta, but I doubt many in the crowd had Judas on
their minds.

I picked my way through the terra-cotta shards,
heading for the bus-terminal, utterly bamboozled.
I'd caught a whiff of old Byzantium and hadn't much
liked the aroma.

8

The most dispiriting thing about failing to be moved by others' rituals is that it brings you face to face with your own *ordinariness*. And, if you're feeling even slightly oceanic, that ordinariness swamps everything in sight. Who doesn't long at times, in the midst of piles of washing or slumped in front of the television set, for something utterly unnatural to happen?

Wanting to take a breather, as my father would have said, before the evening's Resurrection celebrations, I went to Kassiopi – that was where the first bus at the bus-terminal was going. Unnatural things had no doubt taken place at Kassiopi over the centuries – well, for a start, Nero had once dropped in on his way to play his lute at the games in Corinth – but that afternoon, when, the only passenger, I got out of the bus in the ugly little town square and looked about, I had the feeling that nothing unexpected had happened here for years. A dog or two came ambling by; a group of youths sat listlessly outside a bar across the street, hailing a passing friend from time to time, then lapsing into moody silence; and a busful of blank-faced Danes drove by, thinking of beer, by the look of it, rather than the Crucifixion.

Idyllic from a distance, of course, Kassiopi: two tiny, turquoise bays, with a wooded promontory wedged in between, and just across the water, so close you could almost shout a greeting, the fabulous, forbidden fastnesses of Albania's mountain ranges. Down on the palm-fringed bay beneath this wall of mountains, I could see the windows of Sarandë (Forty Saints) glinting in the sun, and tiny, indecipherable movements, like shifting grains of sand, along the waterline – people, donkeys, buses, who could tell? It was eerie, almost spectral, like watching a dead man walk silently by in broad daylight.

Romans came to Kassiopi two thousand years ago to lie about and think and read – great vacationers, the Romans, unlike the Greeks – so no doubt somewhere here beneath my feet were the remains of their baths and vomitoria. In fact, Cicero once spent a week here. Cervantes came as well, before or after the Battle of Lepanto, I don't recall, so with or without his left arm, depending. And so did Casanova. And Princess Margaret – it had been her 'holiday choice', according to the *Corfu Sun*, for several seasons now. And so, needless to say, did the Durrells. Their White House was only a few bays to the south, so they'd have boated up here quite often, I'm sure. No doubt a Durrell had stood right where I now stood, knowing infinitely more about what his eyes took in than I did and chancing, as he clambered about, on a colourful band of Albanian smugglers or some type of *prunus prostrata* previously thought extinct – something extraordinary, anyway. All my eyes saw when I looked around, apart from Albania, was a sprinkling of pretty white flowers.

And the sea, Homer's sea. Ithaca, where Penelope waited for Odysseus, lies just over the horizon to the south. In fact, according to the Durrells, it was almost certainly here, in one of the bays of Kassiopi, rather than in the middle of the island around the airport, that Odysseus was cast ashore for the last time before reaching home. It was a quickening thought, so imaginable.

From Nausicaa's point of view it was a day much like any other. She'd trundled off in her painted wagon at first light to do some washing in a pool some way from the palace. (The stream at Kassiopi seems a long way to go with a load of dirty shirts and blouses, but once Fate has taken a hand in things, as we know, reason counts for little.) Around noon, the washing done and out to dry, Nausicaa and her maids were whiling away the morning tossing a ball around. When it fell into the water, as it was bound to do sooner or later, there was a chorus of girlish shrieks. And that's when the day like any other became enchanted, prose turned to poetry and Nausicaa, the unremarkable daughter of an obscure king on an island so remote that no stranger ever came ashore, soared (as it were) into the empyrean.

Roused by the hullabaloo from his slumbers under some bushes, Odysseus, stark naked, his skin all crusted with brine and his tangled hair caked with scurf, came lumbering out of the undergrowth to accost the white-limbed creatures gambolling in the glade nearby. For seventeen days and nights, ever since leaving Calypso's isle, he'd sailed, all alone, across the seas towards Ithaca – towards home. Just as the mighty mountains of the Phaeacians' isle rose up out of the sea like a vast bronze shield, Poseidon, who bore a grudge against him, piled up wild clouds above him, sent savage storms to pound him, smashed his craft and left him, in the hush that followed, to drift to shore on a single beam. From the gently shelving beach Odysseus set off through the reeds at the mouth of a nearby stream to take shelter in the woods beyond, where 'Athena showered sleep upon his eyes'.

Her maids now scattered at the sight of this naked brute, but Nausicaa was made of stauncher stuff. Sensing, perhaps, some goddess's hand in this encounter, she helped him bathe, gave him suppling oil to soothe his briny skin and, having at hand her brothers' shirts and hose all crisp and freshly washed, she clothed him in princely garments. As we have seen, Odysseus then set off, shrouded in 'an enchanted mist', for the city on the hill behind her painted wagon. His face now, we're told, was like beaten silver washed with gold.

Of course, I do not believe any of this – I don't

believe in Nausicaa's washing or the ball or the
enchanted mist or the 'circling frieze glazed blue as
lapis', at least not in the way I believe in the Nausicaa Restaurant near the Hilton, which rises right
where King Alcinous is said to have once had his
court. I don't believe these are the facts about that
particular morning in the aftermath of the Trojan
War. But I do believe it's true.

Homer was telling the truth, I think, about *going
home*, about that 'pining, all my days, to travel home
and see the dawn of my return'. Odysseus was not a
great traveller or restless explorer, despite what Dante
had to say about him – all Odysseus wanted to do
was to go home. Not even lustrous Calypso, with her
promise of immortality and ageless beauty, not all
the nectar and ambrosia and ardent love-making in
the world, could stanch his pining for home. Not
that every traveller wants to go home in a literal
sense – some are marooned for so long they think
they *are* at home – but every traveller, even the kind
that never leaves his armchair in front of the fire,
wants to find the place where being what he is will
matter. That place is home.

I think Homer told the truth about washing-days,
too, on which, if you've got your wits about you,
you'll see goddesses streaking up out of the waves like
shearwaters. On occasion, anyway, in a manner of
speaking.

The bus-driver had told me the last bus back to
town would leave at four o'clock. The timetable

stuck to the lampost said 4.15. The young man sell-
ing nobody ice-creams in the empty square said 4.30
at the very latest. We actually set off for Corfu Town
just on a quarter to five. By this time in the afternoon the very thought of the Resurrection was
fatiguing.

9

Before Byzantium, before even the Mycenaeans beat their gold or the Minoans leapt over their bulls, long, long ago up in the very mountains on the mainland I'd been staring at for half the day, the heartland of the Hellenes, the birthplace of the tall, blond Dorians, fires were lit in temples on the mountain-tops to the Sun God to pray for a bountiful spring, for good weather and abundant crops. One can imagine that even then as the flames leapt heavenwards, in imitation of the fiery charioteer, the sound of goat-skin bagpipes, lutes and muffled dulcimers would have echoed round the crude stone walls.

This kind of pagan cult is what came to mind at midnight when the glowing purple cross on top of the citadel suddenly burst into dazzling brilliance, blindingly white, great tents of fireworks canopied the sky, and all around me in the park below the citadel tens of thousands of candles blazed in the dark, cupped against the wind, while the bandstand was lit up with strings of fairy lights, choirs began their jubilant singing, bands struck up and Christ was risen. '*Christós anésti,*' everyone shouts at everyone else – a little early from a Presbyterian point of view, but why be pedantic? '*Alíthos anésti*,' everyone shouts back – *In truth He is risen* – and then their minds seem to drift off in the direction of Easter soup and sausages and roast lamb. It had been quite a spectacle. Virtue on a panoramic scale.

Over in Albania in the darkness, where it was just an ordinary Saturday night, I can imagine the inhabitants must have watched this orgy of fire and light with . . . but no, I can't imagine what they must have thought. To them it might as well have been a bonfire on the moon.

Later, in the early morning hours back home in Gastouri, I could hear small sounds of joy that the tomb had been empty after all. Ancient sounds they were, to my ears, accompanied by a kind of distant shrilling – reedy piping, melodious plucking – something very old, almost at one with the wind itself. Still, by that time, to be frank, Athena was busy showering sleep upon my tired eyes as well and nothing I say is to be trusted.

10

Greta, it turned out, lived in a two-storeyed house, all pinks and greens, on the lip of a hill not so far from Gastouri. A suburban villa, I expect you'd call it, with Italian touches and lovely, untidy grounds disappearing on all sides into stands of oak and myrtle.

In the fug of roasting lamb – it was turning on an electric spit in one corner of the walled terrace – I smiled, shook hands and nodded as I was led around the terrace, then through the french doors and into the kitchen. A few yachtsmen and their wives, a consul and his wife, a Dutch couple, an Irishman and his sister, a Greek from Athens (banks or something), someone's grandmother stirring soup. 'Hullo, hullo . . . Pleased to meet you . . . Hullo . . .' Even here, on a day such as this, I noticed that *frisson* of apprehension that always runs from face to face when someone new appears in a room. Oh, yes, they smile, but you sense a sudden wariness: this outsider might catch them out at something – at not being themselves, perhaps, or at being themselves, whichever is worse. Apart from the young woman chopping up shallots and anise, the guests all seemed to be in their middle years, that not uninteresting in-between age when you know at last what it is you want and also know you'll never have it. It shows on the face.

'Didn't you give those up, Bernie?' Greta said as the Irishman's sister shook another cigarette from the packet on the table.

'I was more in the *throes* of giving them up, Greta,' Bernie said with just a touch of peevishness. 'Then I lost my *fear* of giving them up, so I'm smoking again.'

'I see,' Greta said, half her mind on counting plates. 'How's your Chilean, by the way, dear? And why isn't he here?'

There was a distinct pause. 'Is he *my* Chilean, Greta? I think you'd better ask Arthur whose Chilean he is.'

'Ah, yes. How silly of me. But he *was* yours, wasn't he? I mean, at the beginning.'

In the hush that followed, I wandered unnoticed out onto the terrace and tried to take an interest in the revolving lamb, which still had its eyes and teeth. A couple of the sea-captains and one or two other smartly turned-out northerners were gathered around the spit making desultory conversation about summer charter flights back to civilization. Everyone was speaking English, even the Dutch couple to each other.

Greta had been living up there in the hills behind the town for fifteen years or more, it turned out. This was her bailiwick. As we'd darted along the winding roads, in and out of the shadows of overhanging trees, up village streets, past lush gardens, she'd waved to the right and waved to the left, pointing out where this couple or that friend lived – a doctor here, a professor there, a retired publisher, a German businessman and his wife. And why was Greta here? Why had *she* washed up here amongst the cypresses and retired sea-captains?

'Ah, well, you see, it was the sixties,' she'd said with a knowing smile. Expressions like 'the sixties' always stump me. I remember things that happened in the sixties – Cliff Richard, a dog dying, learning Latin at school and so on – but I have no memory at all of 'the sixties' as such. I never woke up in the morning and registered that I was in them.

'And when I first saw it – I remember the morning, I remember the exact smell on the breeze – Corfu just looked like what I'd been waiting for all my life. It wasn't, of course, but that's another story.' She laughed, had a coughing fit and subsided. 'Does that make sense?'

'What was it you'd been waiting for?'

'Are you too young to remember what we waited for then? What I was waiting for in Sydney after the war for *years* was for something to happen – well, it was never going to happen in Australia, was it? So, like everyone else, I eventually got fed up and went to where it was already happening – London.

'And it was thrilling, of course, you can't imagine – filthy bed-sits, men who could actually talk and went to the theatre, plays with buggery in them – or perhaps that came later, it's hard to recall exactly. There'd been none of that where I came from. Books, of course, we'd had books, but that was the other magical thing about London: it was all the books I'd read come to life. It was like dreaming of ancient Babylon and waking up next morning to find you were really there.' She seemed to drift off for a moment, trying to recapture the sensation.

'Then I decided to go home on a visit – you know, remind myself of why I'd left, see people before they died, the usual sort of thing. But I never got there. Got off the plane in Athens – in those days it still had a certain charm – and I thought: I needn't take another step – I'm home. And then I met – But here we are.'

And we swung off the road up the gravel drive towards the house – big, pink splashes through the trees. Over to one side of the house I could see the terrace and a dozen people I didn't know standing about.

'Look, most of us are here, when it all boils down, because we were bewitched,' Greta said, wrenching at the handbrake. 'By someone or something. And now it's too late to move on. And anyway, where would we move on to? Where most of us came from no longer exists . . . But come and meet the gang.'

It was certainly a long time, I'd have thought, since the gang on the terrace had been under any kind of spell. They were mostly just beached there, waiting again. Comfortably enough, of course, Corfu being a comfortable place to wait, even faintly glamorous if you had a part in the local pageant.

There's no glamour without a pageant – I'd seen that in London. Wealth, a smart address, designer outfits, even fame – none of that is glamorous without a part in some pageant or other. To be glamorous you must be playing at kings and queens, you must come out of the palace and wave at the crowd. You must be a sovereign or in the sovereign's entourage. Everyone *knows* you're just a hairdresser from Hamburg, but if you can mark yourself off from the ordinary folk in some way – through outrageous immorality, for instance (although it must go unpunished, naturally), eccentricity of an entertaining kind or even just a *soigné* kind of beauty – and join some cortège, some colourful charade, then the ordinary folk will think of you as glamorous. Or act as if they did – it's all a game. In Hamburg you just cut hair, but here you become extraordinary. Where I come from, even racehorse-owners pass themselves off as glamorous – inside every racehorse-owner we presumably discern the outline of the Queen.

Whether or not that lunch was a pageant of kinds was difficult to tell. And if it was, it wasn't clear if I was one of the minor retainers or really just part of the cheering crowd.

After the soup of tripe and sweetbreads, which was eggy but tart, and before the lamb was sliced, I thought I might explore Greta's garden. Exploring people's gardens allows you to escape without being rude – not, I thought, that anyone much would notice my disappearance. Crossing from the half-walled terrace towards the myrtles, I mooched about for several minutes, examining the peonies by the fence, breathing in the juicy smell of rank grass sprouting anemones – just aimlessly peering about, really, taking refuge for a moment from the babble at the table. I said hullo to a ginger cat snoozing in a flower-pot.

Suddenly I heard a cough from above. Glancing up, I saw a figure in a crimson dressing-gown staring down at me from a second-floor window of the house.

I nodded, smiled and waited. The figure in crimson just kept staring.

'Not joining us, then?' I said finally, waving vaguely back towards the terrace.

'Fuck off!' it said.

A little taken aback, I did. I turned and walked round behind the house.

I was just wondering how to avoid passing the upstairs window on the way back to the terrace, when I heard a voice behind me say: 'Greta tells me you're living in Kester's house.'

Wheeling around, I found Arthur, the Irishman, standing grinning at me, hands in trouser pockets. He hadn't said much during the soup, rather drowned out by his sister, Bernie, who ran a second-hand bookshop in town and was a bird-fancier. She winced every time there was a gun-shot. Arthur was a bit biscuity for my taste – biscuity pullover, biscuity trousers, biscuity hair – but pleasant enough with an engaging smile.

'That's right. Do you know Kester?'

'Indeed I do.'

'Tell me about him.'

'You've never met him?'

I explained how it was I'd ended up in the strange white house down the road from the palace in Gastouri and how I was finding it hard to work out who my landlord was. A voice on the telephone, some books, a few photographs, Krishnamurti, cups and saucers that didn't match, sparse furniture, a doggy smell . . . Who was he? Where was he? And where was the dog? No one except Greta had come to the door and said his name, but sometimes it felt as if he were still living there and I were the ghost. It was a house I seemed to have made no real impression on at all.

'Tell you what,' Arthur said, slouching back against the wall in the sun. 'I'll come over tomorrow afternoon, if you're going to be home, and give you all the guff on the locals. Including Kester. Around fourish, say?' Why not? I was curious.

'Do, yes, four's fine.' The dull popping of hunters out slaughtering wildlife peppered the momentary silence.

'They're a wonderful colour, aren't they, those anemones,' he said, nodding at the overgrown lawn.

'Beautiful,' I said, knowing that anemones were not the point. 'What do you do?'

'I teach.'

'What do you teach?'

'English, of course,' he said, and laughed. 'To private students.'

'Why do you laugh?'

'Well, I started doing it just to fill in time, really, and here I am, fifteen years later, still doing it. It's not quite how I thought I'd end up spending my life, I suppose.' And he laughed again.

Before we could pursue the subject, we found ourselves back on the terrace and were made to sit down and contemplate platters piled with steaming Paschal lamb and sausages. Oregano was in the air.

So untethered to anything was the table conversation that afternoon that I wouldn't have been in the least surprised if we'd all floated up off our chairs into the sky and vanished. The consul's wife embarked on a long story about Abu Dhabi, where they'd spent eight years, but it petered out in a spattering of interjections about other things entirely – the correct pronunciation of Arabic words (her husband was a stickler for the glottal stop), Arab terrorists, bats, Scientology, AIDS, Andy Warhol (who'd just died) . . . this and that. Someone eventually asked me where I came from, and I said Australia. The Dutch said they'd once lived in Indonesia. A Greek man said he had a cousin in Adelaide.

The Resurrection, needless to say, never came up. Should it have, I wonder? Was anyone there having a new life in Christ? If someone was – and that's what the red-painted eggs on the Easter loaves were hinting we should be having, it says so in my *Treasury of Authentic Greek Cooking* – wasn't it at least worth mentioning? Should I have asked the consul's wife as I passed her the sauce if she believed in the bodily resurrection of the Nazarene?

In fact what I asked her, while Greta was inside making coffee, was if she knew who the man in the upstairs window was.

'What man?'

'There was a man in a red dressing-gown staring down at me from the upstairs window.'

'Really? How very odd. Did he say anything?'

'Not really, no.'

'No idea. Arthur might know. Or the van der Weels.' But she was already nibbling at the halva, dropping tiny oily crumbs of it all down her raw silk blouse.

When I was getting into my taxi, not so long afterwards, I looked back up at the window where I thought I'd seen him, but all I could see was an empty black square with a long, crimson curtain hanging out across the sill.

11

Unlike Sisi, I had no fragrant, hunchbacked companion to talk about Homer with on my walk next morning, but I didn't feel solitary in the least. Less invisible, really, than I'd felt for days.

It was a poking-about sort of expedition. As I wound my way down the hill through the village – and it's a snake's nest, Gastouri, with lanes and stepped passageways wriggling off in every direction, slithering down the hillside to a shaded stream – I couldn't help thinking of Sisi, Empress of Austria, wending her way through these very streets and alleyways a hundred years before. She'd have smelt the same fresh-bread smells, seen the great-grandfathers of the very men I nodded to, sitting on their wooden chairs in the sun outside the village store. And when she got to the stream at the bottom, she'd have looked across the valley as I did at the town of Ten Saints (Ayii Deka), huddled like a herd of goats high on the mountainside to the south. And then she'd have made her way along the path above the stream to the stone well, still called Elisabeth's Well, standing to this day by the roadside, a grey, domed affair, surrounded by figs and olive-trees.

Nowadays, of course, carloads of Germans and families from Leeds sweep by, cameras at the ready, but in Sisi's day, presumably, there would have been just the odd passing donkey, laden with firewood, with a boy behind it, urging it on with a stick. You can still see these donkeys on the paths amongst the olive-groves further up the hill.

I stared at the well, trying to imagine what it would have been like to stumble upon the Empress of Austria sitting here, dressed in black, drinking a glass of water, alone except for Christomanos with his hump. Just the two of them. Thinking of what? Poor Sisi, homesick for somewhere she'd never been.

At least Odysseus knew where he belonged, at least he had Penelope waiting for him back in Ithaca, weaving her sea-blue web by day and unravelling it by torchlight every night to keep her swaggering suitors at bay. At least in Telemachus he had a wise and spirited son who loved him in his palace back at home, not some spoilt, spineless, jaded, morphia-addicted wastrel like Rudolf – although he had been Sisi's son and she'd loved him. And when Odysseus was wined and dined by kings in palaces, he knew he was on his way home, a hero. His heart was somewhere.

Sisi, sitting by this well, was nobody dressed up as somebody, going nowhere. Lovely, of course, with her auburn hair and amber eyes, but even that loveliness was now a touch parched, on the verge of sinewy.

Back up at the top of the hill, not so far from her

palace, I came upon a small white chapel. In the green dankness behind it were a few gravestones, but on the southern side, in the sun, dribbles of white and pink spattered the stones – daisies and wild garlic dotted with honesty. Can there be a better place to sit and think than on the whitewashed steps of an abandoned chapel? At least, it certainly looked abandoned: its dark wooden doors, emblazoned with white crosses, hung heavily on their rusted hinges, closed against the world, and high above me its two big bells in their peeling double-arched belltower looked somehow timelessly stilled.

Perhaps, though, this sense of bittersweet desolation wafted over me less because of my awareness of the sealed gloom behind me (in the chapel itself as well as the mossy garden of death just round the corner) than because I had begun to remember another dilapidated chapel surrounded by old tombstones, designed and painted by William for Act II of *The Cherry Orchard*. Lopsided, it was, as if it had sunk down into the earth with its forgotten dead.

What a nightmare Act II was for the actors. All those regrets over misspent opportunities, all that tedious yearning – for love, for something meaningful to happen, for life to stop being grey. All that shilly-shallying about how to rescue the estate from debt, all that frittering away of time and emotion on the thinnest of memories and hopes. We floated on and then floated off again, snivelling about our futile lives, sluggishly sniping at each other, talking, talking, waiting, waiting . . . and I was the worst of the lot of them, in some ways. Droning on at one moment about the appallingly undernourished workers and peasants, their stinking housing, the bedbugs and the vodka binges, and the next moment declaiming to Anya (who was infatuated with me for some unfathomable reason) about the need to '*rise above all the petty, illusory things that stop us being free and happy*' and '*reach for the bright star shining in the distance*'. But what is 'petty' and what is grand? And if reaching for the stars means trampling all the beautiful *little* things in life into the mud, is it worth it? Not one of us – and I least of all, although I'm supposed to be the 'revolutionary' in this play – could get a fix on what really *matters* in life, what is *good* and what isn't . . . what, in other words, to do with our time here. Peasants, pickled gherkins, sunsets, love, billiards, money, work, the shining star . . . all much of a muchness, really, a bland, lumpy pudding of no significance. Not one of us, needless to say, turns to look at the toppling gravestones around the chapel.

When I started holding forth like this, if he was there, William would smile. Not exactly cheekily, but knowingly. I asked him why once, a little tersely, during a coffee break, and he thought for a moment and said he just couldn't help it – I was so *good,* he said, and yet *such an idiot.* I never knew whether he'd meant me or Peter Trofimov.

Like Trofimov, I, too, have never quite figured out the way to work in the gherkins and billiards with the shining star. How do you irradiate the humbly trivial – the sneezes and waiting in bus-queues – with the lofty, and *at the same time* cherish above all in the lofty those things that nourish you here, today, in all your ordinariness? I cannot understand, in other words, what sort of God would bother to count every hair on my head.

Miraculously, in *The Cherry Orchard*, Chekhov has managed to create a wholeness out of all these lost galoshes and great loves. Not his characters, but Chekhov himself. In 1904, the first-night audience in Moscow was seized with a kind of crazed joy at this spectacle of blithe desolation, the applause was tumultuous, at the end of Act III there was practically a riot.

But my life is not a play. Down in the village beneath me, lost amongst the dozing pink tiles, the fig-trees and broom, a dog began yapping, a door slammed, and, jolted back to the present, I hoisted myself to my feet. A cheese sandwich wouldn't go amiss. A sit with a book, one of Kester's, in a comfortable chair. And at afternoon's end an hour or two of playing with the jigsaw-puzzle of Kester Berwick's life. With Arthur.

12

In the event, I couldn't settle on any of the books on Kester's shelves. They were either unappetizing (*The Analects of Confucius*) or dotty (*The Astral Plane*, for example, and *Occult Chemistry*). And then there were the books one feels like reading in general, but not at any given moment – Clive James, *The Bhagavad-Gita* and so on.

So in the end I did what I knew I'd do: I went upstairs, opened the drawer in the writing-desk and contemplated the snap of Kester and William. The whiteness of the wet limbs, the slightly awkward smiles, William's delicate musician's fingers splayed on the rock. And the Horus-eye tattoo, of course, the sky-god's moon-eye inked in just below his right collar-bone. It made me feel as brittle as a wine-glass.

Everyone knows the Horus-eye, it's magic: humped eyebrow, moon-eye ending in a dash, and underneath a curl and a vertical wedge. Seth (god of chaos and confusion) gouged it out in a fight with Horus, his sky-god nephew, while trying to rape him. But Hathor made it wax again, just like the moon, so now – and you really feel this when you stare right into it – it stands for healing, for violation salved and soothed into wise wholeness.

I once asked William why he'd chosen this particular symbol for a tattoo. 'No reason,' he said lightly, 'I just liked it.' Could something so permanent, so rooted in dark myth, really be there for no reason? 'None at all. Always looking for a meaning, aren't you. It's just a cute tattoo.'

But that was long after *The Cherry Orchard* and Clive's Christmas party, nearly a year later, in fact, at a time when I felt free to comment on the skin beneath his collar-bone and he to joust with me a little.

It was bizarre: looking at this photograph, I felt as if I'd been followed here *before* I'd even set out. Stalked in advance. I put the photograph back in its envelope, slid out a sheet of paper and took up my pen. Something had to be said.

Rome. Nothing could be said without mentioning Rome. But what could I say? Which lies should I tell?

～

It was in fact our taxi-driver who had found the hotel. I'd only arrived from Perugia an hour or two before William's train pulled in, so I'd arranged nothing, and with Easter just around the corner rooms were scarce. Eventually we found one in a sort of *albergo* on one of the upper floors of a dingy apartment block. Yellow and purple, with a window onto an echoing light-well.

William sank onto the bed and sighed. Time yawned. I knew it would, ever since that moment at the station, but I'd hoped to stop its mouth. At root, wasn't that why we were in Italy? Wasn't that what Italy was for? It was for dazing time so it wouldn't notice us, for stopping it in its tracks with all the usual feints and ruses – mooching about Rome, popping over to Sicily, perhaps, where William had friends, time-travelling in art galleries and ruins, talking about the future, about Australia (but never arriving there) . . . It wasn't supposed to be about filling in time, but about living as if there were none. That's the kind of enchantment wooing weaves its web out of.

Now, with that sigh of William's on the purple bedspread, time opened its great maws and yawned. It would have to be filled in. It was asking me what I wanted to do with it and I had no answer. That was the very quick of the matter.

So I said to William (although I hadn't smoked for months): 'I'll just duck out for some cigarettes – might pick up a map while I'm out – I'll be back in a jiffy.'

I grabbed my wallet, ran down the stairs and set off looking for a tobacconist's. People, dogs and backpackers surged around me on the pavements, cars roared past in waves, I smelt coffee and perfume . . . but saw nothing, I was blind.

Twenty minutes later I found myself back at the station. As I pocketed the cigarettes, it struck me: I had no idea where I had left William.

Stopped dead in my tracks, I broke into a sweat. My mind was blank. The hotel's name, the building, the street . . . nothing, a void. *Think! Think!* It was like trying to ring a bell that had no clapper.

For an hour or so I tramped the pavements south of the station, peering into vestibules, squinting at names on plaques, trying to recall if I'd seen this café before, that display of bananas . . . Nothing, nothing spoke to me, I was lost. What would William be thinking? Or would he be dozing happily on the bed?

And that's when it hit me: I didn't have to go back to that yellow and purple room. *You should leave now* – the words hung in the air in front of me in lurid, red letters. I had everything I needed in my wallet. I fingered it through my coat. But my clothes, my books . . . was I mad? *Not really. A door has opened into another room. Just walk through it.*

And so I did. I went back to the station and caught a train to Brindisi. I didn't even know where Brindisi was.

I hovered in the corridor most of the way like a ghost, as if unable to convince myself I was really there. I flattened myself against the darkening windows as people squeezed past me.

Yet, as soon as I stepped out into the light at Brindisi station, way down on the far side of Italy's wobbly heel, I felt almost tumultuously alive. And in the squalid little hotel near the ferry-terminal where I spent the night, with sexual cries jabbing at me through the wall in little bursts, I dreamt I was soaring up to heaven on a grass-green ass with a golden bridle, singing songs of joy in Hebrew, songs like whirlwinds, gusting through the clouds of swooning angels – white-robed, tumbling angels. Too much Chagall in Nice the week before, I suppose. Still . . .

A rap at the door downstairs. Arthur. Hovering behind him, even more pear-shaped this afternoon, was Agape.

'*Guten Tag*,' she said, smiling with a hint of mischief and trying to peer in. Then she said something in Greek to Arthur, nodded and set off down the steps.

'What did she say?' I asked as he came in the door.

'I haven't a clue.' Arthur was looking distinctly less biscuity today, quite jaunty, in fact, in a forest-green hand-knitted sweater.

'Why does she speak German?'

'A relic from the days of the casino up the hill, I suppose, when Baron von whatshisname ran it. In the Achilleon. Have you noticed it? Ugly monster of a thing.' His eyes flicked round the kitchen. 'You've been busy cleaning, I see. It's usually a pig-sty.'

'A bit grimy, yes.'

'A pig-sty. I'm sure Kester has the idea that squalor is awfully Zen. But look, I have a confession to make.'

'What is it?'

'I'll tell you on the way into town. Thought you might enjoy a coffee down by the water. And Prue said she'd join us, too, Prue . . . I'm just trying to think of her last name . . . Married to a local. Great friends with Kester.'

Soon we were sailing in the sun up over the crest of the hill past the palace. I could imagine a German baron thinking it would make a fine casino.

As we wound down through the olive-groves towards the sea, Arthur said: 'The thing is this: I'm not much of a fan of Kester's. That's why I thought you might be interested in a second opinion.'

'Why not? What do you think is wrong with him?'

'I wouldn't say there's anything *wrong* with him,' he said, grinning. 'It's just that I think he's a bit of an old fraud. Not that I've got anything against old frauds – I'm Irish, after all, and Ireland's full of them. No, it's more . . .' He concentrated for a moment on a particularly hair-raising manoeuvre on the road ahead of us. I looked out to sea. A milky mistiness was closing in from the east, shimmering in the late afternoon light and blotting out Albania.

'I met Kester as soon as I arrived, you see, at his booklaunch. Have you heard about the booklaunch?'

'No, but Greta did mention a book.'

'Yes. Sank without trace, of course. Dreadful title – what was it now? *Head of Orpheus Singing* – that's it.' And suddenly I remembered seeing its spine on one of the bookshelves back at the house. Blue and yellow. 'It was an amazing evening. It was the day the Colonels seized power in Athens and declared martial law. In fact, Celia – have you met Celia?'

'I don't think so.'

'You will. Her husband was rather famous, but nobody can remember what for. Anyway, Celia, who was having the launch party at her place, you see, wanted to call the whole thing off, she was rattled by the talk of a curfew, but Kester was adamant that nothing was going to interfere with it – this was his hour of glory, coup or no coup. So we spent the evening up at Celia's stumbling around in the dark, with just a few candles, treading on the cats and talking to people we could hardly see. Then half of us got lost on the way home – the hills were alive with sozzled ex-pats trying to find their way back with no headlights. I ended up getting lost with Kester.'

Over to our right, in the milky blue glare, I could just make out a little white church surrounded by water in the middle of the entrance to an inlet. Or perhaps it was a convent. It was almost spectral. 'Beautiful!' I murmured.

'It was so typical of Kester,' Arthur went on. 'I thought *he* knew where we were going and he thought *I* knew where we were going, and we ended up half-way across the island in somebody's vineyard. Not that Kester was fazed at all – in fact, I think he thought it was the perfect end to a perfect evening. We sat and ate some chocolate I found on the back seat until it got light.'

'What did you talk about?'

'Funny you should ask that. We talked about that Krishnamurti fellow.'

'Are you interested in . . . that sort of thing?'

'No, not at all. It just struck me as rather bizarre – an Australian and an Irishman sitting in a car in the middle of a Greek island at three o'clock in the morning discussing some mad Indian.' He grinned again – quite disarmingly, as a matter of fact – but the swerving and cornering on the narrow road above the sea were mostly keeping my eyes glued to the road ahead.

'So is that what you mean by "old fraud" – the Indian guru business?'

'Partly, I suppose, although he claims to be a Buddhist these days, I think.'

'You could claim to be worse things, I suppose.'

'Oh, it's not the Buddhism in itself I object to . . . so much, although personally I find most of the stuff he comes out with as daft as . . .' He hesitated to say as what precisely, not being quite sure what eccentricities I might myself be prey to. 'No, it's more the sanctimonious shit that gets up my nose – the clasped hands, the wise smile, the highmindedness – it's relentless. The man can't eat a carrot without a song and dance about the suffering he's putting it through. I don't believe in any of it.'

'Why not?'

'Because it's phoney. But Prue thinks differently.' A surprisingly gentle smile all of a sudden. 'Of course, he'd only been here a few years himself back when I first met him – he must have got here about 1969. He'd been living on one of the other islands before that – somewhere over on the Turkish side, Lesbos, I think. In those days he had a house off a courtyard just near the old chapel – lovely old place, really, high wooden ceiling, whitewashed walls, with a bedroom upstairs looking out over the valley. That's where he used to sit writing and strumming his guitar.

'That's the other thing that gets on my wick – not that I should talk, I suppose – what does my life amount to, after all? But there's a sort of *smallness* to Kester, if you know what I mean, that really gets under my skin. To hear him talk, it's all Art and Beauty and Truth and Goodness, but what does it all amount to? All he does is sit up there in his room day after day, typing away, *tap-tap-tap*, page after dreary page . . .

'Have you seen his manuscripts? Piles of them everywhere, all covered in minute corrections, whole paragraphs stuck in with glue and sticky-tape, and every second word misspelt. And the lot of it just lukewarm rehashings of his screamingly dull life.'

'How do you know, Arthur?'

'I've flicked through some of it – I baby-sit the dog from time to time, when he wants to go to Athens.'

He was silent for a moment, letting his irritation settle.

'The point is that nobody is ever going to publish any of it. It's simply dead boring. Kester can't write.

He was in the theatre once, too, you know – acting, teaching, writing plays . . . all gone, like a puff of smoke. Who's ever heard of Kester Berwick? Oh, to listen to him, you'd think he was quite the celebrity – the names he drops! He knew everyone who was anyone in the theatre in England – in his day, of course. But where has it got him? He may've known Dame Sybil Thorndike – good luck to him – but the fact is he's a lonely old man stuck in a God-forsaken village on an island most people have never heard of . . . tootling the days away on a bamboo flute he made himself and teaching English to Greek fishermen's sons. He's not even qualified.'

There was nothing I could say, really. I didn't know the man, did I.

'If you find him so unlikeable,' I said, choosing my words with care, 'why do you baby-sit his dog?'

'Well, that's the thing, you see, that's the idiotic thing. We all get roped in. We take him fresh fish, we invite him to dinner, we read his damned manuscripts, we look after his dog, we even go round and spring-clean his house for him. Why? I don't know why.' He was thinking hard as we moved out onto the road along Garitsa Bay, heading towards the Old Fort on its rocky crag. 'Do we feel sorry for him? We certainly don't find him interesting. I just don't know. Ask Prue. Anyway,' he said, as we threaded our way through the park between the town and the citadel, 'why are you interested in him? If I'm not mistaken, you've not even met him. All you're doing is renting his house.'

Now I was stumped. I could hardly bring up William. And in any case, was it just William?

'Yesterday at Greta's,' I said, 'a man in an upstairs window told me to fuck off. Who might that be?'

Arthur laughed and swung the car into a parking space outside the Palace of St Michael and St George, a massive limestone building with a Doric colonnade brooding over the parklands beneath the citadel. Oddly light, given its bulk.

'Well, you never know with Greta, it could've been anyone. Probably her husband, though. Rude bugger. They don't speak. Haven't spoken for ten years. Not a syllable, apparently.'

I wanted to know why, but I once read somewhere that unbridled curiosity is really just a form of indifference – I'm sure that can't be right, they can't be the same thing at all – but anyway, by the time I'd mustered the determination to lead Arthur on, we'd reached the little garden behind the palace and he was waving at a young woman seated at a table near the seawall.

'Prue's here already,' he said, smiling. 'That's good, punctuality is not her strong point.'

Arthur and Prue greeted each other with a special kind of ease – a hint of playfulness, breezy questions – that can only grow out of affection untinged by any hunger. A pleasure to watch.

'So you're living in Kester's house,' Prue said, smiling up at me. 'Have you got everything you need? His cupboards are rather bare.' She was a strikingly good-looking woman in her thirties, even beautiful, with long, silky hair dyed a tasteful auburn. Big, frank eyes.

'She means he's an old skin-flint – hardly a pot or pan to his name,' Arthur said.

'It's fine,' I said. 'It's only for a couple of months.'

'It'll be his teeth,' Prue said, as Arthur tried to catch a waiter's eye. 'Every now and again he pops off to have his teeth looked at. Athens, probably, or London.'

'Yes, he seems to have enough money to go to London alright to have his teeth done, but can't afford to feed himself properly or buy warm clothes for winter.'

'Arthur, that's unfair. He's an old man, he just doesn't . . .'

'What?'

Prue was looking genuinely wounded, but gracefully so. She'd clearly heard all this before. While Arthur dallied with the waiter, she turned to me and said quietly: 'Arthur doesn't understand. He's actually very kind to Kester, but he doesn't understand him at all. He looks at all the small things about him – the shabby things, I suppose . . . and they're there, of course: the darned clothes, the dirty cups, the biscuits and cheese he seems to live on – a few olives, if anyone drops in . . . and the dog always has a rash . . .'

'Where *is* the wretched dog, I wonder?' Arthur said as the waiter sauntered off. 'Perhaps he's had her put down.'

'You're being beastly, Arthur. She'll be with Celia or somebody – Kester would never do that.'

'He might just as well. He doesn't look after her. All this Buddhism business, respect for every living creature and so on – all that palaver about how it hurts him to slice up a tomato – yet he can't even look after his dog properly.'

Prue looked stung. Behind her, curling down the sheer seawall to the rocks below, was the most exquisite spiral staircase, so elegantly elongated it took your breath away.

'How old is Kester?' I asked.

'He must be over eighty. But he's not frail. And he doesn't talk like an old man.'

'Oh, Prue, what's this now?' Arthur was goading her again. 'The man doesn't live in the real world at all. He doesn't even know it's there. He's like a ghost from the 1930s.'

'Why does he interest you?' Prue said, ignoring Arthur. 'Do you have friends in common?'

'It's just one of those funny things,' I said, treading warily. 'I came into his house and it was like hearing echoes.' But of what? 'Of conversations I'd once taken part in, or overheard, I'm not sure. I feel I'd just like to know where these echoes are coming from.' I hadn't known I was going to say that, it just came out.

'Arthur won't like me saying this,' Prue began, although Arthur wasn't even listening – the waiter, as sleek and playful as a seal-pup, was at his elbow, sliding

cups and plates onto the table, trying to feign indifference, even disdain. 'But Kester Berwick is the most
spiritual person I've ever met.' And she blushed slightly
and blinked.

I never know what people mean when they say
things like that. What on earth does 'spiritual'
mean?

'You see, when Arthur talks about the holes in his
pullovers and having no food in the house, what he
sees is an old man living a rather empty life in an
empty house, whiling away his time doing rather
pointless things – playing his guitar, writing plays no
one will ever put on, listening to the radio . . . little
things, aimless things. But what *I* see is someone
who has gone through the attic of his life, as it were,
and thrown almost everything out – all the rubbish,
all the bric-à-brac, all the clutter . . .'

Not quite all of it, I thought to myself, remembering the smell of lavender as I pulled open the drawer
of his desk.

'What *I* think is that he's found the secret of
something.'

'And what would that be of, I wonder? The art of
sponging off the rest of us?' Arthur guffawed.

'Oh, do shut up, Arthur,' Prue said, not without
affection. 'No, the art of . . .'

'Happiness?' I asked.

'No, no, Kester doesn't seek happiness.' This was
obviously something they'd talked about. 'No, it's
something more like *peace*.'

I was getting edgy. Peace, spiritual wholeness – what would be next? Love? A couple of the photos I'd found in the drawer came to mind.

'Kester's in touch with something – he just is. No, he's not happy – perhaps he's content, I'm not sure – but he's found a way to live and think about his life I find inspiring. When my father died – he was a potter here in Corfu –'

'Oh, please, Prue, not the dream!'

'When my father died, I sent Kester a letter to tell him – he was very fond of my father, but didn't have the phone. Well, a week went by and I'd heard nothing from him – he wasn't at the funeral – so one morning I went up to Gastouri to see what had happened. He actually had my letter in his hand when he answered the door – he'd only just got it, it had taken a week to reach him – I mean, it's only five miles, but the postal service here is hopeless.'

'Like everything else,' Arthur murmured.

'And he looked so happy, he was smiling – almost cheerful. And he said: "I knew he'd gone, Prue, I knew days ago, because he came to me in the night and told me I'd hear bad news, but not to be sad because everything was alright. *All is well*, he said to me." And I knew he was telling me the truth.'

'God in heaven, Prue – I don't know how you can fall for that kind of gobshite. The man's batty. Actually, I think he's worse than that: I think he's heartless, he was peddling you heartless claptrap to cover his own bewilderment. It's inexcusable.' Arthur was quite seriously annoyed.

'I noticed a picture of Krishnamurti on the book-case. And there are the books, too – Madam Blavatsky and so on. What's all that about?'

'He knew Krishnamurti – he met him in Australia years ago, apparently, before the war, and then again in London. There was some sort of bond between them – or at least Kester thought so. He was terribly upset when Krishnamurti died last year – that really shook him.'

'Not as cheerful as he was about your daddy, then?' Arthur's lip was curling. 'No nocturnal visits? Not, at any rate, from Krishnamurti . . .'

'That's enough, Arthur – I'm going to get cross with you.'

We lapsed into a charged silence, and then drifted into chit-chat about less contentious things – the almond cake, the flying-boat that used to land in the bay in front of us on its way to Australia (of all places) and what Prue was doing in Corfu.

'Love, of course,' Arthur said. 'Isn't that why we're all here? She fell in love with a Greek sailor, didn't you, Prue? And never left.'

Actually with the manager of one of the marinas, as she explained. She painted.

I thought of Nausicaa again, and her painted wagon, heading off for the palace with its lapis-blue frieze and solid gold doors, the shipwrecked Odysseus in tow. (Chagall has a marvellous green,

pink and white painting of this scene – it was one of
the ones I'd stared at in Nice not long before, until I
was bewitched.)

∿

In the bus back to Gastouri (I didn't want to be too
beholden to Arthur), I thought about the two pictures of Kester Berwick I'd just been presented with
and wondered if they'd ever dovetail, then merge and
come alive as a single image with real depth. Was he
a prurient old trickster, a nobody masquerading as
somebody, hoodwinking the gullible with spiritual
flimflam, or was he some kind of sage, who'd drifted
into saintliness in some mysterious way, high in the
hills behind Corfu Town, in those whitewashed
rooms of his with cold floors and wooden ceilings?
  And just for an instant, as we chugged along the
pot-holed road to Gastouri, horn blaring, sky turning to velvet, I had one of those translucent
moments again, when all of a sudden I felt I'd
become just a fizz of light and sound – of voices,
memories, visions, streaking out of the past from all
directions to cross at the point that was me . . . Nausicaa, Ranyevskaya, Achilles (dying), Krishnamurti,
purple bedspreads, saints and miracles, London bed-
sits . . . A soft explosion and – there I was again, an
ordinary man on a toiling bus in Greece, heading
home, not a burst of light and sound at all.
  Strange to relate, the detonation left a kind of

afterglow, and in that afterglow, to my own bewilderment, I saw images of Adelaide, a blur of muddy
yellows and blue.

In fact, I smelt them. I smelt that soft, warm,
squelchy chook-dirt smell that hung in the salty air
over our sprawling backyards in summer when I was
a child. And the rain on hot asphalt when finally,
after what seemed then half a lifetime of baking heat,
it suddenly poured. And the hot stone and roses in
the still, wide, tree-lined streets where some of the
boys played cricket after school and cats got stuck up
lemon-scented gums. And the dog-turds we dropped
in Mrs Evans' letter-box.

I didn't admit to William that I also came from Adelaide until we'd known each other for nearly a year –
not until the disastrous weekend we spent in a
French hotel together, when it rained for three days
and all sorts of things came out of the woodwork.
And I don't come from Adelaide, except technically.

It's a completely unremarkable city, a city where,
apart from the odd axe-murder, nothing ever happens, or nothing that matters. It's just a flat strip of
land between the gulf and the hills where retired
clergymen and hairdressers, presided over by the
Anglican gentry, eke out their days mulching their
gardens and putting on *Brigadoon* in church halls.
It's true there was a period in the 1970s when we all

thought a new Golden Age had arrived, because the Premier wore shorts in parliament and everyone started potting and weaving and living disordered lives in mudbrick houses in the Hills, but that was quickly snuffed out. The moment my divorce came through, I was off. I blanked it out.

Yet now all of a sudden there were reverberations. There was William, of course, and now Kester Berwick. Among the little piles of pamphlets and obscure magazines on his bookshelves were several articles he'd written about his involvement with some avant-garde theatre company in Adelaide before the war. None of it had rung any bells with me, I must say, although I'd moved in theatre circles there for years – for most of the seventies, in fact – before going to London. Well, I was an actor, after all.

Not that my wife called me an actor when things got scratchy. 'Look at you!' she used to snap in that terribly tight way of hers when I'd failed yet again to make something of myself. 'Always crapping on about the theatre, but you're not an actor, you're just a night porter with delusions. I'm living in Largs bloody Bay married to a motel receptionist.' Sometimes she wept. She'd been to a very good school.

She was being rather unfair. I was also a magician at children's parties, mostly on weekends, and spent a lot of time at the Studio in rehearsal during the week, preparing audition pieces, doing a bit of back-stage work when parts were scarce – that kind of thing, all perfectly professional. I don't suppose it was a frantically exciting life, but you have to begin somewhere.

The catalyst for change was an American called Harold. He was doing research at the Museum in the city, something to do with indigenous cultures, and I'd like to be able to say I thought he was a pretentious bore, but, to tell the truth, he was fascinating, and there was something about his nose and chin I really took to as well. There was something about Harold that said he was going places. And indeed, one hot Sunday afternoon while I was pulling coloured scarves out of my fist, he went to Texas with my wife.

It was a shock when it happened and I won't pretend it wasn't. I'd introduced them, after all. I'd stood next to him at a poetry reading in a bookshop. We'd got talking and I told him to look us up. Which he did. I'd noticed, of course, the little day-trips they started taking together to the hills or the Barossa Valley on days when I was tied up with a children's party, and the concerts Harold would suddenly ring with one extra ticket for on nights when I was on duty at the motel, not to mention the queer girlishness that came over Lisa whenever he dropped by, the little hints at inner commotion. But, if I thought about it at all, I suppose I just thought the arrangement was rather sophisticated, with a touch of the charmingly dissolute about it – after all, we were civilized people and I wasn't above the odd *divertissement* myself, so long as it didn't mean anything. I found the idea of a close friendship with a man who didn't just talk business and offer gardening tips rather appealing. I didn't have many *friends* as such.

To be honest, I always took it for granted that Harold was gay. I mean, the brightly coloured shirts, the choir he'd joined, the tasteful shoes, the . . . well, the deftness with words, the rightness of every syllable. The charm, I suppose, the disarming interest in what Lisa or I thought about things. No men I knew in Adelaide looked or behaved like that. Once or twice when he dropped around while Lisa was at the library and began talking to me about things in that intense, eloquent way he had, it even crossed my mind he might be after something more intimate with me. It was the way he offered me his vulnerabilities for pricking. I even said as much once to Lisa while she was doing her eyes to go out with him.

'No, I don't think so,' she said, studying herself carefully in the mirror.

'Why is there never any mention of a wife or girlfriend, then, do you suppose?'

Lisa said she understood he'd had a 'great sadness' in his life. I left it at that.

I've never seen her since she left. We've only spoken once in all these years – it was on the telephone after Harold had his accident. He was beheaded in the Yukon when a sheet of roofing metal came off the back of the truck in front of him, sheared through his windscreen and took his head clean off. They found it right at the back of his van in a plastic bucket. It was very quick, apparently. By then, though, I was in London and the Yukon seemed a long way away.

13

Did I mention that the staircase at Kester's house was outside? It was an iron affair, beginning by the front door, crossing the front of the house and ending in a little landing upstairs around the corner outside the bedroom. Very off-putting in winter, I'd have thought.

One morning a week or so later I was clanging down these stairs to make some tea when I noticed Greta standing at the door.

'Well,' she said with a smile, 'you've become quite the recluse – as bad as Kester.' Did I have any choice? I had no telephone, no car and knew where nobody lived, except Greta. 'I've come to invite you up to the Big House next Sunday. It's quite a coup – by no means everyone is welcome.'

The Big House – well, fancy that. I'd heard mention of the Michaelís family residence. Corfu is a small island, after all, barely out of the feudal age, so the names of the great land-owning oligarchs crop up in conversation regularly – especially ex-patriate conversation, because no one aches for the trappings of significance, for *notability*, more than nobodies from distant seats of power.

The Durrells, who found the feudal set-up so much fun, were *habitués* at the Big House, I seemed to remember. Kaiser Wilhelm II had certainly dropped over from the Achilleon more than once in the years before the First World War, according to what I'd heard, not to mention assorted kings and queens of England, Greece and Denmark. Someone even thought Edward Lear had lunched there once in the mid-1800s, over from Albania, and left behind a sketch with a witty inscription as a parting gift.

How on earth had rumour of my lowly existence reached the Michaelíses' ears? I hurtled into town and bought a snappy tie and jacket.

The following Sunday, heading off with Greta (who was dressed in a cream linen suit, also from one of the smarter boutiques in town) for the middle of the island, I felt pleasantly on edge. But by the time we'd left the main road and, skirting a deserted nunnery, were winding up a hillside through brooding olive-groves towards the manor gates, I was beginning to feel a little unnerved.

Then all at once the trees thinned out and I found myself looking back over the tops of flowering quince and orange trees into the humming haze in the valley below. And slumbering amongst this sunny lushness, tucked up in the shadows of a crag, all mouldering Tuscan pinks with deep green shutters, lay the fabled Big House.

According to Greta – whose familiarity with Corfiote history struck me as broad rather than deep, so

I can't vouch for the truth of the tale – the Michaelís family first came to Corfu in a galley from Malta in the late Venetian period to help the Christians fight off the Turks. Putting two and two together, I worked out that the Turkish siege these Maltese knights had come to lift, along with the Spaniards, the Tuscans and the Genoese, was the very same siege St Spiridon and his heavenly hosts were credited with smashing in 1716. As their reward, in those deeply feudal times, the Maltese knights were given huge estates on the island, well-stocked with peasants, olive-groves and giant oaks, olive-oil and wood for ship-building being two great sources of wealth in Corfu under the Venetians. As his reward, St Spiridon got *another* procession, every August.

'There are still Maltese Catholics all over the place up here in the hills,' Greta had said to me as we headed inland from Gastouri. 'It's a real zoo, this island.'

In Greta's story, a Venetian countess or two was soon woven into the Michaelís family fabric and this added a certain éclat, a thread of brilliance no mere Maltese could aspire to.

Indeed, the first thing we saw when we came through the door of the Big House, high up on a flaking wall in the gloomy main salon, was a portrait of the first countess to join the clan. Serene, mournful, she eyed us with an insouciance I found quite appealing.

'Maria someone, I think,' Greta said, as the servant ushered us in meandering fashion round the vast oak furniture cluttering the room. 'I have an idea it was she who had this place built.' Martha, the servant, who was ancient and had denture problems, had not stopped mumbling ever since she'd opened the door to us. 'Don't pay any attention to Martha,' Greta said. 'She had a vision of the Virgin Mary about ten years ago, round in the old stables behind the boiler, and hasn't been the same since. Appalling cook, but quite harmless. Thank you, Martha, dear – *efharistó*.'

We'd been shown through onto the narrow balcony running along the far side of the house, overlooking the valley. Across the courtyard below us, half in shadow, was the old family chapel, unpainted now, with faded, brownish tiles sprouting weeds. Beside it, right in front of us, rose the elegant belfry, ropes from its three bells trailing down its splotched façade into the shrubbery below. Nothing stirred. The valley beyond, apart from the occasional flash of sun on glass, was swathed in a blue-green mistiness. Far, far away a child shouted something and then shrieked with laughter.

We stood there together, Greta pointing things out to me. Around to one side of the house, for instance, past the stables where the sons of the family kept their expensive German cars, were the crumbling servants' quarters, a two-tiered wing of empty cells with gaping doorways, half-choked with vines.

'You can see how very grand it must all have once been,' said Greta. 'I'd have loved to see it in its heyday. Imagine the goings-on.'

'When would that have been, do you think?'

'A couple of hundred years ago, I suppose. Then the French arrived and freed the serfs – not that that was of much use to anybody because the serfs still owned no land. As a matter of fact, the peasants were largely uneducated here until well into the 1950s. I dare say Martha's illiterate. Anyway, as far as the Michaelís family's concerned, I imagine it's all been pretty much downhill ever since Napoleon.'

We wandered back into the salon, which smelt of unwashed dogs and rising damp.

'I wonder where on earth they all are. All those cars out in the forecourt – we're obviously not the first to arrive. Perhaps they've gone for a walk in the orchard. I might go and rustle up a gin and tonic in the kitchen. Care for something?'

All I wanted to do was go back out onto the balcony and drink in all that soft decrepitude. Face to face with something very old – a Roman aqueduct, a Dutch master, even your grandmother's wedding-ring – you kaleidoscope, it seems to me, into a different cluster of memories and illusions from the one that empties the tea-pot or watches the news at seven. In the blink of an eye you're engulfed by waves of Goths and Franks, earth-shattering love-affairs and trifling *amours*, war after war, archbishops, miracles, princes, cousins and second-cousins swarming everywhere like ants whose nest you've accidentally trodden on – and, looking at these stones, this painting, this ring, you shrink to nothing, lose all your

significance. And then you shake yourself – and
piece by piece recover it. And if you're in Rome or
some art museum in Amsterdam, you rush off as fast
as you can to the nearest café to gobble down cake
and coffee and talk rather too loudly to your companion, afraid, no doubt, at some level, of being
obliterated again without warning, however
thrillingly. So, standing on that old stone balcony,
taking in the view, I knew once again I didn't matter
– yet mattered utterly and was slotted in. I felt light-
headed with despair and a rush of excitement.

The hush was abruptly broken down below. The
door of the chapel was flung open and out trooped
a gaily attired file of men and women, all blinking in
the sudden sunlight and smiling with a sort of relief.
Jolted back to the present, I waved and called out
hullo. The old man in a suit at the head of the file
stopped dead in his tracks and peered up at me.
Then the others all fell silent and did the same. A
dozen blank faces were angled up at the stranger on
the balcony. Two of them in fact belonged to Arthur
and his sister Bernie, and a couple of the others
seemed vaguely familiar as well, but they all stared at
me as if I were a ghost.

'And who the hell are you?' the old man in front
bellowed up at me. Arthur stepped forward and said
something in his ear. The old man grunted and set
off again, with the others in tow. A young priest
brought up the rear, locking the door behind him. In
a moment or two the whole line had disappeared

into the thicket of broom-bushes at the side of the house. As he vanished, Arthur waved.

It had been a service for all the dead Michaelíses, Arthur explained when he reached me on the balcony. Mind-numbingly boring, he said, rolling his eyes, except for when the consul, who'd converted to Islam while he was in Abu Dhabi, had refused to eat the chunk of bread the priest had offered each member of the congregation. George Michaelís, the patriarch in the suit, had roared at him to 'just swallow the bloody thing and stop being such a prick' – and he had, but was now refusing to stay for lunch. His wife, who was drinking something reviving in the kitchen with Greta, was in tears, apparently. We could hear the consul trying to start his car in the driveway out the front.

In dribs and drabs the crowd straggled out onto the balcony. 'Hullo,' I said to this one and that, 'pleased to meet you . . . No, not long . . . Yes, Gastouri . . . How do you do?' Then they straggled inside again and up various staircases to lunch. I didn't want to make rash judgments, but they didn't look to me like a particularly select crowd, despite what Greta had said.

The house was such a maze of dark rooms, passageways and stairs that Arthur and I got lost and ended up in somebody's bedroom way up in the roof. By the time we reached the dining-room, which seemed to be on a tilt, the priest was already intoning some sort of blessing. It went on for so long that I gathered it had turned into a homily.

I glanced around the long, polished table at the fidgeting assembly, nodded at a couple of familiar faces and lapsed into that embarrassed silence religion tends to hatch nowadays in educated circles. The beeswax was clashing strangely with the smell of dogs and fried meat-balls.

'What's he saying?' I whispered to Arthur's sister, Bernie the bird-fancier and owner of the only second-hand bookshop in town.

'Something about virtue, I think,' she whispered back, rather loudly. 'About feeding the inner man. Personally, I'm an atheist.'

'That's enough of that!' George shouted at us from the top of the table, drowning out the bearded priest completely. 'Show some respect. Sit and listen.' He was still mumbling 'Atheist – what next!' to himself as he passed the *dolmáthes*, once the priest had finished, to the capaciously bosomed woman on his right.

According to Arthur, this was George's Belgian mistress Gisella, who spent most of the meal chatting amiably with the tall, dark man next to her. I thought he might have been Arthur's Chilean, but he turned out to be a car-dealer (amongst other things) from Athens. George's wife was away shopping in London, where she kept a flat. Nobody seemed to have any idea where the sons were.

'So,' George boomed down the table to me eventually, once the meat-balls had started circulating, 'do you sail?' He was a handsome man, in a ravaged sort of way, with thick, grey hair and eyebrows like fat, furry animals jiggling on his forehead. 'Ride? Shoot? What do you do?'

'I'm an actor, actually.' He looked as if I'd just belched in his face.

'An *actor*? Is there money in that?' But no reply was necessary because one of the dogs who'd wandered in with Martha had started peeing against the wall beneath the window. George leapt to his feet and kicked the animal out the door, swearing in Greek. Chewing lustily, the priest gave us all a beatific smile.

'I'm Celia, by the way,' said the woman opposite me, raising her voice above the fracas. She was dressed in that expensively dowdy fashion the English seem to have perfected. 'My husband was a great friend of George Bernard Shaw, you know.'

'Really?'

'Yes,' she said, 'the playwright.' She fingered an errant fake pearl. 'I hear you're a friend of Kester's. I've been lumbered with his dog. I could kill him.'

'Are you a particular friend of his, then?'

'Of Kester's? No, not really – to tell you the truth, I find him rather dreary, I never know what to talk to him about, he doesn't seem to be interested in anything.' Not for the first time in hearing about Kester, I wondered who exactly bored whom. 'But my husband was fond of him – well, quite fond. No idea why. The theatre connection, I expect. My husband knew everyone in the theatre back in England. George Bernard Shaw, of course, Emlyn Williams, Larry and Viv – adorable pair.'

Next to me, Bernie was telling the consul's wife about being almost struck by lightning while out bird-watching the day before in the marshes.

'Sometimes I wish I *were* struck by lightning,' the consul's wife said, tearing at her spicy meat-balls.

'I'm not an ex-patriate, you know,' said Celia. 'I'm an Englishwoman living in Corfu. There's a huge difference.'

When the conversation drifted onto that most Corfiote of topics (how to get out of Corfu), Arthur gave me a nudge and offered to poke about the garden with me. All the familiar words were already trickling down the stairs after us – 'Gatwick', 'Heathrow', 'charter', 'Harrods' – as Arthur turned to me and said: '*Scintillating* company?'

'Oh, everyone seems . . . nice enough.'

'I suppose so – in their fashion. It's just that we're all desperately tired of being ourselves, but don't quite know who else to be. Except the priest, I suppose, but he's not really one of us.'

'So why are we here, do you think?'

'You're wondering, are you?' Arthur laughed. 'It's the *grand seigneur* thing, that's all. George imagines he still counts for something – and he does in some ways, he's got a finger in every pie in Corfu. But the days when you had to have his permission to sneeze are long gone. The little rituals persist, though – the bestowing of favours, the word in someone's ear, and lunches like this one for the fag-ends of the empire. Well, Princess Margaret is hardly likely to pop over for drinkies, is she? She's got the Rothschilds to hobnob with – it's trade that's glamorous nowadays, after all. So it's us or nobody. Even Kester gets an invite at Christmas.'

Venetian it might have been, but the house reminded me of exactly the sort of ramshackled manor Ranyevskaya would have felt at home in, or any of those maundering, rudderless aristocrats, for that matter, in any of a dozen Russian novels I'd read. I wouldn't have been in the least surprised if a booted peasant in baggy pants, clutching his cap, had appeared in the sitting-room to announce a cholera epidemic in the village.

Eventually Arthur and I made our way out of the labyrinth of dank rooms into the unkempt garden below.

'It's all finished, really,' Arthur said, waving an arm at the house, the chapel, the rows of quince and cumquat trees. 'It's all over. *Finito.* Kaput. In a few years from now some German shoe-salesman will be living here with his wife and three children. He'll sell off the olive-groves in plots for more Germans to build their holiday houses on. George will spend his days griping about money and railing at his hopeless sons. Well, it's happening already, really – the family used to own olive-groves right across the island once, but bit by bit they've sold them off, just scraps left now.

'Nobody wants to work, you see, they've no talent for it at all. Oh, they *do* things – the usual things, passing round the tourist cake, hoping chunks of it will fall off into their hands – they wheel and deal endlessly, but they don't actually *work*, not as such. No, it's doomed. All those counts and countesses on the walls inside would die a second death if they could see what the family has become. Way back they were standard-bearers for the emperors in Byzantium, you know. That's the sort of thing they do best. Well, the time for emperors has passed – thank God, I suppose.'

After pottering about in the orchard in the balmy air for a while, we made our way back to the sloping dining-room, where Martha was in disgrace for try-ing to clear the table before everyone had finished. She was singing softly to herself, coming in and out with plates of semolina cake and halva.

'Kester sings, of course,' Celia said, helping herself to a very large slice of cold custard *soufflé*.

'Really?'

'Very badly, but yes, to his guitar. Composes his own songs. Sort of haiku things about love being washed away by autumn rains. I find it most embar-rassing. Always try to dissuade him in company. I wonder where he's gone? His teeth, I suppose. Ghastly business, teeth, at our age. And, needless to say, here on Corfu . . .'

While the cumquat liqueurs were still being served, there was a sharp blast on a horn outside, and Arthur rose rather abruptly and made his apologies. Probably the Chilean. Bernie, his sister, fell glassily silent in mid-sentence – she'd been talking (to nobody in particular) about snipe and woodcock – and then said: 'Perhaps I'd better come along with you, Arthur.'

'Don't worry, Bernie, you stay here – we're not going straight home.' Celia then offered to drop her off and, as happens at such moments at the end of meals, suddenly the whole thing unravelled like tangled wool, with everyone pushing back their chairs and hitching onto someone else, unhitching and then hitching up again.

By the time I got down to the front door, even George and Gisella had vanished, which I thought was distinctly odd, roaring off down the white gravel drive between the banks of golden broom in their sparkling Mercedes. In the end, only Greta and I were left, saying goodbye to Martha in a funny mixture of English and Greek. As we drove away, I watched her grow very small in the blackness of the doorway, the empty house mushrooming lopsidedly around her, all scabby pinks and greys, doomed, baleful, melancholy.

'If we'd stayed until evening fell, we'd have seen the fireflies,' Greta said. But all I could think about as we swooped down through the darkening olive-groves past the abandoned nunnery was Sisi. There she'd sat, a hundred years before, wife of the Emperor of Austria, just a few hilltops away, reading Homer and talking in Greek with her hunchbacked nobody about nothingness and lovelessness and loss and poetry, desperately striving to shake off significance of every kind – or at least of the kind her world fought for – while here, at the same time and so close by, amongst these hunched olive-trees the scions of Byzantine courtiers had struggled to do the very opposite: hang on to significance where there was none, ending up, now, with one crazed, toothless housemaid serving meat-balls to failed actors and local shopkeepers and their wives. Was there no middle path? Was Chekhov's 'work, work, work' the answer? If so, what exactly ought we to be working at? Anyway, working hard never rescues anyone's life from futility in Chekov's plays – it's vision that does that, a certain kind of homespun wisdom.

'It all looks so civilized and *normal*, doesn't it?' Greta remarked as we took off down the main road along the valley floor towards the coast, supermarkets and suburban villas flashing by. 'But you know, up there in the mountains to the north – not twenty miles away, probably, as the crow flies – it's still 1000 BC. Up there, believe me, Homer is alive and well. And I don't just mean cures for the Evil Eye, which they say can knock a donkey into a ravine at fifty paces. In some of those stone villages up on Mt Pantokrator, for instance – can't see it today, too cloudy – the old gods and goddesses are still running riot, large as life. I wouldn't be surprised if they were still sacrificing goats and rams at the winter solstice.'

'How amazing.' I gazed back at where the mountain should have been – the 'hilt of the scimitar' that was Corfu, in Gerald Durrell's phrase. (A sickle, in the myth, rather than a scimitar – Saturn used it to lop off Uranus's testicles, so we're told, providing the Venetians with the two rocky outcrops in Corfu Town to build their fortresses on.)

'Yes, and just a stone's throw from Princess Margaret's helipad, too. They still bring in the New Year with old Dionysos sitting up in a painted wagon, I hear, and the men still gad about in women's clothing on Shrove Monday (I think it is), goodness knows why. And those huge what-do-you-call-them ... *phalluses*, they still strap those on in early spring, apparently, and stride about singing obscene songs by torchlight.'

'Are you sure?' I asked. It all sounded terribly unlikely to me.

'No,' she said, 'but I believe it's true. Don't be deceived by all the flash hotels and Paris boutiques. Corfu is still a primitive place, it has a wonderfully pagan heart.'

How paper-thin everything seemed back at Kester's house that evening after listening to Greta, how almost banal the tracts on astral travel and table-rapping, how positively hum-drum, how light as air Clive James' memoirs of his childhood in suburban Sydney. And as for Kester Berwick's pale existence – his notes in old envelopes, his yellowing playscripts and chipped cups and plates – it was little more than a faint smudge in the corner of the last page of history. I blew on his ghost and out it went like a light.

14

Through the letter-slit next morning dropped a card
for Kester. Michaelangelo's *David*. Not a perfect body
– in fact, with a real peasanty thickness here and there
– but perfectly rendered. Breathtakingly naked in a
way no man would ever appear, yet unerotic because
his nakedness we see (miraculously) as our own.
Should I read the card? Postmarked Florence, ten
days earlier. I hadn't the slightest compunction.

> Dear Kester,
>   Greetings from Florence. Isn't he divine? I'm
> on my way home at last and thought I'd drop
> in on you – hope you'll be there. In about a
> fortnight. I'll get the ferry from Brindisi. It'll
> be great to see you again.
> Love,
> William

Good God!
Frantic calculations. He could turn up on the
doorstep at any minute. He could be striding down
the road from the bus-stop in his blunt-nosed boots
at that very moment, as I stood there, gazing up the

hill. Was that the bus revving its motor right now at the top of the rise? What would I say? What would *he* say? Thunder-struck, he'd vanish back up the hill in silence. He'd get that sullen look and say something wounding, horrible. His eyes would widen with surprise, he'd give me an impish grin (always wide open to the unexpected, our William) and move in.

No, no, it was impossible. I'm no coward, but I know what I can bear without falling apart and what I can't. Suddenly in Rome, to put it bluntly, it had been cherry-tree chopping time and (as Clive had once tried to tell us, right at the beginning of our rehearsals) that need not be a tragedy. If those cherry-trees hadn't been chopped down at the end of Act IV, for instance, we'd have all kept circling each other like a mob of silly sheep, bleating on and on about 'love', until we drowned in our own fetid quagmire of it. Or gone mad and shot each other. At the first thud of those axes in the orchard off-stage, off we'd all flown like startled birds, out into the big world. Three cheers for the axemen!

Throwing a few clothes into a bag, I wondered where I could escape to. A couple of weeks should be enough – William wouldn't hang around. I admit to a pang or two – wanting to see those tender, bluish hollows just below the eyes, the knees poking at the jeans, hear the chirpy wise-cracks, just for five minutes, just long enough to start to lose my reason – but I quashed them by searching through Kester's bookshelves for something to take with me, reading out the titles one by one aloud. *Head of Orpheus Singing*, Kester's novel set on Lesbos – why not? And some Sappho, too. She seemed appropriate. Perhaps I could get a nice English murder mystery at the airport, something with a vicarage in it. And at the last minute I threw a few of Kester's dog-eared manuscripts into the bag as well – interesting to see what sort of thing this man (this elderly scribbler William seemed to find so fascinating) laboured away at.

Leery of the ferry-terminal, I got a cab to the airport. When I finally got to the head of the queue and had to say where I wanted to go, my eye lighted on the Sappho sticking out of my bag and I heard myself say 'Lesbos'. You couldn't get much further away from Corfu than Lesbos – it was practically in Turkey, having indeed been Turkish within living memory.

'Mytilene,' the clerk with the swallow's-wings eyebrows said tartly. 'Nowadays we don't say "Lesbos", we say "Mytilene".'

How oddly squeamish of them. 'Whatever,' I murmured.

'Just one?'

Just before we boarded, a fit of good manners overtook me. I tried to resist – there should be no *shoulds* for the lone traveller – but my upbringing got the better of me. I rang Greta.

'Just thought I should tell somebody that the house will be empty for a week or two. I suddenly felt like a change of scene.'

'I was wondering when boredom would strike. Where are you off to?'

'Lesbos.'

'Then you must meet Zoe. You'll adore her.' I didn't want to meet anyone. I wanted to float free. I especially didn't want to get entangled with someone called Zoe.

'Who is Zoe?'

'We've been friends for years. She's actually Kostas's wife . . . didn't I mention Kostas? You know, my *síndrofos* in Athens. What's the polite English word?'

'I don't know. But please don't bother her, Greta —'

'"Lover" sounds so messy, I always think. "Gentleman companion"? But you must meet Zoe. Sometimes I think I'm fonder of her than I am of Kostas. Pots of money – she owns a chain of beauty parlours. Born and bred on Lesbos. Knows it inside out. A Communist, of course, like Kostas. I'll telephone immediately. She'll be tickled pink – she'll probably pick you up at the airport.'

Why this fetish for connections? It was almost as if Greta feared that, unmet by Zoe, I might fail to exist. However, as we soared above the harbour where Alcinous had once moored his sleek, black ships, up and off towards the mainland (Ithaca a burst of yellow to the south), what my mind came to rest on was that blue-black Horus-eye just under William's collarbone. 'My *wedjat*,' he used to call it – one of his little affectations, knowing as he did almost nothing about Egyptian mythology. He's just a magpie.

I'm always prey to strange fixations in aircraft cabins – it must be the air pressure. When chalky-brown Athens appeared beneath our wings at dusk, tinged with a deceptive rosiness at that hour, the Horus-eye was still imprinted on my mind. And the silky skin around it. And other things. But Athens airport is no place for dreamers – neon-lit, foul-smelling, raucous – and I raced off to find the gate for Mytilene.

Untethered again. Panic and pleasure. I shuddered. Suddenly, from the top of my head to my toenails, I was totally, electrically alive.

— PART TWO —

I MORE THAN ENVY HIM

He is a god in my eyes, that man,
Given to sit in front of you
And close to himself sweetly to hear
The sound of you speaking.

Your magical laughter – this I swear –
Batters my heart – my breast astir –
My voice when I see you suddenly near
Refuses to come.

My tongue breaks up and a delicate fire
Runs through my flesh; I see not a thing
With my eyes, and all that I hear
In my ears is a hum.

The sweat runs down, a shuddering takes
Me in every part and pale as the drying
Grasses, then, I think I am near
The moment of dying.

Sappho

1

This was sheer sorcery. When I awoke the next
morning in a town I'd never heard of and gazed from
my window at coastlines whose beauty cut me to the
quick (although I somehow *knew* those piercing
blues, those jagged silhouettes, they were an old
dream come to life); when I stumbled down the
stairs and crossed the cobbled street to stand and
stare down at those ancient roofs tumbling in crazed
zigzags to the bay below, I felt I'd been spirited there.
I felt as if, in the hours of darkness, I'd been mag-
icked away to a place that had been waiting for me.
This was Molyvos. This, as it turned out, was ancient
Methymna. This was where the head of Orpheus,
still singing, had drifted to shore. This stony hillside
village, in other words, was where Kester Berwick
had lived for eight years before moving to Corfu.
Sorcery – no other word will do.

Or was it happenstance? Bucketing along across the
Aegean (the winds from Turkey can be vicious), I'd
fallen into conversation, against my better judgment,
with the two women belted into the seats beside me.
Elvira from Portland, Oregon, was large, especially
in her red wind-cheater, and had a startlingly blond

helmet of hair I couldn't take my eyes off. It gleamed, almost supernaturally. Her friend Andy, who was jammed up against the window, a bit tight-lipped and greenish, was not exactly wispy, nor was she mousy, but beside Elvira looked like a glove-puppet waiting in the wings. Elvira was a witch.

'You were expecting a pointy hat and a broomstick, right?' Elvira snorted. 'Not these days, my friend. As a matter of fact, at the professional level, I prefer the term "goddess theologian", but I have no problem with "witch". In Lesbos – you may not know this – access to the Earth Mother in her various guises is particularly direct. And that's what we're all about: connecting with the Earth. We say *yes!* to the body and *yes!* to the Earth!' She paused to observe Andy, who was being sick in dainty spasms into a paper bag. 'I see you're reading Sappho,' she went on. 'Like most people, you probably think it's all just myth and legend – those hymns to Aphrodite and Hera, the smoking altars, the burnt offerings . . . *Form in a dream, my lady Hera, sweetest shape, O come before me . . .* Well, you couldn't be more wrong.' A knowing smile. 'I've been there.'

'Where?' I asked, genuinely interested.

But at this point the plane lurched violently, Andy groaned, I dropped my Sappho, and it wasn't until we were waiting by the baggage carousel on the ground that we got talking again, this time about Australia. Elvira, it transpired, felt a very strong connection with Aboriginal spirituality. And that's when things went seriously wrong – or right, depending on how you look at it. That, as it were, is when the spell was cast.

Someone tapped at the Sappho under my arm. 'That Australian accent – it's a dead giveaway.' I swung around. Just for a second I thought it was Greta – the same smart cap of greying hair, the same smile and *soigné* stylishness. I grasped her warm, dry hand and felt the rings. That Kostas fellow clearly knew what he liked.

Shouting above the hubbub in the echoing hall, I said, 'How kind . . . you really shouldn't have,' not quite catching what Zoe said in reply – and then I was whisked outside to a waiting taxi. A wave to my witches and in no time at all Zoe and I were heading along the seafront towards the lights of Mytilene.

Chatting to Zoe was easy. She had a sort of American affability, even an American accent, faintly Bostonian. It wasn't until we'd cleared the ramshackled ugliness of Mytilene and seemed to be heading out into the moonless countryside beyond, that the chit-chat petered out. I wondered where she was taking me. Perhaps she had a villa in the hills to the north of the town, or perhaps there was a cosy little hotel out here amongst the olive-groves by the gulf she'd decided would be just perfect. On and on we purred through the blackness. Drowsiness crept over me. And then suddenly, on a mountain pass in the middle of nowhere, she said the most peculiar thing: 'I'm really looking forward to your paper, you know.'

'My paper?' Perhaps I'd misheard. My mind had long since lost its compass.

'Yes. What's the exact title again? Something about recontextualizing the body in late Sapphic texts, isn't it?'

I went cold. 'Excuse me, are you Zoe?'

'Zoe? No.' I couldn't see her face in the dark, but the voice was not alarmed, just puzzled.

'Stop the car.'

'What?'

'Stop the car,' I said, 'there's been a terrible mistake.' We drew over onto the gravel. The silence was drumming in my ears.

'Who do you think I am?' I spoke as evenly as I could.

'Why, aren't you Steven Werner from Sydney University?'

'No.'

'Well, who *are* you?'

'Who are *you?*'

'Oh, God . . .' She sank back into her seat. There was a very long pause. Then she laughed. 'I think I've just screwed up!'

So there we were, two complete strangers, sitting together in the dark in the wilds of Lesbos, one imagining she was ferrying an Australian classics scholar to a conference on Sappho, the other thinking he was safely tucked up under the wing of a Communist hairdresser called Zoe. And presumably, back at the airport in Mytilene, there was a very cross

classicist from Sydney, pacing up and down in the
cold outside the terminal.

'So what do we do now?' I asked. The driver sat
quietly smoking while the two foreigners sorted
themselves out. My Sappho expert from Massachusetts sat and thought. Then she sighed. 'Let's just
keep going. Let's go on to Molyvos. We'll call it fate.
I'm sure Sappho would have.' Then, as we pushed
out onto the road again, she added: 'Anyway, to tell
you the truth, the very *thought* of recontextualizing
the body in late Sapphic texts bores the shit out of
me.'

2

So. Shadowed – that's how I felt that morning in Molyvos. Shadowed by the ghost of a man I didn't know and wasn't sure I cared to. Like the head of Orpheus, ripped off by the Maenads in far-away Thrace to float, still singing, to this bay below me, Kester Berwick would not fall silent. Wherever I went his disembodied voice pursued me.

As I soon learnt, the Molyvos I was gazing down at – this brownish, Turkish-looking town falling away across the hillside like a crumpled skirt – had actually been almost *created* by Kester Berwick. Well, not literally – Achilles rampaged through it on his way to Troy, after all – but, at the very least, he was midwife, so to speak, to its rebirth. To put it another way: the blond-haired tourists ambling along the seafront far below me would not have been there without him. Nor would I.

Not that I knew any of this when I walked up the empty, cobbled street that first morning to the café hanging out over the drop. It was a sort of closed-in, wooden-verandah affair, perched on the cliff-edge just where the street became a tunnel beneath a canopy of wisteria. From the lilac gloom I stepped into the sweet-smelling café, hoping to give the ghost pursuing me the slip. But another, as it happened, was hovering, ready to pounce.

When the roughly shaven waiter stretched out his hand to put my coffee and baklava on the table, I could scarcely believe what I saw: traced onto that tender web just where the thumb and forefinger part was a Horus-eye. I stared at it. It stared at me. It twitched. And was gone.

I first saw William's Horus-eye the autumn after *The Cherry Orchard* closed. Late September, possibly October.

Summer had raised my spirits – Leila had got me work in a touring company putting on plays for children in a string of towns along the south coast. Still Ranyevskaya to my Peter Trofimov, she pricked at me now and then with remarks about William – 'William rang last night, he's off to Sicily with friends' (*what friends?*) or 'William might drop in on us tomorrow, he's in Torquay, something of Joe Orton's, I think it's *Entertaining Mr Sloane*' (but he didn't) – just little niggles, hoping I might unzip and tell all. But I didn't. And after all those months with few reminders I actually quite enjoyed the tiny spurts of pain she caused, like little jabs at a tender gum.

Then I saw the Horus-eye. Late one evening on Piccadilly station. William was leaning against an advertisement for Silk Cut, chatting with two friends. Lanky, at ease, one booted foot crossed casually over the other. One of the girls, the one with red curls with her back to me, was almost certainly Alex from *The Cherry Orchard*. I looked away. The girls laughed. When the train came in, the three of them squeezed on, but when I got to the doorway my courage failed me. The doors snapped shut. I stared through the glass at the bodies jammed against the door. William lifted an arm to grasp a strap. His shirt ballooned and there it was, just six inches from my nose, looking straight at me from its hiding-place under his right collar-bone: the Horus-eye. There was a jolt, then they were gone.

It was like an omen. A day or two later, flushed with the success of our *Cherry Orchard* the previous winter, we were to plunge into rehearsals for *Three Sisters*.

Most of the old gang was in it: Gareth was playing the drunken doctor, for instance, and Alex, with her wild, red curls, was playing that minx Natasha, while I got the part of Andrei, her husband, who means to become a professor in Moscow but ends up working for the local council in a provincial backwater, married to a grasping, unfaithful wife. (Again, I was a wee bit old for it at nearly thirty-five, but Andrei goes to seed so rapidly – marriage always has that effect on Chekhov's characters – that by Act II it hardly mattered.) Leila, not entirely with good grace, took the part of the eighty-year-old nanny. 'Yes, it's a small part, Leila, sweetheart,' Clive kept saying, 'but utterly *pivotal.*'

On the second or third night of rehearsals, when I walked in the door of Clive's living-room, there, lying back on the beanbag in the corner under the lamp, looking at me through his knees, was William. He raised one hand from his knee in a casual wave.

'Wait till you see his sketches for this one!' Clive said. 'They're brilliant!' William grinned.

The first time I ever saw *Three Sisters*, as a teenager in Adelaide, I was bored witless. Even in my twenties, when I went to an English production with Lisa, I was nearly frantic with boredom by interval, and we argued, I remember, about whether or not we should skip the second half or stay the distance. Almost all the characters in the play are bored as well – numb with boredom, occasionally even hysterical with boredom. '*Who cares?*', '*What does it matter?*', '*I'm tired of it all*' – the play is peppered with these cries of desperation between random silences. The only escape from boredom the sisters can imagine is moving back to Moscow.

The first read-through – at Clive's again – had been a dispiriting experience. What we had to work with, after all, was three sisters – a school-teacher, a post-office clerk and the bored wife of a Latin master – and a gaggle of army men, scratching around for something to make sense of their shallow lives in a nameless town in the steppes where the height of sophistication (they think) is to speak a little halting

Italian. (No wonder I'd found it a bit close to the bone in Adelaide.)

'Listen to me!' Clive had said when we'd come to the end that first night, the room a virtual morgue of broken lives, failed dreams and lost loves. 'In real life these people might have been tedious nobodies leading drab, trivial lives. So what? This isn't life, this is theatre, this is art. This *play* is beautiful.' We all stared dully at the carpet. There was a stale curry smell in the air, too, mixed with the acrid tang of Leila's cigarillos. 'They may be unhappy and not know what the point of living is, just flying on blindly like migrating geese; their loves may all go awry and happiness escape them; they may chatter on about working for the poor and future generations (as if drudgery, even in a good cause, could really bring contentment); but one thing they are is honest – they look their failed lives right in the eye and name things by their proper names.'

'What about the "*Moscow! Moscow!*" business?' Gareth asked, quite reasonably. 'How honest is that? They were obviously stuck out in the boondocks for life.'

'Yes, and what about all the adulterous love-affairs?' Leila said, drawing on a fresh cigarillo. 'What's honest about them?'

Clive was having none of that. 'What's dishonest about the adultery? Everyone knows, everyone understands, everyone forgives. Wouldn't you commit adultery if you were married to Andrei, for example? It's a lot more honest than the sort of tacky hypocrisy you get –'

'Careful!' said Leila.

'And as for Moscow,' Clive went on after a minute pause, 'well, of course the sisters know they'll never get there, obviously it's just a dream – what's wrong with dreaming? They never lift a finger to actually go there. Moscow doesn't really exist.' We all coughed and shifted in our seats, thinking about adultery and our own private Moscows. 'On the whole they're good to each other, too. Love may prove an illusion, but there's affection and warmth in abundance in all that muddle, and very little bitterness. That's what we have to bring out.'

Clive thought for a moment, not unmindful, I imagine, of how gossamer-thin the veil was between the lives he was describing and most of the ones in his living-room. 'And one other thing: did you notice how it's the least important of these characters, the least self-regarding, even the most clownish – the ones Gielgud and Olivier would never have dreamt of playing – who seem to have lit on the secret of contentment. Like Masha's silly husband. It's her husband, the Latin master, spending his days teaching a dead, useless language to bored schoolchildren, who understands, as he puts it, that *without form, life is over. Form* (and isn't that what "beauty" means, the "poetry" the sisters ache for in their workaday lives?) is something he finds in the smallest, most deeply ordinary things in the life he's actually living in that shithole of a place. He even finds it in Latin verb endings. The rest is all just words.'

This was sobering and quite unexpected from Clive. By the time he'd finished we were all looking at him rather than the carpet. 'So,' he said, as we rose to leave, 'I want our audience *riveted* by your provincial school-mistresses and empty-headed lieutenant-colonels. I want them bringing down the rafters with their applause. I want them to feel they've never seen anything so fucking *beautiful* since the day they were born.'

A couple of days later in Clive's kitchen during the break, making a show of looking for tea-bags while William made the coffee, I told him what Clive had said that first night. It was the first time we'd found ourselves alone together, and it was my way of being friendly without being intimate.

'I'm riveted already,' he said in that slightly broken-voiced way of his.

'Really? Why?'

He grasped the plunger. 'Do I really have to analyse it?' But he wanted to say something. 'I suppose I like it because it's so raw and so gentle at the same time. How's that?' He glanced up almost shyly and grinned. 'Not good enough? It's an irresistible combination, though, don't you think? OK, what else?'

He considered the dishmop. 'I love the way every-thing seems so all over the place in Chekhov, so out of control – it sounds like an orchestra with no conductor at first. Actually, you all sound deaf – you sound like an orchestra of deaf musicians. And then it hits you: there's a score alright, and every note's in place, not a single one's wasted. It's just not the kind of music you're used to, that's all, like Chinese opera or something. You have to learn how to listen to it. No, not Chinese opera – it's more like Debussy or someone the first time you hear them. Do you know what I mean?'

Then he plunged. And, as I watched his wrist push down on the plunger, at the instant it hit the bottom, something inside me tautened, almost to breaking point. For just a speck of a moment, as we stood motionless at Clive's sink, a bubble of understanding ballooned around us. The wrong word, the wrong tone and it would burst.

'I saw you the other night,' I said at last, 'at Piccadilly station.'

'Why didn't you say hullo?' His eyes were on the swirling coffee.

'You were with other people.'

Still looking down, he picked up the pot of coffee. 'Well, the next time you see me with other people,' he said, and then looked up at me, with the faintest of teasing smiles, 'you must promise me faithfully you'll come and get me.'

3

The best place to read a book in Molyvos is not down by the toy harbour behind the break-water where all the cafés are huddled and the fishermen mend their indigo nets – there's too much coming and going down there, too many Danes and Dutchmen filling in time. Nor is it on the pebbly beach beyond the old olive-press – the mussel-blue bay, the bobbing caïques and strolling, half-naked bodies are too beguiling, the eye wants no words, it just wants to look. No, the perfect place to read a book is in the ruins of the old Genoese fort.

Built by the Gateluzzi family from Genoa over six hundred years ago, before the Turks came, it crowns the cone-shaped hill Molyvos is draped over. Nobody much seemed to go there – at least not while I was there, during the lull between Easter and the full onset of summer – so I could perch up on the crumbling battlements, with a view across the empty straits to Turkey, with nothing but the fragrance of a few violets and wild roses to distract me, drifting off into other times, listening to long-dead voices. Occasionally I'd hear the cracked clanging of church-bells far below, and now and again the watchman would saunter out of his little stone hut and blow his nose noisily, but by and large it was just me, the warm stones and, distantly, Turkey.

The more you read about it, the more Lesbos appears to abound with miracles and with love. Every stony village on the island seems to harbour a wondrous icon, every tree to hide a cupid with stretched bow. And if you were to believe the stories that are told, the Lesbian forests of pine and oak were once alive with lissome nymphs, the glades with goatish shepherds; in Sappho's day the altars were thick with the rich, burnt fat of she-goats offered to Aphrodite, goddess of love; in her day 'Love the limb-loosener' loosened limbs and 'Love the honey-bee' swooped and stung until half the island was mad with love – the very sails of the ships off-shore were lovesick, Sappho tells us.

It is somewhere between Mytilene and Molyvos, I realized – not far, probably, from where I stopped the taxi that fateful night – that Chloe is supposed to have first watched Daphnis wash his naked, sun-burnt body in a spring and known in a flash that there was something she wanted to *do* with this goat-boy with hair as black as myrtle-berries – but *what*? And so she'd kissed him. Instantly set on fire, Daph-nis knew there was something more he wanted to do with pink-and-white-skinned Chloe, too, apart from pelting her with apples and teaching her the Pan-pipe – but what could it have been?

As it turned out, what he *wanted* was to 'lie down',

'get big and ready for action' and then be 'guided into the passage that he had been trying so long to find'. (The author, Longus, is quite specific about this in my modern, unexpurgated edition.) This comes as no surprise to a modern reader, but what is disarming is the length of the passage from inno-cence to knowledge: it takes a year and a half of dalliance and tomfoolery to get to it. Then the story abruptly ends with Chloe going to her wedding a virgin.

Perhaps that is miracle enough, but the same woods and mountain slopes where Sappho mooned with her 'violet-tressed maids' and youths 'like tender saplings' also teemed with miracles of a more abrupt kind: here St Paul struck the earth and a spring bubbled forth; there an icon of the Virgin ('Our Lady of the Sweet Kiss') flew from a ship's mast to the top of a rock on shore (twice); here Saracen pirates were foiled by a phantom wave miles from the sea; there a mosque kept falling down until a Christian cross was placed on the minaret; here an icon made with the blood of mur-dered monks casts out devils and heals the sick; there a ploughman who had lost his ox simply vanished into thin air every time a Turkish bandit tried to shoot him; and everywhere the bones of saints have been unearthed through the extraordinarily accurate dreams of the faithful. (One of the saints was the Byzantine Empress Irene, who had had her son's eyes stabbed out in her lust for power, although this misdemeanour must have struck the saint-makers as forgivable.)

Down in the village the echoes of these wonders were now faint – at least, to my eye. The landscape of Lesbos, as every writer keeps telling you, has changed remarkably little over the millennia – the pines, chestnut, oak and olives are still thick on the hills, herons still stalk the salt-flat beside the gulf and goat-herds amble across the fields munching on pistachio-nuts as if Daphnis might still be smooching with Chloe among the poppies behind the next barn. But down at the water's edge in Molyvos love and miracles wear modern dress. The sleek youths slouching across the handle-bars of their motorcycles in the sun would, I imagined, find Daphnis contemptible – poor, patient Daphnis, wooing Chloe with his eyes, and then his lips and hands, season after season, not even knowing (despite the antics of his goats) what else to woo her with, just knowing there was more; and it was hard to picture the surly waiters in the tavernas by the harbour calling on Christ to shield them from a Turkish onslaught except in the most perfunctory way, as a kind of superstitious tribal oath. Nor could I see the slightest link between the Texan lesbians striding about in their shorts and boots, thumbs in knapsack straps, all gender-theoried up to the eyeballs from courses they'd completed in Houston or Dallas, and Sappho of Lesbos, doting mother, dead for love of a handsome ferryman. She was tumbled like oak-leaves (as she put it) by love, she shuddered, 'pale as the drying grasses' from love . . . for girls in apple-groves, certainly, girls with 'violet-sweet breasts', girls in saffron blouses and purple dresses, 'high-flying swallows' lured to earth by her lyre . . . Still, I can see no connection – I don't think any of these sturdy modern women, brimming over with well-being and bits of Foucault, could write a poem which simply said 'Pain drips.' Besides, down to the last crone on her death-bed, this is a fiercely heterosexual town, there's a phallus rearing from every window in Molyvos. Texan lesbians don't belong.

Apart from Achilles and Odysseus (who came here long before he reached that beach on Corfu), the Romans, Franks, Catalans and Genoese were here (indeed, I was sitting in their castle); and the Turks were here for over four hundred years, leaving behind them a bath-house, a mosque, all those hanging verandahs and (some would say) a certain cast to the eyes of the locals. Oddly enough, though, I had no sense of this Lesbos, let alone of Sappho's or the saints', while reading Kester's book, *Head of Orpheus Singing*, set in that very town. It was bizarre.

He must have begun to write it, I now imagine, in his room down near the very wisteria-covered, cobbled street where I was staying, although he finished it on Corfu in the house with the high, wooden ceiling and whitewashed walls that Arthur had told me about. It appears to be about a middle-aged Australian widower who comes to Molyvos to teach English, becomes the inseparable friend of a teenaged peanut-vendor called Euripides and then, when Euripides and his weeping mother move to Australia, gets married to a tedious, clinging woman he feels no passion for (a student of his from Australia called Claire – a pretty but watery name) and settles down in Molyvos forever. He has a few ricocheting sorts of encounters with a clutch of other characters – a retired headmistress, the police, assorted foreigners – but basically that seems to be the story. Not for a moment, of course, did I think that that was what the book was *about*, so I quickly read it twice.

Pain certainly drips. Little by little, page by page, everyone drops away. Gradually, the gentle widower from Sydney loses everybody: his American painter friend, his wild, footloose German friend Monika and her drugged admirer, and, of course, Euripides (a sort of male Eurydice, spirited away to the underworld of Australia) . . . everybody leaves, dies or disappears, one after the other. He even loses his homeland, in a sense, marooned at the end in Molyvos with a 'wife' he feels nothing but a vague affection for and his humble 'lyre' – the voice of Orpheus singing on and on in his greying head. At certain moments and in certain places, he also had what he curiously describes as Unitive Experiences.

So it's about loss and the kind of inner grace you need to bear it. It's about contentment, even though life's most precious gift – friendship – slowly seeps away. Everyone grows smaller and smaller and then disappears.

This is the nub of it – friendship in its many guises. All those meat and onion stews in the book, all those fishermen he writes about with their wine-red nets, the green figs in syrup, the molten sea – none of that is what it's about. Nor emigration to Australia or never going home.

It's about that many-hued, subtle, fragile art we call in our hale and hearty way 'friendship': the teacher's for his pupil, the adept's for his guru, the neighbour's for the man next door, one villager's for another, even the casual diner's for some bird of passage at his table. And woven in and out of all these friendships is an erotic thread – barely perceptible, except, perhaps, when Euripides turns somersaults on the beach and rushes over to sit beside the English teacher, shining and dripping, his naked chest heaving – but it's there. Erotic like a peacock's tail, erotic like red shoes – not sexual. (Perhaps in real life the erotic and the sexual overlap from time to time, but not in this book – not even in marriage.)

In an ancient Greek village there was little space for friendship in the delicious, modern, urban sense of the word – that completely voluntary sense of 'I just like you, that's all, and feel more fully *me* when I'm with you'. In ancient Methymna – and I suspect things aren't as different in Molyvos today as one might think – there was kin and there was the village, walled against a hostile world.

Odysseus, we notice, doesn't seem to have had any friends in the modern meaning of the word at all, just his household and his companions in adversity – his 'mates', we would have said in Adelaide when I was younger. I suppose that's why in *The Iliad* the passionate friendship of Achilles and Patroclus (the 'dearest life' he has ever known) seems so shocking – people have been sniggering and smirking about those two, calling them sodomites and lovers, for over two thousand years (especially the Romans).

I suppose, too, that this lack of space for voluntary friendship in the traditional village accounts for that surge of delight we foreigners often feel at the sudden intimacies that flower as we pass through on our travels. Of course such attachments flower – we're neither kin nor comrades, we're a virgin space in which innocence can be lost simply because of *liking* somebody. Old habits die hard, though: the locals usually find it difficult to think beyond friendship as a mutually advantageous arrangement, while the foreigners' minds are apt to drift towards sex. No wonder the result is all too often bonking for payment (a gift or a stolen wallet) on the beach.

No wonder, too, that the Romans, with their love of great cities, glimpsed other possibilities and marvelled at them. In a city like Rome there were lots of spaces for attachments outside the family and the 'village' – that tight little hub of comrades, colleagues and associates every life revolves around. Cicero, I remember from my brief flirtation with the classics, called friendship 'the greatest thing in the world'. The pleasure to be had in a friend, according to Cicero, left wives, orgies, fame and wealth in the shade. Horace too, a few years later, said that so long as he was in his right mind, he knew he'd find nothing to compare with a 'pleasant friend'. Nothing!

In Adelaide, when I was young, none of us would have said a thing like that, even under torture. Nor, I suspect, would anyone in Clive's North London flat. Health, a good job, a loving family, even money . . . none of those things would have raised an eyebrow. But *friendship*?

We had friends, naturally – people we just liked – or would have said we had. If we'd been pressed to say why we liked them, though, we'd have been nonplussed. Cicero, two thousand years ago, was astonished by precisely this carelessness: everyone takes great pains to select their sheep and goats, he wrote, and knows exactly what qualities to look for in their livestock, but ask them what they look for in a friend, infinitely more precious, and they're struck dumb. It would have been much the same in Adelaide – not that anyone ever asked: we'd have happily rattled off our requirements in a dog, a house, a car or a good accountant, but why we liked somebody . . . it would have seemed too obvious and at the same time too vague to bother finding words for. So-and-so is *fun*, we might have said, if really nailed down, so-and-so is *interesting* (not *boring*, in other words) – clued up on football, wine, rock music, fishing, whatever subject was thought to be *interesting*. Easy to get on with, too – good-natured, tolerant (of us), reliable (wouldn't let us down), generous . . . Then we'd have tried to change the subject, obscurely anxious that someone might think we had a lurking desire to do to this friend what Daphnis eventually did to Chloe.

If we were clear about anything at all, it was that 'love' for a friend had nothing whatsoever to do with 'love' of the kind that climaxes in 'getting big and ready for action'. I'm not sure that women have always *quite* understood the difference, but we males have no doubts.

4

Who should I see waving at me from a restaurant table on the cobbles down by the harbour the following evening but my witch, Elvira!

'Why, hello!' she called. 'Come and join the coven!' At her elbow Andy giggled. Together with half a dozen other women, Elvira was waiting for the moon to rise before setting out for the site of an ancient temple to Aphrodite, somewhere in the mountains to the south.

'What's going to happen?' I asked, squeezing in at their table.

'A major ceremony. Obviously I can't tell you the details, but believe me, we're expecting big things tonight.' I glanced around at the eager faces of the women at the table, all rosy in the early evening light. The sky was an extraordinary green, streaked with orange.

It was details I wanted to hear, though. What would these witches actually do at the temple under the swollen moon? Chant ancient litanies? Summon up the goddess in her shell of foam? Sacrifice a she-goat? Would spells be cast? Images of flaming torches, blood-smeared foreheads and drifts of aromatic smoke flicked across my mind. Here on Lesbos, in point of fact, the aroma of divinity traditionally reaches the nostrils well before the tapers are lit: if a goddess has a mind to make her presence felt on some mountain peak or in some hallowed grove, she's wont to charm her worshippers with a whiff of something sacred as a curtain-raiser. It's a Lesbian speciality, apparently. Or so I've been told.

'We'll be worshipping the Mother Goddess – that's all I can tell you,' Elvira said. 'She's present everywhere, of course' – and here she gestured at the mountain ridges etched against the sky, the gleaming bay, the postcard stands, the empty coffee cups – 'but we have ways of making her presence real in our bodies now.'

'Yes,' said Andy, all in blue tonight, 'ancient ways.' Everyone smiled at me in a knowing manner.

'The veil between the worlds is very thin tonight, you see,' Elvira said. 'We aim to pierce it.'

I wished, when they set off, I could have stowed away in their minibus, under the pile of black-handled knives, star-spangled gowns and hazlewood wands I imagined they had lying at the back. I'd have loved to see the piercing of the veil. I'd never really had a truly Unitive Experience.

And then I had one.

Well, it wasn't exactly Unitive, but it was definitely an Experience. Right there on the quay in Molyvos I suddenly saw Leila. In fact, I smelt her first, catching the whiff of her cigarillo. I looked up and there she was, candle-lit, risen up before me in the flesh.

'Darling!' she said. 'Just been talking about you – and all of a sudden there you are! Are you sure you're not an apparition?' She bent to kiss me, and in a flash, in the cloud of warm Leila smells I knew so well (the perfume, the smoke, her lightly powdered skin), I saw the blue neon glare of the Shalimar, heard the thud of axes in the cherry orchard, caught the squish of the coffee-plunger, glimpsed the Horus-eye, the spiky hair . . . in the blink of an eye I was in North London, looking back at Leila on the waterfront in Molyvos through a spyglass across months and even years.

'Leila! What are you doing here?'

'I'm having a dirty weekend, darling. Well, a dirty week, actually. I met this *delicious* man – literally edible, let me tell you – in a phone-booth on St Pancras station. Terribly Greek and masterful. He said I simply *must* go to Molyvos with him before the summer hordes arrive – he's got a house here, up near that ruin on top of the hill. Pops over all the time.'

'Who were you talking to about me, then?'

'Why, William, of course, the poor dear is absolutely – But here's Yanni!'

Still looking through my spyglass, quite dazed now, I stood up to shake the hand of a middle-aged, slightly pudgy man I took an instant dislike to, partly because he'd broken off Leila's sentence, partly because I didn't find him remotely edible and partly because of that irritating animal tautness that grips men while they sniff the air for a rival.

'Have you eaten? Let's all have dinner together here, then,' Leila said, 'and catch up on the gossip.' Yanni said nothing, but sat down anyway, calling out and nodding to this one and that on the busy quay. He was at home. 'God, it's amazing, running into you like this! It's like seeing a ghost. Now, you must tell me *everything*, absolutely every little thing that's happened since I last saw you.'

As it turned out, I had very little chance to say anything at all during the first course, what with Leila's tales about who was doing what, and to whom, in London, and Yanni's long and lively discussions in Greek with every passing male. I also suspected that in some mysterious, Leila-like way she already knew every little thing that had happened since she'd last seen me.

Then suddenly, just as the waiter dropped my almond fingers onto the table, Leila caught sight of the book beside my plate. '*Head of Orpheus Singing*! Fancy that! So you've been reading Kester.'

'Yes, have you read it?'

'Read it when it first came out, darling. I've known Kester for years.'

So. All of a sudden things were kaleidoscoping into place.

'It's set here, you know, in Molyvos, although he calls it something else.'

'So I gather.'

'It's not very good, is it.'

'It's interesting.'

'That ghastly wife who pops up at the very end . . . God, I laughed!'

'That amused you, did it?'

Leila considered me for a moment, a tiny smile at the corner of her lips. 'A wife drops down like the final curtain at the end of practically everything the dear man's written. Needless to say, there's never been a wife, wives aren't his thing. That wife's a penance. Kester's a lovely man – the gentlest, sweetest man, a saint, really – not my type, of course, but lovely.' Leila's 'type', as we all knew, ran more to Costa Rican shark-fishermen and Brazilian cattleranchers. She was always off on package tours to South America.

'I was a student of his, you see, at the acting studio he ran in Hammersmith years ago – in the late fifties, just before he threw it all in and moved here, as a matter of fact. I grew quite attached to him, really. But no, Kester isn't the marrying kind.' She doodled with her fork in the honey oozing from her baklava. 'The whole book's a sham, really. I thought he'd have more courage.'

'What do you mean? It's a novel.'

'What I mean is, Kester wasn't here to teach English, darling – that was an accident. He was here to escape. And somehow or other, I doubt he was just a father-figure to the peanut-sellers of Molyvos.'

'But you're fond of him.'

'Oh, yes. I adore him. So does Yanni, in his fashion. It was Kester, believe it or not, who taught him his first English. Half the town went to his classes in the early sixties.' She glanced over at Yanni, who was deep in conversation with a passing local, telling beads as he talked. 'Do you want to know why Kester really came to Greece in the first place?'

'To escape, you said.'

'Well, obviously to escape – why else would anyone come to Greece? To live a more fulfilling life? Just look around you.' We both turned our heads to peer into the gathering dusk. Knots of tourists wondering where to eat. Greeks smoking. Iridescent water. A molten horizon. 'No, what I meant was: would you like to know what he was escaping *from?*'

It grew quite dark while she told her tale, sitting beside me in a pool of yellow light on the cobbles. The moon came up behind us, high above Turkey, and one by one the fishing-boats stole out of the harbour, lanterns swaying, to prowl for octopus across the bay.

5

Not long after the war, Leila told me, in a large, coastal town near Sydney (it must have been Newcastle, but Leila was vague about anything south-east of Suez), Kester Berwick had been teaching drama at some sort of 'adult education outfit'. There was lots of Movement, apparently – 'Form and Movement were the core of good theatre for Kester, as well as Voice, but not words' – with rehearsals like African tribal gatherings, performed to the beat of the tom-tom. 'They had nothing, of course – no props, no real rehearsal space, no money – some mining town out in the bush just after the war, you can imagine.'

'Newcastle isn't out in the bush, Leila,' I said, but I could tell from the look she gave me that she thought I was being pedantic. The whole town was stripped for props – landladies found their chairs and tea-services gone, wives missed their quilts and slippers, light-bulbs disappeared from landings and hallways, wedding photographs vanished from their frames. Books, gramophones, tables, violins – all over the city things just kept vanishing into thin air. 'It was like some divine curse. Kester would've been

in his element, of course – he positively relishes con-
juring something out of nothing.'

They tried a bit of Ibsen, a scene or two from
Wilder, but it was the staging of a French play –
Martine, by Jean-Jacques Bernard, just a touch
avant-garde, exquisite but numbing – which turned
Kester's life upside-down. No, not just that – it
picked him up and flung him right across the world.

One night during a black-out, while Kester and his
actors were huddled around hurricane-lamps reading
their lines, a boy nobody knew walked out of the
shadows and stood in the hissing glare, his eyes fixed
on Kester. Just a boy, no more than sixteen. Thin,
with a long, strong face and remarkable eyes.

(I like to imagine a sort of *twang* in the room – the
gentle plucking of a string – when Kester looked up
from his script and into those eyes. In those days, as
I know from the photographs in the drawer in Gastouri, although Kester was in his mid-forties, there
was a kind of drilled playfulness about him, a sort of
honed sexiness – in a word, a foxiness – that I like to
think locked into something in that raw but promising face on the edge of the circle of light.)

What Kester was looking at for those few seconds
before the boy spoke was his joy and his doom. It
was the rest of his life.

Young John Tasker had come to ask about 'doing
something', if there was something for him to do –
anything, really, he just wanted to get involved in
theatre. Acting, props, sound effects – anything.

On opening night, as his innocent parents proudly noted, there was his name in the programme – twice:

Assistant Stage Manager: John Tasker
Prompter: John Tasker

Martine was a moderate success. A play about a French peasant girl's infatuation with a city journalist by 'the master of the pause' was not, perhaps, an ideal choice for Newcastle just after the war. And the sky ended up green instead of blue owing to a dyeing accident in somebody's bathtub. Still, the reviewers, while they didn't rave, were not unkind.

After the final curtain fell, John did not go straight home with his mother and father. Instead, against their better judgment (actors had some funny habits), he joined the cast in the kitchen at the back of the hall for a little celebration. He waited, glass of cordial in hand, while the crowd around Kester thinned. Gradually (would they never go?) the dishes were washed, the chattering school-teachers, shop-assistants and secretaries drifted off home, lights were turned out and John said to Kester, alone now by the sink, under a bare light-bulb: 'Let's do something mad.' And Kester went hard and soft in that way we all do, knowing this was it, he was on, and they went out the back, got on his motorcycle and roared off to the beach. And John wrapped his arms around Kester, huddling with his nose at his neck behind him, shouting insane, boyish things into the bitter wind, and when they got there, way down near the crashing blackness far from the lights, he wrapped his arms around him again, for warmth and because he was ready. And they stayed there on the cold sand a very long time. He was an angel – a loose-limbed, wicked angel – and that night after the streetlights went out Kester took this floppy-haired angel firmly, but gently, in hand.

'It depends who you talk to, naturally,' Leila said (now onto her second retsina), 'but it's hard to avoid the impression that John was in some sense using Kester, as a stepping-stone to bigger things. Perhaps that's harsh – I suppose we all "use people" in the early stages of an affair: after all, there must be something we want from them or we wouldn't be attracted to them in the first place.' She looked across at Yanni, who was inspecting a friend's new car in the shadows some distance away. 'But I know John. He's a passionate, stubborn, ambitious, rather wounded man. There he was, a small-town boy with talent, and no real father – his father never spoke, crushed by all the things my father was eventually crushed by . . . the wars, the depression, their failed lives . . . and all of a sudden a father-figure appeared, a teacher, a good man, who talked to him about Ibsen and Chekhov and God and London and Paris, and promised to take him there on a ship. The perfect lover – for a time.' It sounded almost Greek.

The Newcastle community was shattered in 1951

when Kester told them he was off to Europe. He'd been a pioneer. If any eyebrows were raised when it became known that their youngest member would be accompanying him, if any knowing glances were exchanged or vague qualms voiced, we'll never know. Off they sailed, John just eighteen, to Italy, then on to the Tyrol (where Kester had lived before the war), and finally to London.

Everything John saw, though, everything he tasted – the chaos of Genoa, the emerald-green slopes of the Tyrol with its red window-boxes, steeples and tiny castles, tea at the countess's in Paris, the circus that was London (and its pubs and clubs) – he saw and tasted through the bars of a cage. But Kester loved him too much (as he put it to Leila) to keep the door shut and, after some time, off John flew. There were arms open wide for him all over London.

'That was all rubbish, of course,' Leila said, flicking ash into a handy saucer.

'What was?'

'The "loving him too much" business. I never believed in that for a moment. Mustn't clip the fledgling's wings, mustn't stand in the way of Destiny, mustn't want, mustn't hold on. It's nothing but self-delusion.'

'It might be the Buddhist thing.'

'I don't know what it is, darling, but it certainly makes him miserable. To tell you the truth, I don't think it's got anything to do with Buddhism, I think it's the teacher thing. It's invariably fatal. Always the teacher – that's Kester's trouble. Always wanting to bring light, always wanting to bless. And that's always a disaster. What is the pupil supposed to do, once he's been taught? What is the acolyte to do, once the mysteries have been revealed? Anyone with an ounce of self-respect will obviously stand up one day, say, "Thanks very much, it's been a real education", and head for the door.'

Sometimes, too, I thought to myself, like Sappho's simple ferryman, who panicked one day and took off for Sicily, the pupil begins to choke on the teaching, leaving the master to his refined delights (and wrinkles) for other, often earthier, philosophies. Unlike Sappho, Kester didn't set off in pursuit or throw himself off a cliff, but took on more pupils. According to Leila, all you ever saw at the studio in the days following John's defection was a kind of measured calm:

'Of course, he believes in reincarnation,' she said, grinding out her cigarillo with a couple of vicious stabs, 'so I suppose for him it's all part of a longer story. Personally, the idea of reincarnation frightens hell out of me. The thought of having to go through the whole damn thing over and over again . . .'

We sat there for a while, the two of us, listening to the lapping water and thinking (Leila, too, no doubt) of the unequal bargains we had both struck in our own lives, afraid to be left with nothing – all the times we'd said 'yes' when we'd meant 'no', fed someone when we'd been famished ourselves, laughed at jokes we didn't find amusing, been sisters, uncles, fathers, friends and lovers to people who in the end had needed something else. And the slow unstitching that had followed, endlessly painful, an infinity of wounding rents and jabs.

'It was the third time for Kester, you see, that's the point,' Leila went on. 'The first time, just before the war, he'd taken a young man called Alan Harkness to England with him to break into the theatre there. Kester would only have been . . . what? In his mid-thirties, I suppose. They'd been running a sort of experimental theatre company together in Adelaide. One day Sybil Thorndike had popped along to some performance of theirs – or so the story goes – something Japanese, I seem to recall, Kester always had a penchant for masks and robes – and after the performance Dame Sybil had said to them both, as one does at such moments: "Do keep in touch," or "If you're ever in London . . ." – you know the sort of thing. Well, you should never say that to Australians, as we know, because they almost certainly will. Not that she was much help when they eventually got to London – she probably had difficulty remembering quite who they were. They ended up at Dartington Hall down in Devon – do you know about Dartington Hall? I've never got to the bottom of it all myself – it's one of those idealistic sorts of set-ups . . . you know, a bit of pig-farming and pottery in a medieval setting, all terribly umbilical and spiritually improving. It's still there as far as I know.

'Anyway, Michael Chekhov, the playwright's nephew, set up a theatre-workshop there in the mid-thirties to teach his famous Technique. Don't roll your eyes – everyone thought he was a genius . . . Yul Brynner, Gregory Peck . . . a lot of very fine actors have been devotees. Actually,' she said, opening her tin of cigarillos but not taking one, 'Marilyn Monroe once said that working with Michael Chekhov was the most spiritual experience she ever had.'

I could just see it: the hand-picked students improvising Living Statues on the lawn beside the banqueting hall, all searching for their Higher Egos, radiating Invisible Essences and striving to please their Russian master – a dangerous cauldron of rivalries, infatuations, alliances, betrayals and arcane beliefs. And bobbing around in this soup (according to Leila) was Kester Berwick, watching his friend Alan falling under the Russian's spell.

'Won over body and soul, he was, while Kester, one gathers, began to sense that he didn't belong. Well, that's not quite how he explained it to me – what he told me was that he decided he didn't want to be an actor after all, locked into somebody else's method, he wanted to teach. As for Alan, it wasn't just the Technique that won him over. Bit by bit he was won over by some of the young women in Chekhov's collective as well.'

Taking another sip of retsina, Leila eyed me over the rim of her glass in the hope that I might ask for details.

'Really?' I said. I would not be teased.

'Yes,' she said, enlivened as always by the prospect of airing a spot of dirty linen. 'Let's be brutally frank – Alan was spreading his wings – which is what Kester would have said he wanted him to do, but still, to have to watch it happen, day after day . . . the empty bed night after night, the glances over breakfast . . . well, it must have been torture.' We both sat in silence for a moment, picturing it in vivid detail.

'To tell you the truth,' Leila went on, 'reading between the lines, I get the feeling that Kester was a dud at Dartington Hall. Chekhov, after all, wanted to create a troupe of first-class performers, he wanted to reinvent the theatre, he was a guru with a world-wide mission, and this young Australian, I think, failed to impress him in the end. Not a complete washout, just not up to the mark. Basically, although Kester's an excellent teacher (partly thanks to Chekhov), I suspect that he can't act. So, gathering up his skirts, he said he'd leave the studio and get on with his writing. Well, as we know . . .'

Reaching across for Kester's book, she flicked through a few pages, reading a few sentences at random, then snapped it shut. She sighed. 'Life's a let-down for almost all of us, let's face it,' she said, with a sudden rueful smile, 'but in Kester's case, ever since he was booted out of Dartington Hall, it's been downhill all the way, really, an endless anticlimax. I shouldn't say that, should I? But, to be honest, what has he ever achieved? Where are the plays and novels he was going to write? After all, he's had fifty years. Where's the recognition, the trickle of students who've gone on to fame and fortune? Yanni would put it even more brutally: Where (he would ask) is the house, the car and the wife and kids?' She paused, lowered her voice, and examined her mauve fingernails. 'Yet I know that's a cockeyed thing to say. I know it, but I can't quite put my finger on why.'

We both sat and contemplated the night beyond the hubbub on the quay. Leila finally lit the cigarillo she'd been fiddling with.

'The word that comes to mind,' Leila said after a smokey pause – it was almost a murmur – 'is *beauty*. It's got something to do with beauty. But for God's sake don't ask me what I mean by it.'

When Chekhov decided to move his studio to America to escape the looming war, Kester tried to talk Alan into going to France with him instead. 'Damned if I know how he thought they'd survive – writing radio plays and teaching method acting? In the south of France in 1938? They'd learnt their French in evening classes in Adelaide, for God's sake. No, Kester didn't have a hope in hell. Alan went to America with the studio, naturally, and after the war got married – to a Swiss woman, I think, one of the members of the collective, with a strange name I can't recall. Mathilde, was it? Something like that. Alan became quite a successful theatre director later on, apparently, somewhere over on the West Coast.'

'How did Kester react? He must have been distraught.'

'Why even ask? He didn't believe in wild displays of feeling, except on the stage when called for by the script. Kester took himself off to France and Austria collecting folk-tales for Michael Chekhov – and Alan Harkness – to turn into uplifting plays over in America. Pathetic, really. Until he got a telegramme to tell him his services were no longer needed. In Austria he taught English for a while, mostly to Jews, I think, wanting to get out to England or America. When war finally broke out, he got himself onto the last ship to leave Italy for Australia.

'He taught again on board, of course,' she said, pouring herself just a little more of the yellow-coloured wine. 'It's a curse with him, this teaching business. A bit of English during the day, some ball-room dancing in the evening. He'd have been in his element, obviously – a whole shipful of rootless people. Teachers adore the rootless, have you noticed? The moment they clap eyes on them they yearn to give them roots. I dare say at this very moment he's broadening the mind of some bored young recruit he's picked up outside the barracks in Athens. Is it Athens he's gone off to?'

'Nobody seems to know.'

A scrawny ginger cat slunk out from beneath the table to rub itself against Leila's legs and she bent to stroke it, but distractedly – she was still remembering. 'The Alan Harkness story ended rather sadly, I must say. One day, when Kester was on his way back to England after the war – with John Tasker in tow, as it happens – the ship put in at some small port on the west coast, and Kester ducked into town to buy some fresh fruit. Last chance to stock up before the long haul across to . . . wherever ships stopped in those days. India? Africa? He's always been a bit of a health nut, you know, terribly picky about what he eats. Funny, isn't it, how so many "spiritual" people are. Have you noticed? Anyway, he brought the fruit back to the cabin and started to unwrap it. One of the sheets of newspaper it was wrapped in fell to the floor. When he bent to pick it up, he saw a little headline near the bottom of the page: AUSTRALIAN ACTOR KILLED. It was Alan. Car stalled on a railway crossing. I believe Kester wrote a very gracious note to his widow.'

A sudden gust of wind off the water sent napkins, ice-cream wrappers and scraps of paper scattering across the cobbles, then just as abruptly died away. We just sat quietly and thought our own thoughts. From somewhere behind the restaurant came a muffled burst of bouzouki music.

'You said there were three . . .' (I searched for the word) '. . . failed loves, Leila. The first was Alan, the last was John – who was the second?'

'Number Two was an Austrian soldier, killed in the war, fighting for Hitler. Just a boy, really. Raymond. Kester showed me his photograph once – Raymond's parents sent it to him with the most touching letter after the war. Not exactly handsome, but open-faced, guileless. I'm not sure which trip he met him on, or how – all those Franzes and Willis and Rudis he kept in touch with, I could never keep up. Anyway, by the time I met him at the studio in Hammersmith in the mid-fifties, he must have been riddled with grief. Not, as I say, that you'd have known to look at him. Still, inside, the sense of sliding without a companion into old age, not having made much of a mark in the world, must have been almost unbearable, don't you think?'

To be honest, I wasn't sure. It depended on what Leila meant by 'a companion' (although I had a fairly good idea). Uncompanioned by a spouse or lover, was one really a failure as a human being? And as for 'making a mark in the world', almost all of us had to bear passing through it without trace.

'At any rate,' Leila said after a thoughtful pause, 'he seems to have felt defeated.'

And, in his defeat, he drifted south, like thousands of others, looking for nothing more than some work to pay the rent and a measure of tranquillity. Just an ordinary little boat, much buffeted, in search of a quiet anchorage.

Athens looked promising in 1959 for someone with Kester's inclinations – plenty of idle young men for him to draw out, to take a Socratic interest in; cheap rent; an Australian climate without (as he'd have seen it then) the disadvantage of being a cultural backwater at the end of the world. (Greece was, needless to say, a cultural backwater of the most stagnant kind, and still is, as bad as anything the three sisters suffered, but it was not at the end of what was thought to be the world, it was dirt cheap, it conferred a certain status on foreigners who would have been nobodies at home, and turned a blind eye to the kind of prowling which would have been scandalous at home. And if you ever woke up one morning and wondered what on earth you were doing there, you could always think of Pericles or Plato, which was out of the question in Turkey or Tasmania.)

One hot morning in Athens Kester overslept. When he answered the banging on his door, he found himself standing groggily in his pyjamas in the presence of one of the city's most powerful, and colourful, men. It was Michael Goutos, tall, grey-haired, and no doubt elegantly suited, with rough edges to his suaveness that Kester must have found appealing. While Kester perched on his crumpled bed, a little flustered, Goutos strode back and forth across the room, outlining his plans for his native village, Molyvos – the tourist hotel, electricity, sewage pipes, the new road (at that time the bus from Mytilene took hours to grind across the mountains to the northern coast) . . . and English-speaking locals to milk the expected hordes of foreigners of their dollars and pounds and marks and francs. And Kester Berwick (or so Goutos had been told at the British Council in Athens) was the perfect man to teach the town officials, the shopkeepers, hotel-managers and knick-knack sellers the English they'd need for the job. Single, keen to stay in Greece, desperate for a work permit, a teacher by profession ... *Mr Berwick, come to Molyvos, come immediately. You will fall in love with Molyvos.*

Kester smoothed his rumpled pyjamas, considered the chiselled, smoothly shaven features of the towering Greek beside the wash-stand and thought to himself that he indeed might.

It was a graceful forking of the ways for Kester. With John Tasker now back in Australia (stranded there, ironically enough, when his English lover failed to follow him to the antipodes), Kester's homeland was like a haunted house to a child – alluring, almost unbearably so, but threatening as well. By taking the boat to Lesbos, then rattling across the mountains in that bus stuffed with peasants in Turkish pantaloons, bleating goats and half-dead chickens, Kester was turning his face in a new direction. Over the next eight years, Molyvos, with Kester's help, was transformed into a smartish, although still sleepy, resort, and in his various barely furnished rooms, in his class-room and on the grassy headlands and tiny, pebbly beaches around Molyvos, Kester slid with as much dignity as he could muster into white-haired middle-age.

Yanni had disappeared altogether by the time we reached this point in the story. 'He'll be in one of the tavernas round the back,' Leila said, her mind switching suddenly to more immediate matters. 'I think I'll go and drag him away.'

'But you still haven't told me,' I said, as she fussed with her drachmas and told me I absolutely *must* come up to the house for coffee ('you'll die when you see the view'), 'how it is you came to be talking about me to William.'

'I'm sure I told you – you've just forgotten. He rang me here from Corfu – such a sweetie. He's staying in Kester's house, as a matter of fact. Didn't you know?' She kissed me on the cheek. 'Must run, darling, or I'll turn into a pumpkin.'

It wasn't quite the witching hour as I watched her hurry off around the corner, but it was late. Climbing up the hill in the chilly dark, I wondered what my goddess theologians were up to at that moment, whether or not they'd pierced the veil. Would they be dancing wild-eyed around a roaring fire in a Bacchic frenzy or would Aphrodite come to them in a rush of silence? More to the point, where was William at that instant? Lying in my bed in Gastouri? Dreaming of what? Could he see this selfsame moon that I could see? Was there a ghostly triangle in the sky at that very minute: William–moon–me?

I stood for moment by the café at the mouth of the wisteria tunnel and gazed up at the sky. The gods were certainly busy that night with their signs and portents. Around the moon, in fading circles, were haloes of pale rainbows, the faintest, most perfect pencillings in red and blue.

But I don't believe in signs, I told myself, turning back towards the stepped alleyway to my hotel. Just in things as they are.

6

Pinned to the back of the toilet door in his bed-sit in North London William had a Rilke poem (which I could make neither head nor tail of), an old *New Yorker* cartoon, and a Monet print: *The Beach at Trouville*. Vivid, light, momentary. Ochres, smoky blues, a dash of vermilion. Nothing remarkable about any of that – just an ordinary North London toilet door. But one day during the *Three Sisters* rehearsals, when I dropped in on him for lunch, the Monet gave me a brilliant idea.

Since the moment of the ballooning bubble and the plunged coffee in Clive's kitchen, I'd felt an urgent need to find the right words to describe what was happening. New words, my own words, today's words, not last week's or Hollywood's – and not Leila's, either. ('So where's your *friend* tonight?' she'd whispered huskily right into my ear the first evening the beanbag under the lamp lay empty. And once when I completely forgot my lines in Act IV, Gareth snorted: 'I think the poor possum must be *in love*, girls and boys, don't you?' And everyone – except Alex – giggled. With these words they were railroading me into feeling things I wasn't sure I felt.)

Anton Chekhov was of absolutely no help in sorting out what was happening. Night after night we
tossed the word 'love' backwards and forwards across
Clive's living-room – *Three Sisters* is crawling with
'love'. I 'love' my wife Natasha, for instance (or so I
keep saying), although not for herself – she *herself*, as
I finally admit, is petty, boring, vulgar, barely human
– but as one might 'love' old furniture one has grown
accustomed to and can't be bothered to throw out.
She for her part 'loves' my boss, the chairman of the
town council – or at least has an affair with him, a
bit of slap and tickle in the troika – while also 'loving' her children, naturally enough. (Our children
are very likely my boss's, too.) The Latin teacher
'loves' his wife Masha (madly), while Masha 'loves'
the battery commander, who in turn 'loves' her
(although not his own wife, not even as old furniture). Masha's sister Irina is 'loved' by the baron with
an embarrassing passion, as well as by a young
poseur of a staff-captain whose 'love' comes straight
from the pages of romantic novels. Irina, however,
'loves' neither of them, although she quite likes the
baron – enough to marry him, anyway. And they all
'love' the old nanny and each other (more or less).
It's not a play, as Chekhov himself said – it's just a
tangle.

Yet, as far as I could tell, what happened when
William plunged the coffee that night mirrored none
of these 'loves'. It didn't feel like a rush of sibling
affection, for instance, nor did I want to be his mate

(who would we close ranks against, exactly?) or his teacher *à la* Kester Berwick. It had something to do with an unbidden bolt of pleasure that he was who he was and I who I was, it's true; but something had also been laid dangerously, enticingly bare. In North London at that time – and in the Adelaide Hills when I was younger – *laying bare* often blurred quickly into unclothing, and disclosure into undressing, but what I felt was not as straightforward as the steamy desire to ravish his body – like Daphnis, I couldn't quite picture what that would entail – nor was it even run-of-the-mill romantic passion, that giddying technicolor jumble of every kind of love in the world that ambushes all of us from time to time and for a season sends us mad. It was a puzzle.

In Act IV of *Three Sisters*, trying to explain to the baron why, although she's happy to become his wife, she does not 'love' him ('it's not in my power to'), Irina says: 'I've dreamt about love, I've dreamt about it day and night for years, but my heart is like a beautiful piano which is locked shut, and the key's lost . . .' One night, a couple of weeks into rehearsals, I heard these lines as if for the first time. To tell the truth, they'd always struck me as rather mushy. I mean, did anyone ever really talk like that – 'my heart is like a beautiful piano' – even unmarried post-office clerks in provincial Russia a hundred years ago?

That particular night, though – I'd just wheeled

the wretched pram off and was standing in the kitchen doorway, listening, acutely aware of William in his beanbag, listening – for some reason, what Irina said that night made perfect sense. All the words I'd tried to open the piano with had turned out to be old, blunt keys to something else, so it had stayed locked up. What were the right words?

A few minutes later, as we know, the baron is shot to death in a duel, Irina weeps for fully ten seconds, and the idea of love and locked pianos flies straight out the window. Instead of looking for the key, she decides to go away and become a school-teacher – 'to work, just work'.

Nobody shot William, though, so I kept scrabbling about erratically for the Key to the Piano of my Heart. Stupidly, I said something along these lines to Leila a day or two later in the Shalimar. I thought she might be touched and say something wise. Instead, she rolled her eyes disdainfully. 'You know what Picasso said about looking for things, don't you?'

'No. What?'

'*I don't look for things, I find them.*'

Arrogant bugger. But perhaps he had a point.

I'll bring it to a head, then, I thought. I'll put it to the test. I'll find the word for what we are, William and I.

The very next afternoon, wandering back into the kitchen from the toilet as casually as I could, I said to William, who was frying fish for our lunch: 'What do you think about going over to France for the weekend? Normandy, say – Honfleur, Trouville, somewhere like that.'

'Great idea – let's do it.'

'You don't need to think about it?'

'No. I've sort of been expecting it.'

This was odd. I'd only just thought of it myself.

'Why is that?'

'Alex read my cards last week.'

'Did she, indeed.' *Keep the curled-lip tone out of your voice.* It was the one thing that annoyed me about William – this penchant for horoscopes and Chinese herbs and reincarnation. 'And she said you'd meet a handsome stranger from across the seas and go to France with him?'

'No, not exactly. In any case, you're not a stranger, are you? But France did come into it, as a matter of fact.'

'I'll bet it did,' I said, a little too sharply. 'Her mother has a house near Honfleur, doesn't she?'

'Yep.' He turned the fish on its bed of sizzling onion. 'Right on the beach.'

'Have you been there with her?' I hated myself for asking.

'Yep. Once.' He started scooping the soft, white flesh onto plates, sprinkling it with the curls of onion. Was he waiting for the next question or busy with the fish? 'How much sauce do you want?'

'Lots,' I said. We carried our plates over to the table in the sun.

7

Hotels have an amazing effect on my libido. The games with the desk-clerk, the key in the lock, the smell of the sheets, the fluffy towels, the glances from strangers . . . I feel a spring in my step the instant I hoist my suitcase out of the taxi. On the ferry from Portsmouth, queasy with indecision about what part to play, I'd brought up my cheese roll and Fanta quite spectacularly all over a West Highland terrier on the upper deck. Roué, scoutmaster, big brother, pal – what was my role in this scenario? (Perhaps 'scout-master' covered it nicely, I thought dolefully, recalling three weeks in the scouts when I'd been fourteen.) Not that William had seemed troubled by any doubts: he'd been in high spirits from the moment we'd met at Waterloo all the way across the Channel. He'd nosed around the ferry like a frolicsome puppy, bantering with strangers, sniffing the damp air, gobbling down pies and doughnuts with pink icing, and chatting with me about anything that came into his head.

One sniff of the floor-wax in the vestibule at the Hôtel Flaubert, however, and I perked up. I flirted with the desk-clerk (*Bonsoir, messieurs! Vous désirez?* – the tea-party manners of a duchess, heart of ice), I took command, I slid the key into the lock and twisted, threw back the curtains, took possession of the room. And it was vast, with ante-room and alcoves, lamp-lit corners and shadowy doorways. We peered out at the blackness beyond the windows. Strips of grey sand in pools of light, ghostly façades with tall, glowing windows, a man with a dog on the boardwalk beneath us, rugged up against the gusts of rain. It wasn't quite Monet, but it *was* Trouville. I stood there for a while, nose against the glass, pleasantly on edge, half bewitched by the inky possibilities beyond the pane, then turned to find William stretched out, eyes closed, on his bed.

'William!' I said softly, perching on the edge of the bed beside him. 'What do you feel like doing?'

'Sleeping,' he murmured, not even opening his eyes. 'I'm stuffed.' He smelt of salt air and damp wool.

'I might go and get something to eat.'

'Sure,' he said, and nestled into the duvet. 'I don't need anything, I'm full of pies.' I studied his peaceful face for a moment, thought of lightly kissing one eye-socket, decided against it and quietly let myself out.

When I got back an hour or so later, he was dead to the world, buried deep under the duvet. I was relieved, up to a point, to have been let off the hook.

⌒

There's only so much mooching around a seaside resort in the off-season you can do, especially in the rain. A walk along the deserted beach, looking across from time to time at the yellow-grey waves; drinking coffee in a beach-front café, a few white hulls glimpsed bobbing mistily through the steamed-up window; idle window-shopping in dim, stony side-streets; another coffee; lunch.

Waiting.

For the sky to clear, for something to happen, for dinner, for bed. It's vaguely threatening, like mid-afternoon in the home they put my mother in. It's your everyday life stripped of all the little distractions that hide its emptiness: the telephone calls, the trips to the corner store, the evening news, walking the dog, work.

That first day William seemed to revel in it all. He wondered about everything – why there were no fishing boats out today, what everyone was *doing* in those shuttered, narrow houses in the side-streets, why the impressionists loved the sea. 'Look at the colours now,' he said, nudging me when the sun came out for a moment, dissolving all the brownish greys in a wash of blues, pinks, whites and emeralds. It was just slightly irritating.

When the rain squalls hit again soon after lunch we went back to the hotel. Time yawned. William flopped on the bed. Had the moment – or at least *a* moment – arrived?

'I wonder if this is where Flaubert stayed,' William said. 'I mean, I wonder if that's why it's called the Hôtel Flaubert. It looks old enough. We should ask.'

He rolled onto his side. 'He wanted to write a novel about nothing, you know.' How did he know that? '*Un livre sur rien.*'

'So you speak French?'

'I can get by. I told you: I went to a very expensive school.' He grinned. 'This would've been the perfect place to write it, wouldn't it.'

And so we began to circle each other, motionlessly, me on the floor, William lying back on the bed. Flaubert, Emma Bovary, love, disappointment, my marriage, Harold's head in the bucket, Adelaide (at last), his stuffy school, his pushy father (a suburban chemist), his painting, his drift into the theatre, the escape to London, Chekhov, failed love, boredom, suicide, Emma Bovary, Flaubert. There was a pause.

Inside I was coiled like a spring. Flurries of rain hissed on the windows. I was ready. I'd open my mouth and say it – something, anything . . . *I think I may be falling in love with you . . . Feel like a fuck? . . .* anything to make the spring snap. I looked across at him. He smiled that funny smile of his – a little jet of impish warmth. I cleared my throat.

'Feel like something to eat?' I said.

'Sure,' he said, swinging his legs down onto the floor. 'Where will we go?'

Bloody William. At the table next to us was a shaven-headed soldier. Some distance from his plate, safe from splashing wine or drops of sauce, lay a snowy, white cap. Outrageously white. William kept casting furtive glances at it as he ate his crêpes.

'He must be a Legionnaire,' he whispered, nodding at the cap. 'A Foreign Legionnaire. The cap! God, how romantic!'

Trim, square-jawed, self-possessed, even sexy – but not, I thought, romantic. A well-trained animal, feeding. He caught William's eye and nodded. Then, leaning back to enjoy a cigarette with his wine, he casually opened a newspaper. The front-page headline read in English: US HOSTAGE FREED IN BEIRUT. Further down there was a picture of a familiar face under the headline: EX-PM CAUGHT OFF STRIDE IN MEMPHIS.

'Don't tell me he's English,' William said, quietly agog.

When I got back from the loo, as I half expected – half wanted, perhaps – William and the Legionnaire were deep in conversation. Max was from Manchester and had been in the Foreign Legion for five years. He had the weekend off. (So why was he kitted out for the jungles of South America?) He regaled William – and bits splashed over onto me – with tales of derring-do in French Guiana and the mountains of Djibouti. William was transfixed. I had the impression that Max was starting to think of fresh-faced William as the *plat du jour*.

'Feel like going on somewhere, guys?' he said eventually, stubbing out his fourth or fifth cigarette. 'I know a couple of places —'

'Sure, why not?' said William, with that little spurt of eagerness I was getting to know quite well.

'You go,' I said, getting to my feet. 'I'm a bit whacked. I'll head back to the hotel.'

'Come with us, it'll be fun,' William said. The square-jawed Legionnaire said nothing.

'I'm not in the mood. I think I'll call it a night.'

I strode back to the hotel in the freezing drizzle, so angry – with myself, with William, with Max the Legionnaire, with Trouville – that I rang my brother in Adelaide and tore at him like a fighting-cock for twenty minutes. I do this once or twice a year, often around Christmas, and always feel much better for it. He's a complete shit – a real estate agent up in the Hills. Then I turned out all the lights and went to bed. When William crept in, smelling slightly odd, well after two, I was still wide awake, but lay still and said nothing. Needless to say, he was sound asleep in seconds.

If I'd imagined a bit of limb-loosening boyishness in the bathroom of a morning – nothing too vivid: a flash of soaped flesh through the steam, a moment of vigorous towelling, a bit of playful banter while we shaved bare-chested at the sink – I couldn't have been wider of the mark. By the time I opened my eyes, William had had his coffee and croissants, gone for a run along the boardwalk in the icy wind, and was now standing quite unsheepishly at the end of my bed, ready for action.

'So where did you and Jungle Jim go last night?' I said, as evenly as I could, hoisting myself up on my pillows.

'The casino. Is there anywhere else to go in Trouville at midnight?'

'And was it . . . *fun*?'

'The casino? Well, slot-machines are much the same anywhere, I guess. The casino's themed – you should see it – it's all cartwheels and cowboy hats, it's hideous!' He laughed. 'It's stopped raining. Do you feel like getting some bikes and going for a ride?'

An image of quaint, half-timbered Norman barns and wagon-sheds flashed through my mind. I could just picture the two of us, sailing along the clifftop road towards Honfleur, waving to rosy-cheeked peasants herding geese among the apple orchards . . . green, the rolling hills would be a deep, juicy green, the air heavy with the smell of mud and hay . . . we'd shout into the wind, swooping like larks uphill, downdale . . .

'No, I think I'll stay here and read a bit,' I heard myself say. 'But you go.'

'Are you sulking?' A mischievous glint in his eye.

'Sulking? Why would I be sulking? No, it's just too bloody cold, William. You go, though, while the rain holds off.'

I didn't read, of course – in fact, I didn't have a book. I tramped up the hill behind the town, past all the mock-Norman villas with their prissy gardens, feeling foolish, nettled, crabbed and elated all at once. Later, down in the Sunday market, jostled by the seething, garishly dressed crowd, I felt nothing at all. Sitting eating a sandwich where the fishing-smacks were moored, I flailed at the seagulls. Disgusting birds, seagulls, with their greedy, yellow eyes and vicious squawk. Turning back towards the crowd, I noticed two cyclists propping their bikes against a lamp-post beside the ice-cream cart. It was William and Jungle Jim. I pulled my scarf up to my nose and set off for the Flaubert.

'*Ah, monsieur! Votre ami vous a téléphoné tout à l'heure . . .*' It was Lemon Lips, offering me a small slip of paper and a very thin smile. Why she thought a chartreuse blouse was flattering to a woman of her complexion was beyond comprehension.

Rendez-vous Brasserie Le Central six heures.

Such decorum in one so young! And would the Legionnaire be joining us, in full regalia?

'*Merci, madame.*' A twitch of the lips, no more.

'*Je vous en prie, monsieur.*'

The bang of my door, when I slammed it, came to her, I'm sure, as no surprise.

I was running a little late. Not so late as to appear inconsiderate or ruffled, but just late enough to make a point. The restaurant wasn't crowded. An uncluttered pre-war décor which felt oddly modern. Shaking my umbrella at the door, I scanned the faces for *mon ami*. No sign of the spiky hair and slender neck anywhere. Just Alex. Good grief!

She was alone, at a table near the bar. Red curls, white scarf, blue jacket – quite nautical, in fact. A little wave (as if I could miss her).

'Hullo! Having fun?'

There was that word again. Fun. What was it? Whatever it was, I wasn't having it.

'Yes, we're having a great time.' I settled gingerly across from her. 'Despite the cold.'

'Where's Will? You haven't lost him, have you?' She giggled, but tightly.

'*Will?* Oh, William. Actually, I'm not sure. He's been out cycling all day.'

'He got my message, though, didn't he? He knows we're meeting here at six?' So this was the friend who'd rung to suggest a rendez-vous at six.

How infinitely tempting it was to say 'yes', wait for an hour, watching her keeping her eye on the door, her pale, English fingers starting to drum after a while, and then say: 'God, he's so unreliable! Sorry you've come all the way from Honfleur for nothing . . . see you back in London.' And then dash back to the hotel and lock William in for the night. I could feel myself flushing pink at the thought of it.

'Just let me call the hotel and check what's happened,' I said.

William answered the phone. That little catch in the voice. 'Hi!'

'William – or should I say "Will"? – it's me. Look, Alex is here –'

'Where is she? She said she might call.'

'Well, we're in a brasserie called Le Central, down on the quay near the town hall –' There was a sudden crash on the other end of the phone.

'Shit!' said William under his breath. And then giggled.

'What was that?'

'It was just the ashtray falling off the um . . . bedside table. It didn't break.'

'What's Alex doing here?'

'She's been staying with her mother. She said she might pop down. Look, I'll be there in twenty minutes. I'll just take a shower.'

'OK.'

But William didn't smoke.

⌒

It was pure *butoh*: a painfully slow, long-drawn-out dance of tortured souls, miming feeling. It began as soon as William and Max pushed the door open: we all smiled, ritually, and then quickly froze over, settling into a subtle, almost imperceptible shuffle this way and that – excruciatingly tedious, mesmerizing, coolly febrile.

Alex froze at the sight of shaven-skulled Max, as

did I (already frosty over Alex), while Max in his bright yellow ski-jacket stiffened slightly at the sight of Alex. William went as taut as a cat. A chill descended. We all smiled and began to dance.

Slowly, Max warmed towards Alex, and she to him, so William inched his way in my direction. I shrank from him towards Max, William from me to Alex. We all took a minute, malicious step forward, one to the side, then back again, eyeing each other through the slits in our masks. We ate our *fruits de mer*, our *moules* and *marrons glacés*, we passed the salt and cider, all infinitely bored, as alert as cornered rats.

'So, Will, what have you decided?' Alex said finally at about seven. 'Do you feel like a couple of days at Honfleur?'

Decided? The dance stopped. We all stood stock still. Max lit another Gitane.

'Would you mind?' William asked, turning to me. 'The thing is, if you're coming, you may as well drive back with me now, don't you think? You were leaving in the morning anyway, weren't you?'

'Honfleur,' said Max, 'I've never been to Honfleur.'

All of a sudden I realized I was acting in the wrong play. This wasn't a gut-wrenching tragedy, this was a farce.

I stood up. I was about to say 'Would you excuse me?' or 'I'm suddenly dog-tired – must go', but nothing came out. I made a little fish-mouth to say something, but then turned on my heel and walked out onto the street.

'Where are you going?' It was William's voice behind me.

'Just fuck off, William,' I said, not even turning round. For one exciting moment I considered facing him and having a scene, but decided against it. Those four words more or less covered it.

Back at the Flaubert, I stuffed William's things into his knapsack and took it down to reception. Lemon Lips was almost rigid with suppressed delight. Soon afterwards there was a knock at the door, but I ignored it. The telephone rang, but soon fell silent.

Next time you see me with other people, he'd said, *you must promise me faithfully you'll come and get me*. So what the hell had he meant by that? Was it just a cute line he'd read in a book?

During the long, rainy night I began to understand. My eyes were on the gleaming, empty boardwalk below my window, but my mind was on that speck of an instant in Clive's kitchen. William had reached out towards me, coaxing me to reach out towards him. Mystifyingly, drawing together meant much the same as drawing apart, and I had no idea how to step into the space between us. Indeed, I had no idea who should step into it.

The next morning, while I was waiting for the taxi, a little boy was spinning a top on the pavement near my feet. I was transfixed. In a flash, as the taxi pulled in, I stretched out my foot and stamped on the whirling cone. Then I slid into the back seat and was gone.

8

Perched on a rock in the sun behind the ruined castle, I'd just sunk my teeth into a cicada when I heard the holler. I nearly bit its head right off.

'What on earth are you doing?' It was Elvira, aglow in her red wind-cheater and all alone.

'I'm biting my first cicada of the season for luck.'

'Really? Is that what they do here?'

I threw it up into the sky. We both watched it lurch off drunkenly towards the cliff-edge and Turkey. It would drown before it got there.

'So how was the ceremony?'

Elvira looked at me with such intense joy that I felt embarrassed. I knew that my question had been inappropriate and banal, but I never know how to approach these things. If I show too much interest, I'm likely to be mistaken for a seeker after truth, whereas all I want to know (genuinely) is what happened, what it *felt* like to be there. When I was a teenager, I once asked Mrs Evans, our neighbour, the one whose letter-box we used to put dog-turds in, what happened at her New Thought meetings, and for years after that she dropped pamphlets in our letter-box – pale-green, misspelt invitations to lectures on 'The Secret of a Beautiful Life' or 'Our Godlike Humanity', with music by Miss Sarah Codd. But I didn't want to know about any of that (we were Presbyterians) – I just wanted to know what it felt like to be Mrs Evans. In the end my mother had to have a word with her.

'We scried her,' Elvira said at last. 'We scried the goddess!'

'Scried?' *Careful here.*

'We don't usually say "see", we say "scry".' She considered me for a moment, as if pondering whether to say more. Was I worth saying more to?

I bent and picked a red poppy, twiddling it while I waited.

'I'll just say this once,' Elvira said, 'so don't ask me to say it again. Once, when I was a small girl, eleven or twelve, I was waiting with my brother on a railway-station for a train. We were going to visit an aunt in another town. I was sitting staring at the puddles on the platform, thinking about nothing. Suddenly there was a brightness – not a light, it had no source – and in that brightness there was no measurement any more, no now or yesterday or tomorrow, no movement or stillness, no me and them, no here and there, I was everywhere and everything and nothing at all – the puddles, my brother, the chocolate he was eating, even you now, and also none of it, just the point where everything crossed, the flying of an infinitude of arrows to their target, never to be reached, yet already hit.' She was very fluent, and I wondered how often she'd told this story just once. 'And I heard a vast sigh, and then myself saying to my brother in the brightness: *I am dead, you should go home.* And then we *were* home, and the brightness faded, and everything could be measured again, with some things behind us and some ahead, and my mother came running to the front gate, as white as a ghost, telling us she'd had a phone call to say that our aunt had died. I said: *None of us was ever born.*' She paused. I smelt wild rosemary. 'Well, that's what it was like last night. There's nothing else I can tell you.'

I couldn't help thinking, being who I am, that it would be interesting to have a chat one day with Elvira's brother.

'You're wondering about my brother, aren't you,' Elvira said, with a laugh. I felt pierced. 'You're wondering what his version of the story might be. Well, he says we never left home. That doesn't bother me. In a sense he's right.'

'What I don't quite understand,' I said, still twiddling the poppy, 'is whether you believe that Aphrodite actually exists.'

'Oh, only in the sense that you do,' she said, staring off towards Turkey. 'Feel like a walk? It's such a marvellous morning.'

A little way off we heard the dull clunk of goatbells and we turned to see an ancient goat-herd ambling across the road with his goats towards his stone shelter. Just a few hundred yards away behind us, beyond the fort, people were telephoning Berlin and Barcelona, booking flights to Singapore, watching people talking in Athens live on television screens, reading about what had happened in New York the day before – I could hear their doors banging and their motorbikes starting up from where we stood. Yet, looking the other way, I was in a world so ancient I'd not have been surprised to see a bunch of Lydian pirates come scrambling up over the edge of the cliff, waving iron swords, to loot the town, or a trireme go scudding past, headed for Egypt, oars thrashing the blue-black waves, loaded with corn and sacks of figs.

Elvira set a cracking pace.

9

'They *scried* her?' Leila thought the whole thing preposterous. 'I wish I could scry Yanni once in a while
– he's been gone since breakfast. Down by the harbour, I suppose, yacking with his mates. What am I
supposed to do all day? Arrange the flowers?'

Sappho was right about love the limb-loosener: it's
not bittersweet, it's sweetbitter. In time the honey
burns.

'Kester's a bit prone to that sort of thing, you
know,' Leila said, taking me out onto the tiled balcony to enjoy the late afternoon sun and the view.
Yanni's house was indeed spectacularly situated, high
on the hill just below the fortress, although, as usual,
it was furnished in that comfortless, very Greek way
– a rug here, a chair there, a vase, an icon, no books
– as if life were essentially to be lived elsewhere.

'What sort of thing?' I asked. I was drowning in
the blueness of everything below.

'Well, not goddesses, of course, but, you know . . .
spirit presences, the odd spot of table-turning.' Leila,
as I knew, was not above reading her stars in the local
newspaper herself, and was ready to excuse all sorts of
eccentricities in herself on the grounds that she was a

Taurean with Libra in the seventh house or some such nonsense. 'We sat for hours once in his flat with one of those planchettes, waiting for a message from my brother Giles, who'd just drowned in France.'

'Nothing?'

'Not a thing. "He's there," he kept saying, "I can feel he's there." And he'd put his fingers on the planchette, and it would shudder a bit and scrawl a bit of gibberish – there's a pencil stuck through a hole in it, you see – and Kester would sigh and wait and try again. Eventually it wrote VA TE FAI and then stopped and wouldn't move. Kester was sure this was significant, but I was jack of it by then and went home. Of course, I never really got on with my brother, perhaps he was just sulking.'

Leila looked across the bay into the blue haze, remembering. 'Then there was the time, back in the thirties, quite soon after they arrived in London, when he took Alan Harkness to one of those dance performances that were all the rage in those days – you know the sort of thing: women floating about, draped in white, expressing the lost rhythm of the cosmos. Anyway, well into the evening, with the audience all Apprehending Being or whatever it was they did with *great* intensity, one of the dancers, a woman with a withered arm, suddenly stopped and pointed at Kester and Alan in the front row (with her good arm, I presume) and said: "I can see you many lives ago . . . you were together then as you are now . . . I see you both in Persia, at the court of the king, at Isfahan . . . one of you is a master of music and dance, the other his assistant . . . you're travelling players, you've come across seas and mountains to entertain the king and queen, I can see the flaming torches and hear the drums . . . *and as it was, so it shall be*."

'Kester was thunder-struck, naturally. "It all *tallied*, you see," he said to me (that was the sort of slightly wishy-washy thing Kester *would* say). He and Alan *were* travelling players, they *had* come across seas and mountains – well, seas, anyway – to the seat of empire, and Kester *was* in a sense Alan's assistant, and had been even back in Adelaide. So Kester naturally saw it as a sign.'

'Well, you would, wouldn't you.'

'It was certainly a sign that madam had done her homework. But she was wrong: Alan went to America, as I told you, got married and died on a level-crossing. Kester's such a treasure, but heart-breakingly easy to swindle.'

'You really have a great affection for him, don't you,' I said. I was moved.

'It's not hard. Even Yanni feels a fondness for him – I can tell. Amazing, isn't it? The man I meet on St Pancras station turns out to have been taught English by the man who first taught me to act. It's as if we're all caught in this huge web of connections spread across the globe, and right in the middle, arms folded, quietly waiting to see what butterfly or gnat might fly into it this time, sits Kester Berwick.'

'You make him sound like a spider.'

Leila just smiled. 'Do you know the word the locals all use about him? "*Evyénikos*", they say. The mayor, the village policeman – they all say the same thing: *tóso evyénikos*, so good-hearted, such a gentleman, so . . . kind, really. Such a good man.'

'It makes him sound a trifle dull.'

'Dull . . . Must goodness be dull?' Leila lit a cigarillo and examined her gleaming fingernails – a vivid fuchsia this afternoon. Far below us in the village cats started fighting. Someone somewhere was frying fish. 'Few women I know would call Kester dull. Men tend to draw a blank with him, it's true. Even Yanni never knows what else to say about him except how *evyénikos* he is – and a marvellously patient teacher. I don't think he was ever popular with the taverna crowd. But there's another side to him, you know.'

'I've been thinking there might be. Not quite so *evyénikos*, this other side?'

'Kester has a night side, yes.' Leila blew lazy plumes of smoke out over the narrow laneway below. The blue haze was thickening. 'I had to laugh when I read what that Australian writer friend of Kester's wrote . . . Betty someone . . . wrote a book about Lesbos, half in love with Kester herself, I always thought . . .'

'Betty Roland?'

'That's the one. Never liked her much myself – a tiresome mixture of the wanton and the twinset and

pearls, I always thought. But that's precisely what
appealed to Kester, I think. They saw a lot of each
other in London in the fifties, when she was working at the BBC and writing bits and pieces for the
dailies. Then she came to Lesbos, more or less at
Kester's invitation. I can just imagine it: "Why don't
you call in to Lesbos on the way home?" he'd have
said to her. "It's beautiful, the people are friendly, life
is good . . ." She'd have been convinced there was a
subtext. So sophisticated, yet so blind.'

I could tell from the vicious jet of smoke she blew
across the table that Leila relished this failure in
another woman.

'Anyway, when Betty went to Athens for Easter,
Kester put her in touch with a couple of his young
friends. She found them captivating, of course – lean,
handsome, with eager young minds – it's all in her
book. They climbed up Lykavittos Hill with her at
night to join in the candle-lit procession, and sat in
cafés with her, lamenting their hopeless futures. This
was the early sixties, you see, there were no jobs, these
boys had starving widowed mothers and unmarried
sisters in need of a dowry, university fees to pay, and
God knows what other demands on them – which
they no doubt regaled Betty with, as she gazed into
their melting black eyes. And then, in that insufferably
prim way of hers, she adds darkly that some of these
boys were driven to the point of taking money from
"certain types of tourist" who came to Greece to satisfy
their "particular requirements". I could practically see

her hand going to her throat in horror, pearls caught up decoratively in her fingers.'

Rolling her eyes, Leila shot me another curious glance to see if she'd snared my interest.

'Just how exactly did the silly woman think Kester had met these charming boys?' She snorted, blowing more smoke over me in pleasurable irritation. 'What type of tourist did she think he was? Did she think he'd met all these Theos and Georges and Spiros in the public library or that they'd spent their time poring over Plato together while their mothers dished them up lamb stew? (What, for that matter, were *her* "particular requirements" when she travelled? Why did she really come to visit Kester in Molyvos?) Kester met these young men everywhere – in barber's shops, in public parks, at the beach, in the bushes around the Parthenon late at night. And took them back to his hotel room for a bit of whoopee. Night after night. And, after he and Betty had spent the evening down at Nick's taverna, chatting intimately about life, love, art and the whole damn thing for hours on end, where on earth did she think he went? Did she think he went back to his room to mull over marrying her? Or dip into some Buddhist tract before drifting off to sleep alone in his chaste bed? I don't think so, darling,' Leila chuckled.

'What he probably did after kissing her cheek,' she went on, wrapping her shawl more tightly around her throat against the first chill of evening, 'was wander off along the seafront in search of a hungry-eyed young sailor or two to spend the night with. In those days he didn't have far to look. I can just see him, wafting off into the darkness with that funny walk of his. He used to walk as if he were caught in an undertow. I saw him walking like that along Oxford Street once – miles away, on the other side of the street. You couldn't miss him. It looked as if someone was pulling him along by a string attached to his navel.'

Leila sighed and glanced at her watch. The sky above us was turning the palest of greens, streaked with orange clouds. 'Have you read Betty's book? *Lesbos: The Pagan Island,* it's called!' Here she cackled and had a brief coughing fit. 'I think the penny may've dropped eventually. A distinctly miffed tone creeps into the story after a while, as if she'd suddenly put two and two together and realized she'd be catching the boat home alone. Rather abruptly, I seem to remember, Molyvos lost its charm for Betty Roland.'

Although I'd obviously been putting two and two together myself over the past few weeks, what I didn't understand was why Leila saw these appetites as Kester's 'night side'. I was about to say something along these lines when the door was flung open and Yanni came into the room, with that slightly grumpy, yet elated, look on his face that men have at such moments. It's time, I thought, to make a move.

10

'It's not a tragedy,' Clive said, looking us in the eye one by one when we gathered for rehearsal after the weekend in Trouville. At last we were in the church hall off the Holloway Road. Typically, William had not shown up. 'That's the whole point, don't you see: it's not *even* a tragedy.'

'It's hardly a barrel of laughs, either,' Gareth muttered. He was having trouble with the drunken doctor. Lines like '*We don't exist, we only seem to exist . . . Anyway, what does it matter?*' didn't come easily to him.

'I heard that, Gareth,' Clive said, 'but that's not the point, either. My point is that the three sisters and their hangers-on are so ordinary that they can't even rise to tragedy. That's why our hearts go out to them. Do you see what I mean?'

'*The point? Look, it's snowing. Where's the point in that?*'

'Thank you, Gareth. Perhaps you should be playing the baron. Where *is* our baron, by the way? It's nearly ten o'clock.'

'*The baron's a fine fellow, but one baron more or less – what does it matter?*' Gareth took aim with an imaginary pistol and shot the absent baron dead.

'OK, places, everyone, we'll start without him. Olga, Masha, Irina . . . Irina, sweetheart, you're not looking *lost in thought* – remember the stage directions? – you're looking bored witless. Alright. It's midday, it's sunny, the atmosphere's almost *cheerful*, Chekhov tells us. The table's being set for lunch. Olga . . .'

> OLGA: It's exactly a year since father died, one year today, the fifth of May, your name-day, Irina. It was very cold, it was snowing. I thought I'd never live through it, and you lay there in a faint, dead to the world. But now a year's gone by and here we are, remembering it all without any heaviness of heart, you're even wearing white again, and your face is glowing . . .

And we were off, tracking in interminable, broken-off conversations, the minute shifts in our aimless, futile lives – with remarkably good humour. At that stage it didn't have quite the 'riveting' quality Clive wanted brought out – 'Think of Monet,' Clive kept saying, 'think of the impressionists, think of van Gogh's bedroom, think of those boring haystacks and rows of poplars, all those women with parasols sitting in deck-chairs on beaches or picnicking . . . and think about why you can't take your eyes off them' – but *something* was starting to shine through the haphazardness, the happenstance of our characters' lives. I wondered if Gareth's eyes, or Alex's, for that matter, had ever rested on a Monet or van Gogh, except on the back of a toilet door in Islington, but even they seemed to intuit what Clive meant. Something was working.

All of a sudden, right after lunch at that rehearsal after Trouville, like a vision of the Virgin Mary, it struck me: in *Three Sisters* the key number was three, it wasn't about a tangle of meandering lines, it was about overlapping triangles.

Nothing ever looked the same again.

What I mean is this: *Three Sisters* wasn't a play about dispossession, hope and despair, or lives petering out in failure and death – or not just about those things – it was about people bending the straight lines of their lives into triangles, trying (as we all do, it dawned on me) to make a space in which to play with their deeper desires. In other words, I don't sneak off at night with the doctor to gamble just to get away from my vapid, baby-talking wife, but to give my life a different shape, to stop it turning into a one-way ride into a dead-end, with Natasha and our two children trailing along behind. I *make a triangle*. We all do. All the time, everywhere. Natasha starts her ludicrous affair with the chairman of the town council (my boss – even better), the baron and the bilious staff-captain use each other to make a triangle with Irina, who triangulates with her pathetic fantasies about working for the masses, while Masha creates an amazing lopsided triangle with the battery-commander and her Latin-speaking husband, the battery-commander zigzagging between his suicidal wife and Masha, and the husband between his wife and his Latin verbs.

Only Olga, I suppose, the most solitary of all the characters in the play, the least touched by passion, the most strikingly ordinary, whose words open and close the play, makes no effort to conjure up a triangle. She just stands at the apex, as it were, of the triangle of the three sisters.

Seeing the play in this new way (for me), as a jagged maze of interlocking triangles, I felt suffused that afternoon for the first time with a real warmth for these lost souls. Even if there were no meaning, no point to anything – 'Look, it's snowing. Where's the point in that?' – there could at least be a pattern, straight lines could be twisted into new shapes, trembling with possibilities for new tugs-of-war, new balances, new sorties into new territory.

Olga, Masha, Irina, the baron, the doctor – I didn't see them as shallow any more. Ordinary, but not empty or shallow.

Walking back to the Underground that evening in the biting cold, I held that vision to my chest like a guttering candle. Gliding down into the roaring, fuggy depths on the escalator, I kept thinking of something the lieutenant-colonel says in Act II. It sounds banal unless it's delivered with just that balance of lightness and ardour Chekhov demands – and I'm not sure, a century after Chekhov, we quite know how to capture that. The lieutenant-colonel (saddled with a suicidally miserable wife and point-lessly in love with married Masha) is gently trying to explain to Masha that all dreams of finding happi-ness in Moscow are an illusion: once there, everyday life would be as bland and stale as it is in the provinces. Moscow is *not the point*. So he tells the story – so trivially true it's barely worth repeating – of a French government minister jailed over the Panama swindle who writes in his prison diary about the birds he sees sitting on his window-sill outside the bars. Just ordinary birds – sparrows or pigeons or something, not toucans or peacocks – so common-place they're not even worth naming, birds he'd never even noticed when he'd been busy being a gov-ernment minister, although no doubt they'd sat on his window-sill at the ministry just as they did at the prison. And he's seized with a kind of intoxication, a joyful wonder at the mere thought of these sparrows and pigeons. Then he's released and, of course, again these utterly ordinary birds just fade into a blur. And that, I knew, is what the theatre is about. That was why I was there. There are no toucans in Chekhov. But intoxication and joyful wonder . . . well, bit by bit, day after day, we were reaching for it.

11

There was no reply when I first knocked on the door. But I could hear the muffled jabbering of the television set just inside it, and tried again. It was the Friday night of the week after the Trouville fiasco. Although I hardly expected William to be home on a Friday night – weren't the young always out having endless fun on a Friday night? wasn't it social death to be caught at home watching television? – I'd suddenly leapt to my feet in the middle of the BBC detective drama I was watching (who gave a toss who'd robbed the gaga pensioner of her life savings?), threw on my overcoat and set off to have it out with William. He'd never appeared during rehearsals at the church hall – perhaps he was busy painting the scenery somewhere – and Alex, my ruthless, simpering, bat-brained wife, had not once deigned to mention Honfleur, the French Foreign Legion, William or anything else. During breaks she'd sat twittering away in French with Mireille, who was Costumes. I was buggered, quite frankly, if I was going to ask.

By 8.08 on the clock on the stove I'd had enough. Something (although I wasn't sure what) had to be straightened out. To be honest, though, in the Underground, my eye alighted on one of those Silk Cut advertisements and it was all I could do not to turn around and go home.

Now I banged on the door a third time. The chain jingled, the door jerked open and there was William in his floppy blue sweater, grinning at me nonchalantly as if I'd just been out for ten minutes buying cigarettes. I could've knocked him to the floor, but I kissed him lightly on the cheekbone and walked on into the room. Sitting on the couch, her feet scrunched up beneath her, was Alex. No one spoke. Alex's hair flamed red in the lamplight.

'So,' I said, refusing to mention France.

'Take your coat off, sit down,' William said. Was he flustered or just a bit unfocused, as usual? 'Although, actually, Alex and I have to go out fairly soon. But there's time. Do you want a coffee?' The accent, the timbre, the easy gestures melted something inside me.

'No, thanks, William. I really just wanted to have a talk.'

'What about?' He was genuinely interested. So was Alex. The mass of red curls under the lamp was boring into my right eye.

'Things.'

'OK.'

'Maybe now's not the best time.'

Silence. *Alex, piss off.* More silence.

'Tell you what,' William said, reaching down to

turn off the television. (A tiny squeak from Alex.) 'Why don't you come with us? We're just going to see a friend of mine, someone rather special. Then afterwards maybe we can talk.'

'You go,' I said. 'I'll come round another time.' Melting, hardening, stung, soothed, I made for the door. Alex still hadn't spoken, although she'd uncurled her legs. 'Have fun,' I said, reaching for the door-handle.

But I went with them, naturally.

Seb lived in a depressing terrace in a cul-de-sac not far from Tuffnel Park station. An abandoned plastic tricycle stood in the middle of the path to the front door. There were chimes, which whimpered like a very small animal in pain every time there was a gust of wind.

'We're just getting under way!' Seb said in a loud whisper, beaming at us as he greeted us in the cluttered passageway. Dressed in an ivory cotton caftan (which took me straight back to the Adelaide Hills in the seventies), Seb was almost ravishingly handsome, with gleaming blond curls and a clipped, blond beard like a chisel. His eyes seemed to be a disconcerting violet. Perhaps it was the purple light-shade. I took a deep dislike to him on the spot.

There must have been a dozen or so people filling the low-lit living-room at the end of the passage. There were smiles and nods as we came into the room, and several of the young men and women sitting cross-legged on the floor squeezed up to make room for us. Jammed between William and a gypsy-beautiful young girl swathed in batik, I kept my eyes fixed on the golden figure of Seb, glowing like a Burmese buddha in a high-backed, red-plush chair beneath a yellow lamp. The odour of long-dead geraniums was wafting through the air from smouldering tapers. I sneezed.

'A wise teacher once said to his eager pupil,' Seb began, after a pause to allow deep calm to settle, 'that, if he wished to follow him, he must first be beheaded.' Seb smiled – my God, he was handsome, in that way that kills desire in a flash – while his eyes moved lightly from face to face around the room. No one stirred. 'Tonight, my friends, I invite you to your own beheading.' Since my left buttock was already going numb – the gypsy's trailing beads seemed to be wedged in tight under it – I shifted up against William. He smiled.

'Tonight, in other words, we'll be taking a journey deep into the heart – not, of course, into that ball of beating muscle in your breasts, but into Being . . .' I knew it had a capital B from the way he lightly pursed his lips. 'I want you to close your eyes and let your everyday self slide down, down, down . . . and into your hearts . . . Breathe deeply, let your breath sweep your mind clean . . . don't rush it, just let your minds empty out, throw open every window one by one and let the winds of Being blow through . . . Your bodies are beautiful, you must cherish them, but they are just the echo, not the Voice itself. Let your self become faceless, let your features dissolve . . . eyebrows, nostrils, lips, chin . . . let them thin into nothing . . . This is the First Merging.' William's knee relaxed against mine. Somewhere in the house, I was aware, there were dirty nappies.

'Down . . . down . . . slide slowly down into the heart, into bliss, into love, into Being. Relax the neck, let the neck become liquid; relax the throat, let the throat thaw out and soften; relax the shoulders, let the shoulders sleep . . .' The pale-faced young man on William's right lolled against his shoulder, his long hair dangling down onto William's arm. On the couch in the corner Alex looked still and waxen. I tried to edge my buttock off the beads.

'Are you all relaxed? Are you all coming down? Take it slowly, leave the head behind, merge down . . . Watch those shoulders, just let them float into noth-ing . . . In a moment, when you're ready, we'll drop down into Being, we'll let go and just drop into pure Being . . .' William's long thigh quivered warmly against mine.

All of a sudden there was a sharp chill in the air, a tiny hiccough in the merging, something I sensed, rather than perceived. 'Are you all relaxed?' A new tautness in the voice, although it was now a murmur. 'Someone is not letting go. Someone is not relaxing. Please, everyone . . . *everyone* let go . . . gently . . . gently . . . no need to bully yourselves . . .'

My left buttock was killing me. I had to get off the gypsy's beads, but when I tried rolling to the right, I jerked her lolling head smack into my shoulder. 'Sorry!' I whispered. It ricocheted round the room like a bullet.

'*Someone* is not with us,' Seb said quietly. 'I'm sorry, but *someone* here is not merging. *Someone* here is kicking against his beheading.' Surreptitiously, I knew, the whole room was trying to catch a peek of who it might be. I was rigid with shame.

Silence.

'No, I'm sorry, someone is holding us back.' Seb was sounding brisk all of a sudden. 'I can feel it in my body. Someone here is refusing to come down out of his head.'

Silence, then a cough or two.

'Sorry, I didn't catch your name.' I opened my eyes. Seb was staring straight at me. I didn't speak. 'I truly regret this, but I must ask you to leave. We can't merge while you're amongst us. I'm sorry, but you'll have to go.'

I clambered to my feet in a lightning-strike of anger, knocking William and the gypsy sideways. Without looking at William, I headed for the passageway. Alex was staring at her feet with what I'm convinced was a distinctly unspiritual smirk at the corners of her lips.

Striding off down the front path, I kicked the tricycle savagely into the pansy-patch, stumbled over a plastic duck by the front gate and fled into the fog. As usual after any encounter with the self-consciously spiritual, I felt an immediate desire to behave very badly indeed.

12

Quivering just above my toes one morning, as I floated, shivering, in the sea at Molyvos, was a quick, white butterfly. So painfully small in that vast arena, so startlingly fragile, so momentary in the face of that sea's timelessness. A flicker of silvery white against the blue and it was gone. Back to its quinces, probably. A fluttering, summery note from nature's orchestra tuning up.

Molyvos, as summer wakes, puts on new clothes. It's not just a matter of figs ripening, or hornets buzzing at the thistle-heads, swifts shrieking, blue-grey flax flowers and delphiniums dotting the roadsides. The light changes, becoming burnished, doors and shutters are thrown wide open, the sound of bouzouki bands practising for the season peppers the night, restaurant courtyards are swept, painted and dotted about with geraniums. Everyone is sprucing up. The boys on their motorcycles, revving their engines, are getting that look in their eyes. The hordes are coming – the Dutch, the Swedes, the Finns, the Germans – they're all packing their shorts and suntan oils up there in the fog and rain, and dreaming of Molyvos. Time for me to go.

Bit by bit my friends were already dribbling away. Elvira and Andy left soon after their encounter with Aphrodite, making for some ceremonial site in the Andes of Peru – 'spiritually *very* dynamic', Elvira claimed – to take part in a midsummer get-together of goddess theologians from all over the planet. Then Leila and Yanni went back to London – they disappeared without saying goodbye, leaving me wondering if the phone-booth romance had suddenly lost its zing.

One afternoon while I was walking out near the Delphinia (the first hotel to be built in Michael Goutos's reinvention of ancient Methymna), I was startled to see strolling (just as aimlessly) towards me down the road my Sapphic abductor of nearly two weeks before, in a sun-hat, twirling a yellow poppy. She too was about to leave.

The conference itself, she said, had been infinitely boring – 'I can't remember a single thing anybody said' – but highly productive in terms of invitations to give guest-lectures, publishing opportunities and new alliances against deadly enemies. 'Networking – it was great for networking,' she said with an American smile (genuinely warm, but calculated).

'And what did you speak about?' I asked, as we stood by the roadside in the humming silence.

'Well, my paper was on just one of Sappho's poems, possibly her last, we can't be sure. It's one of the most beautiful poems ever written. Almost Chinese!' And she laughed.

'Would I know it?'

'Do you know Greek?'

'No.'

'Then you don't know it!' It wasn't said mockingly, but was deeply meant.

'Well, tell me about it.' I felt quite enlivened.

She glanced at the watch on her slim, brown arm. 'Tell you what: let's sit on the beach for half an hour and look at the sea. Does that sound good to you? I have to leave at four, and I can't think of a nicer way to end my stay. The sea and Sappho.'

So, while I stared at the red and blue caïques bobbing on the horizon – a scene Sappho herself would have found utterly familiar – my still nameless friend from Massachusetts, after collecting her thoughts, began to tell me about Sappho's perfect poem.

'*Déduke mén a seléna*,' she began softly, sifting pebbles through her fingers,

'*kái Pleiiádes mesáide
núktes pará derket óra
égo de móna katévdo.*'

'It sounds beautiful,' I said.

'Do you think so? What do you hear?'

I was stumped. Was this a test? 'Perhaps you should let me hear it again.' So again I listened to the trickle of simple syllables. *Déduke mén a seléna* . . .

'Well,' I said, wishing I'd said nothing, 'it sounds liquid, like water trickling over stones. What does it mean?'

'That's the problem, isn't it. That's what I meant

when I said that, if you don't speak Greek, you don't
know the poem. And that's what I was talking about
at the conference. Oh, I can give you a version of it
in English, if you'd like me to, but it partly means
what you just said: it's partly about trickling away.
All those vowels, so few consonants. Yet, as soon as I
try to tell you what the poem says, you'll hear my
mouth fill up with lumpy English consonants, you'll
lose the sense of something flowing.'

'I wish you'd have a go.'

'*Gone is the moon, gone*
the Pleiades, it's past midnight,
and time's flashing by, yet
I lie alone here.'

Was that all? It sounded so ordinary. Moon, stars,
midnight, time passing – hadn't I heard it all before?

'You're disappointed, aren't you?'

'A little.'

She laughed. 'I'm not surprised. You see, what's
miraculous about these lines in Greek is that they're at
once so limpid – even you could hear it – yet so
tightly, so seamlessly knit. Let me put it differently:
they're like a drop of water on a leaf. Now, that's something you've seen many thousands of times, and, if
you paid attention in your physics class, you know
that a droplet on a leaf has the shape and colour it has
for a myriad of complex reasons – all sorts of tensions
are at play on the waxy surface, and there are angles to
the sun to consider as well. Yet what could be simpler,
more familiar than a drop of water on a leaf? Well,

when you speak Greek, and read this poem of Sappho's, it's like becoming instantly aware of all those angles and tensions, as well as of the everyday beauty of the droplet on the leaf – simultaneously. So it's a wonder – there's no other word.'

We sat in silence for a moment or two. I felt touched by an unexpected melancholy.

'There's more to it than that, of course. Somehow, in just sixteen words and thirty-two syllables (eight a line), Sappho has been able to make a distillation of sadness sound almost like the jaunty plucking of a lyre. It's about stillness – lying alone in contemplation – as well as about movement – towards old age and death, presumably, but also, from the wider world's perspective, a new day. It's about desire, clearly, and waiting – it's drenched with the anguish of hopeless waiting – yet only one tiny, insignificant word, *móna*, 'alone', hints at this. Sappho has taken plain, worn-out old *móna* and somehow, by uttering it at just the right instant, perfectly angled to the poem, she's turned it into a knife in the heart.

'It's pitiless and tender at the same time, this poem. As is the sea we're looking at now, I suppose. Or those swallows up there – are they swallows? Swooping about above the old olive-press, killing things. So, when I recited those lines to you in English . . . *Gone is the moon, gone the Pleiades, it's past midnight* . . . and so on, I knew I wasn't reciting Sappho's poem for you.'

'Still, it was worth doing.'

'Oh, yes. Absolutely. An impossible task, but none the less worth doing.'

'I really have to speak Greek.'

'Yes, I'm afraid you do.'

'I still don't know your name,' I said awkwardly, as she stood up to go.

'And I don't know yours, for that matter. Shall we leave it that way? We don't really need to know, do we?' It was said with a kind of knowing warmth I found touching.

The deserted beach, as the sun dropped behind the hills, was the perfect place to sit and think about setting off for home myself. Or, at least, Corfu. Sometimes you just know that everything has been said, the conversation is at an end and it's time to move on. In the morning I'd be packing my bags.

13

Chugging up over the rise to Sisi's palace two days later, I really did feel as if I were coming home. There was Gastouri, tumbling away down the hillside into the valley below, and, as I walked down to Kester's house from the bus-stop outside the palace, the postcard sellers and waiters in the kiosks around the entrance greeted me, old Spiros, edging his way up the hill on his walking-stick, called out *Kaliméra* (and a few other things I couldn't understand), the neighbour's cat rolled over to have his tummy scratched – I was home. It's so comforting, in a small village like Gastouri, to have all the *little* things you do remarked upon. Even Kester's disarmingly ugly little house on the bend of the road seemed to be watching me approach with a kind of benign somnolence. And how much greener everything was since I'd left! The trees and bushes all seemed to have thickened and grown lusher, while the roadside was a mass of white daisies.

I pushed open the door and surveyed the kitchen. Nothing seemed to have been touched. No unfamiliar odours, no half-drunk cups of coffee. William seemed to have left no trace. Even in the bedroom upstairs nothing at first betrayed his visit. Krishnamurti still

lay face-down on the bookshelf, *The Iliad* and a couple of Kester's unpublished novels were still on the
bedside table just as I'd left them. It was only when I
went over to the desk by the window, where I'd left an
unfinished letter or two and a shopping-list that my
eye fell on the sheet of paper covered in William's
unmistakable looping scrawl.

It was cheeky. If it didn't make me sound like a
school-master, I'd say it was even impertinent:

φίλε μου [*Phíle mou* – 'Dear Friend' – even I
knew that – cute.]

I've missed you. It's all my own stupid fault, I
suppose. I didn't really know what I was doing. Still,
your habit of disappearing into thin air at the drop
of a hat can make things a bit awkward at times.

Are you OK? I've spent a few days here (Agape
let me in), but didn't feel quite right about it, with
you not even knowing I was here.

All the same, seeing your things around the
house – books we'd talked about, clothes I'd bor-
rowed, notes you'd written to yourself – memories
came flooding back. And that was good, really.
Made me a bit sad as well.

I'll hang around for a few more days, just in case
you come back and we can meet again. It would
mean a lot to me. I'll be at your friend Greta's. She's
amazing.

Love,
William.

So Greta must have told him I was there. *There's another Australian staying here at the moment – he's theatrical as well, not a* cobber *of yours, I suppose? No, I'm sure he won't mind if you move in for a few days, he's gone to Lesbos.* I could just see her at the door, reassuring him. Probably then whisked him away to show him off to the gang.

So what was I expected to do? Ring him at Greta's? Have it out? Perhaps he'd just show up. I was trapped.

⌒

In every corner of Kester's house that first day back I seemed to see a ghost. The dank, bare rooms of my early days there were filling up with presences I could now put names to. The very air in the rooms was softening, taking on a kind of melancholy warmth. It wasn't just Kester Berwick who was becoming flesh, although, needless to say, his home-made bookshelves were now a babble of recognizable voices: E.M. Forster's novels, Clive James' memoirs of an Australian childhood, Annie Besant and the host of Theosophical pamphlets, slim paperbacks on Buddhism and the Tao, *The Odyssey,* Michael Chekhov's guides to actors – they all now fitted in. Not just tattered spines on unvarnished planks, these books were Kester's companions on his journey from flat, suburban Adelaide – I could picture its stony, low-roofed dullness, baking in the sun, so clearly I was almost there – to this house among the straggly oaks and olive-trees of Corfu.

That portrait on the wall beside the window – nothing out of the ordinary, just a yellow and brownish picture of a rather gawky young man in an open-necked shirt – must be of Alan Harkness. The photograph in the drawer of the young man in shorts sitting on a stone wall with his arm around a blonde young woman in long trousers must be Alan, too, somewhere in America. Too painful to frame, but too precious to throw out.

Was the smooth-faced angel in the suit – with, incredibly, a lace handkerchief peeping out of his top pocket – perhaps the Austrian boy Kester had so taken to just before the war when, leaving Alan to his wife-to-be (and the overpowering presence of Michael Chekhov), he'd found a niche for himself in the Tyrol? Was this Raymond?

Werter Herr Kester Berwick! the letter began – I'd seen it that first day, rifling through his desk drawer, but had paid it no heed. But here it was, typed on a failing typewriter on a single, thin sheet:

Ihren überaus lieben Brief haben wir vor einigen Tagen erhalten . . .

We received your extremely kind letter a few days ago and are happy to know that you still think of our dear Raymond. How sad you will feel, however, to learn that Raymond is no longer living. He fell in 1944, on 3rd August, in Lithuania. His commander wrote that Raymond had received a bullet-wound to the head . . .

He often spoke to us about you and said how well you were getting on. We often had the impression that he was very much attached to you. How happy he would be to be able to read your letter, but fate decreed otherwise . . .

I skipped the next bit about how difficult life was in Austria – although there was not a shadow of complaint.

Lieber Herr Kester, wir schicken Ihnen ein Photo von Raymond . . .

Dear Herr Kester, we're sending you a photo of Raymond, which he had taken on his last leave. In this way you too will have a last memory of our dear Raymond. Should your path bring you once again to our beautiful Tyrol, be assured that you will find here a heart-felt welcome.

It would give us pleasure if one day we might receive an answer to this letter.

Here we close, wishing you with our whole hearts all the best for the future.

The Muigg family.

The letter was written from Innsbruck on 26 April

1946. It was, I thought, an astonishing letter for its time and place. Perhaps I had misread it.

A curious letter too: it was not at all clear who had fired the bullet into Raymond's head. Could it have been Raymond?

It was just a few years after this frail message reached Kester that John Tasker had wandered into the light of those hurricane-lamps in post-war Newcastle. The snapshots in the deskdrawer of yet another lanky young man on the steps of a weatherboard house, on a bed in a room hung with tribal masks, on a motorbike under a clothes-line in a suburban backyard – these must be of John. I was beginning to recognize the coltish features.

This was no old man's cabinet of curiosities, not any more. Whatever it was, it was alive, its tendrils snaking out to pull me in.

⌒

That night I dreamt I'd gone downstairs to the kitchen to make a make a cup of tea. But when I opened the door and stepped inside, I was in Java. The kitchen, which appeared to open out onto night-shrouded gardens choked with vines and palm-trees, was seething with brown bodies – children, old women in sarongs, sharp-eyed men in cotton shirts with knives at their waists, some cross-legged on the floor, some huddled by the open windows, talking in low voices, some smoking, some slipping in and out of the garden.

Gusts of laughter swept across the crowd.

Suddenly I saw why: where the sink had been there was now a huge glowing screen, across which flew the hard, black shapes of shadow-puppets. Voices shrilled from behind the screen in jagged, foreign syllables. Everyone rocked with laughter. A gamelan crashed. Madly, although the words were incomprehensible, I understood every one. It was *Three Sisters*. And word for word it was my life. And every time I spoke, there were hoots of laughter, gales of it. Almost swooning from the heat and press of bodies, I seized a knife, strode across the squirming bodies to the screen and slashed it from top to bottom. The gamelan fell silent. The voices vanished. In the torchlight behind the screen, lifeless cut-outs in their hands, sat Kester in his overcoat, as prim as a princess, Sisi, Leila, the Austrian soldier, Krishnamurti, Alex, my wife, John Tasker, my witch and William . . . eyes fixed on me, a flicker of evil on their lips.

'Get out of my house!' I roared in the silence.

But there was no house. Just a dark garden, with white-clad figures slipping away into the blackness. And it wasn't Java after all. It was Adelaide. And Kester wasn't Kester, he was my mother, dressed in the beige pants-suit she always wore when I was a boy, although even then she was far too old for it. 'Happy birthday, darling!' she said. 'It's so good to have you home at last.' She was smoking one of the du Mauriers that killed her.

14

Next morning, finding my cupboards bare, I caught the bus down to Corfu Town to browse in the market. Markets, like fairs, parades and possibly theatre foyers after the performance, allow us to loiter deliciously with intent, staving off the need to trudge on into the future, stiff-backed with purpose. Intent is not purpose – a purpose can be satisfied. In a market, time starts to move in circles, losing its thrust, although Corfu's vegetable and fish market, ranged along either side of the dry moat of the New Fort, soon pushes you back out into the new town and the business of life.

Under striped awnings near the bottom end of the market lay trays of cockles, crabs, octopus and shrimp, which I was engrossed in inspecting when I suddenly heard a familiar voice.

'What about a nice piece of mullet, dear? I'm sure mullet don't suffer. Or some *barboúnia* – these little whatsits here – heaven when they're fried.'

I spun around. It was Greta and William, strolling towards me past the trays of fish. But William wasn't listening to Greta. He was staring at me as if I were a walking corpse. Spiky hair, striped t-shirt. Stunned.

I saw Greta swivel, heard her exclaim. As if floating on the salty waves of fish-smells, words drifted
past me from her mouth: '. . . you're back . . . Zoe,
why didn't you . . . William . . . Kester's . . .' But
they meant no more to me than the cries of the fish-
mongers, shouting from beneath their awnings.

'Thank you for your letter, William,' I heard
myself say eventually.

'Letter? What letter?' He still looked shocked, not
altogether pleasantly.

'The letter you left on the desk upstairs,' I said.

'Upstairs? Where? I didn't leave you any letter. I
didn't know you were here.'

What was he playing at? 'What do you mean? I've
read it. *I've missed you, I didn't know what I was doing
. . .*' Greta looked sharply away in embarrassment.

'That was for Kester. He went away before he got
my card and I missed him. Is it you staying at his
place?'

'You didn't know?'

'How would I have known? All Greta said was —'

'I gather you boys know each other.' Greta looked
pleased with herself, as if our meeting up like this
were just one more in a string of minor miracles
she'd been tossing off of late. While she was rattling
on about how small the world was, and lunch, and
Terpsi, who had had colic and nearly driven poor
Celia mad with worry, William and I tussled silently
with each other, sparring with our eyes. We looked
away at the zoo milling around us in the smelly heat,

at the trays of dead fish, at Greta's mouth, the sky,
our feet, and back into the eyes again. Who or what
was winning, it was impossible to say. Eddying
between us were vicious little currents of pain,
streaked with anger, blame, guilt and hunger. It was
a tug-of-war, with the rush of defeat, as it always is,
almost more rapturous than victory.

'I told Celia she should have her put down,' I
heard Greta say. William winced. 'I mean, she's just
a bag of skin and bones, a burden to Kester and herself . . . I think Kester would be secretly relieved. But
she's a Buddhist or something and won't hear of it.
No, wait a minute, Kester's a Buddhist, she's something else. A follower of whatshisname, the one who
killed Katherine Mansfield. Well, what do you say to
the bream?'

In a light haze of sweetbitterness – Sappho knew
her stuff – I trailed off after them towards the
carpark. I'd been swooped on and snatched up again
by a woman with strong wings.

William's knees were showing, I noticed, when he
turned to make sure I was following, through the
frayed fabric of his jeans. I have a weakness for knees,
ankles and wrists. Elbows are so vulnerable I can't
even bear to look at them.

15

'So,' I said, once Greta had left us alone on the terrace to go and grill the fish. I admit to a certain *penchant* for words which lead nowhere while throwing the door open to a larger space. 'So' and 'Well, then' were great favourites of my father's. His whole life, of course, led nowhere.

On dates as a teenager, *this* was what I wanted more than anything in the world: to be left alone in the dark at the cinema, in the car or in the living-room with whoever I was courting. To have time. When it actually happened, though, this *being together* with no script, especially if desire was frolicking somewhere in the wings, caused unbearable anxiety. It meant you were face to face with the question: *What do you want now?* To see this movie to the end? Or listen to music? Talk about the kids in your class? Discuss plans for the next weekend? No, but what? In *Daphnis and Chloe*, every last apple Daphnis threw at Chloe, every note he plucked on his lyre, every kiss, every touch, every word he spoke, was leading towards the ultimate intimacy, being 'guided into the passage he had been trying so long to find'. Pirates, kidnappings, snow-drifts, the antics of the gods – nothing could stop the lovers' progress to the marriage bed. Everything, even attempted rape, was just a delicious apprenticeship for the final loss of innocence. In real life, though, things are less dramatic, and those ancient goat-herds' innocence a rare commodity. Getting 'into the passage' is a very skewed answer to the question of what we want. It's like saying that what Monet wanted to do when he painted those women on the beach at Trouville was to paint those women on the beach at Trouville.

Apart from in Rome, William and I had never really sat in a puddle of unmapped time before, waiting to see what happened next. After the fiasco with the Golden Guru, our paths had hardly crossed until the night of the final dress-rehearsal of *Three Sisters*.

We were all in high spirits that night – 'knackered', as Leila put it, and tetchy with one another, at the end of our tethers, but in a weary kind of way elated. We knew it was good. We'd found the transfiguring 'truth' of it, as Clive would say. Not that Clive had any time for method acting – he never had us standing around finding our psychic centres or radiating our essences through our chins, as some directors do – but somehow or other he knew how to get us to say Chekhov's impossible lines ('It's exactly a year since father died' and 'Our sufferings will bring happiness to those who come after us') in ways that were believable. And William's set-design was brilliant – light, impressionistic, leaving the play's centre of gravity with the actors.

When the lights went down on the final scene at that last rehearsal ('*Ta-ra-ra-boomdeeay . . . None of it matters! It just doesn't matter!*' – that's the old doctor holding forth, and then Olga says: '*If only we knew, if only we knew!*' – CURTAIN), there was a burst of applause. Thin, but loud. A rousing staccato. The lights came up and, smiling broadly some rows back, were Clive, William and (I'd have known that skull anywhere) the Foreign Legionnaire.

'What the fuck is *he* doing here?' I hissed at Alex.

'Max? He's been helping Will knock the set together – he's got a couple of weeks' leave.'

'But . . .' But what? Anyway, Alex was already half-way down the steps into the hall. A fetching trio: red-haired Alex, purring, Max, looking like a pirate with his Captain Kidd bandanna, and William in an army great-coat, hand on Alex's arm. He looked up and flashed me a smile. *Right,* I thought. *This time, my friend, I really am coming to get you.*

So, when everyone started drifting off into the rain, I put my hand on William's shoulder and said: 'Look, can we talk?' And he said: 'Sure!' in that maddeningly accepting way he had, as if the unexpected were just what he'd been waiting for. He waved to Alex and Max to go on without him – 'I'll catch you up in a minute,' he called – and I said: 'No, not in a minute, William, I want to talk,' to which he said:

'Why don't you come with us?' 'Because I want to talk to *you*,' I said, 'I don't want —', but he broke in with: 'I really don't think you know *what* it is you want.' And it was true.

'Come on,' he said, putting up his rainbow-striped umbrella, 'you're getting wet. I'll walk you to the station.'

We sloshed along in silence for a moment. 'The trouble is that I don't know what *you* want, William,' I said, treading carefully. 'You said that if I saw you with someone else, I should "come and get you" – but in the end you always go off with the others. I don't know what *you* want.'

'I went to France with you.'

'And look what happened.'

'What happened? I thought we were having a great time until you threw that tantrum and stormed off. What were you expecting to happen?'

The short answer seemed obvious. 'I suppose I was expecting to find out what sort of relationship . . .' I couldn't finish the sentence – the word 'relationship' always makes my mind go blank, I heard it once too often in the seventies.

'Me, too,' he said, without a hint of rancour. We'd come to the first lighted shop-windows on the Holloway Road. Retro furniture, second-hand clothes. Just ahead of us, Alex and the pirate were dawdling, glancing back to see where we were. The streetlamp, shining through the coloured panels of his umbrella, was bathing William in a strawberry light.

'Well, what I think,' he said, quite softly so the others couldn't hear him, 'is that until you know what you want to *be*, you won't know what you want me to be. When you work that one out, we might be in business. I can wait.'

'You're sounding a bit like a self-help manual. Or your friend Seb. Is that one of the Golden Guru's little gems?'

He twirled his umbrella and went blue-green. 'The others are waiting. Sure you won't come?'

'Quite sure.'

'See you tomorrow then. The big day.'

'There's just one other thing,' I said, suddenly emboldened. 'Are you sleeping with the Legionnaire? Or Alex? Or both?'

He laughed, twirled again, went purple and said: '*None of that matters! It just doesn't matter!* Isn't that what the good doctor would say?'

Yes, but as the old maid Olga replied: *If only I knew.*

Psycho-babble infuriates me. I did all that in Adelaide in my teens. *Until you know what you want to be, you won't know who you want me to be.* I could just see Seb in his caftan, piercing William with his violet eyes and then leaning forwards to murmur this sort of tosh into his ear. For twenty pounds an hour, no doubt.

Oddly enough, though, William's words kept buzzing inside my head. Sitting on the Underground or making toast, walking in the park or shopping for groceries, I'd find myself mulling them over. It was much easier, for instance, to think about what I wanted to have than what I wanted to be, to rehearse in my mind what I lacked and what I needed to fill the blank spaces. Was I a Daphnis without a Chloe, for example, I thought to myself after seeing the ballet that winter. Or a Chloe waiting for a Daphnis? Was I wooing or being wooed? Perhaps what I really needed was a close friend. Perhaps I was an Achilles without a Patroclus. But I had friends – well, people I liked, anyway, people I could call up and go out with if I was at a loose end. Nobody *transfiguring*, it's true – Leila was sweet, in her fashion, as was Rupert, who did all our lighting and liked to go to a movie with me occasionally, but neither of them stood as mirrors to my soul, neither of them made me feel the world was new each time we met, as Emerson's friends made him feel – or so he claimed. Emerson was right about one thing, I couldn't help thinking: that kind of friendship, like the immortality of the soul, was simply too good to be true. When it announced itself, you didn't believe it and laughed in its face.

Everything in between Daphnis' limb-loosening passion for Chloe on the one hand (or Sappho's love-sickness – scorched, shuddering, sweating; she thought she was dying) and the 'perfect union' of hearts and minds all those high-minded philosophers enjoyed with their friends on the other – everything in between seemed so prosaic, dull and unfulfilling, yet it was the stuff of daily life. I'd look around the carriage in the Underground and wonder if the man in the fawn jumper opposite, say, or the punk reading some lurid tabloid next to him, knew what it might mean for a friend's absence to turn the world into a wilderness, or if the young girls chatting by the door knew what it felt like to want some tender sapling of a boy at the office until fire ran through their flesh and the rest of the world was just a mindless hum? And did any of them know both? And was everything else just a grey kind of waiting?

In sloppy March – it was a foul day like any other, with no signs or portents that I noticed – I ran for a train at Victoria and just missed it. Bad busking echoed round the station. I started to read the hoardings. To my astonishment, when I got to the lethally clever Silk Cut advertisement, there was William, standing right in front of it. Army great-coat, beanie, boots, delectable. And utterly ordinary. It was the sudden ordinariness that made the heart leap.

'I'm thinking of going home,' I said, once we'd squeezed aboard a train.

'Really? Back to Adelaide?' He looked at me intently. The tender skin around his eyes was bluish.

'Why not? I'm sick of pulling rabbits out of hats for brats in Hampstead.'

'I thought you were making piles of loot teaching English to Swedes.'

'Norwegians. I'm sick of them as well. In any case, most of them speak better English than I do.'

'But why Adelaide? You always said how boring it was, how you'd rather live in New Zealand than Adelaide.'

'I'm starting to think it was me I found boring.'

'Why would it be any different this time around?'

'It mightn't be. I'm just starting to feel that I want to go home. I want to start again. And that's where I need to do it.'

'Now who's sounding like a self-help book?'

'Besides, if I don't go soon, it won't be home any more.'

'When will you go?'

'I don't know – soon.'

I knew what he was going to say next before he said it. 'How about I come with you?'

Just six words, all commonplace. They were a cluster-bomb.

Two weeks later we said goodbye at Charing Cross, I went to Italy, with William to follow when he'd finished a job he had to do in Brighton.

~

Now, on Greta's terrace, while she fried the bream, I knew William was waiting for me to find the words to explain why I had left him in that yellow and purple hotel room in Rome. I said: 'How is it you know Kester?'

'How is it *you* know Kester?'

'I don't. I'm just renting his house for a couple of

months. But I know you know him – I've seen the photograph of the two of you. Naked on that rock. So obviously you know each other very well.'

He wasn't exactly sulky, but he was quiet, wary, hurt. How to reel him in?

'You know your trouble?' he said, fixing me with those bruised eyes of his. 'You want to pull everything apart all the time to see how it works. You're like those teachers we had at school who pulled poems and plays apart until they were dead. You murder everything, did you know that? Why can't you just let things be what they are?'

'Because I want to *know* what they are. That's the way I am.'

'*Am I fucking Max? What's going on with Alex? Do I know what my tattoo means?* And now you want to know if I've been having it off with Kester Berwick! He's eighty-five years old, for God's sake. It's a photo of two guys sitting in the sun, it doesn't *mean* anything.'

'Nothing seems to "mean anything" to you, William. What do you think life is? One great shopping mall you can just drift about in, listening to the muzak? Pick up a bit of reincarnation here, grab a bonk there – Chekhov, Cher, the Rolling Stones, Beirut, it's all the same to you, it's just background noise.'

'That's crap. It's not like that at all.'

'So where did he pick you up?'

'Who?'

'Kester Berwick. In some bar on Cromwell Road?'

'Is that all you can think about? What if he did? As

a matter of fact, I met Kester in Adelaide years ago –
I'd just left school. I'm not telling you how because
you'll only sneer.'

'Try me.'

'OK, it was at a lecture on TM.'

'The Maharishi whatsit?'

'See? I knew you'd sneer. You're so closed-off.'

'If I'm so closed-off, so boringly conventional, why
did you make me feel I was special in some way? And
you did, you singled me out, you made me feel . . .'

Greta darted out of the french windows towards
us, a tray of plates and glasses in her hands.

'Because,' William said, just as she reached the
table, not lowering his voice in the slightest, 'I
thought I could love you.'

Greta gave a jerk and let the tray slip clattering
onto the table. 'Love' – how I loathed that spongy,
sickly-sweet word, especially after *Three Sisters*. It's a
voodoo word, a meaningless incantation, mumbo
jumbo like Seb's spurious spells. I stood up and
pushed back my chair. It fell over.

'I'm going to take a walk,' I said.

'Why don't you stay and finish this?' William said.

'Yes, and what about the fish?' said Greta.

Rounding the courtyard wall, I glanced up at the
window where I'd seen the figure in the crimson
dressing-gown at the Easter party. I gave a start: it
was there again, leering down at me.

'Why don't you fuck off?' it roared at me again,
waving a bottle of Glenfiddich out the window.

'Why don't you fuck off yourself, you drunken old bastard?' I called back and kept going, round to the back of the house, round to the shimmering quiet of the lawn fringed with cyclamens, right over to the myrtles in the corner. I hate scenes. Faintly on the breeze I heard the old man call after me: 'Who said I was drunk?'

When I turned round, it need hardly be said, William was standing right behind me. Neither of us spoke. I could hear bees humming in the cyclamens.

'Well?' he said after a longish pause, still nettled, but with a softer, huskier edge to his voice. When I said nothing, he sat down cross-legged on the grass to wait, his t-shirt hanging open at the neck. Just below his collar-bone I caught a glimpse of the Horus-eye again, staring up at me. This time there was no escape.

'I'm sorry,' I said. 'It was an unforgivable thing to do.'

'Why did you do it?'

'I panicked.' And there was that stomach-turning yellow and purple room, too, I thought of adding, but wisely didn't. Just picturing it made me queasy.

'I thought something terrible had happened to you.'

'I'm sorry.' I ground a violet or two into the grass with the ball of my foot. 'All of a sudden it just hit me, when you got out of the train: I didn't want to spend the rest of my life with you.'

'I hadn't asked you to.'

That was true, he hadn't. All I wanted from you (I should have said to him then) was what we had: the swerving towards and pulling back, the whirling, the breathless tumbling, the stumbling, the jabbing pain, the solace, the sport – not *life*. Departures, not arrivals, in other words. And as for love – I still didn't have the faintest notion of what people meant by 'love'.

'We're just too different, William,' I said eventually, dry-throated.

'That's what I like.'

'You like *fun*.'

'Sometimes. What's wrong with that?'

'I'd like to be friends, you know,' I said, flashing him an impromptu smile.

'I wouldn't,' he said. 'I've got friends.'

'What would you like us to be?' I fervently hoped he wasn't going to come out with another embarrassing word.

He cocked an eye at me. 'Oh, I don't know,' he said. 'You're the clever one, you think of the right word.'

'We'd better go back and have our fish.'

At some point between the fish and the promised rose-petal *glikó* – 'a favourite of Kester's, actually, he always has a second helping' – a line of Emerson's came into my dry-as-dust, analytical mind, an expression I'd found puzzling when I'd first read it: 'beautiful enemies'. That is what Emerson said friends (in the most life-enhancing sense) should be to each other. All of a sudden it made some sort of cockeyed sense: friend as admired invader, desired (for the sweetness of capitulation) yet resisted, endlessly withstood. It was so much less syrupy, so much more dynamic, than 'soul-mates', 'close friends' and all the other words I'd been trying to choose between.

I was about to try 'beautiful enemies' out on William while Greta was inside getting the *glikó*, when there was a dull thud, then the crash of glass on stone and a curious cracking sound, like a large flower-pot rolling over.

'What in God's name was that?' I said.

William cocked an ear. 'I'll duck round and have a look,' he said.

In the kitchen Greta was singing along to 'Kiss Me, Kate' on the record-player. '*Why caaan't you behave?*' There was a clatter of cutlery and dishes. 'Oh, bugger!' I heard her say brightly to herself. Perhaps she'd dropped a fork on the floor.

I sat, thrumming on the table for a while, then went inside to see if Greta needed any help. The kitchen was empty. The rose-petal *glikó* was gathering flies on the sideboard. '*So in love with you am I . . .*'

When William came into the kitchen a few minutes later to use the phone, I already knew. Some silences – well, after two Chekhov plays, I'd know – are much richer in meaning than mere words.

After the funeral (the usual non-believer's sort of affair: a few well-meaning speeches in the Reading Society rooms, Strauss's *Four Last Songs*, finger food) Greta said: 'It's funny, isn't it. Now the old bastard's dead, I feel a silence has been broken. Dreadful way to go, though . . . across the flower-pot like that. Can't bear to think about it. If he'd only waited another six months, he'd have died of cirrhosis of the liver anyway.' Everyone remarked on what a brave face she was putting on it. There was a strong smell of furniture polish, dead flowers and dust.

'Now perhaps you'll find some peace, dear,' Celia said to her gently, the remains of a mushroom vol-au-vent nestling on the pearls on her bosom.

'Peace? That's the last thing I want,' Greta snapped. 'Come on, William, let's go home. I'm going to put on some very loud music and get drunk.'

While Celia was talking to me about reincarnation, and the sound of Greta's puttering Volkswagen faded into the larger cacophony of Corfu's midday scramble, I suddenly had an idea. A distant Chekhovian beacon lit up. 'Peace. Now you'll find some peace.' Sonya at the end of *Uncle Vanya*.

'What Rudolf Steiner used to say whenever anyone brought up reincarnation – and my dear husband once wrote the most inspiring poem, which captured the essence of it . . . I could show it to you one day, if you'd care to see it . . .'

'Celia, have you got any of Chekhov's plays amongst your books?'

'Chekhov? All of them, I'm sure. My husband knew Michael Chekhov, you know, when he was teaching down in Devon before the war. Very close, they were. Michael Chekhov was a follower of Steiner's, of course – I expect you knew that. Had to keep it a bit hush-hush, naturally, when he went to America, but the fact is –'

'I need to get hold of *Uncle Vanya*, Celia. Straight away.'

'Well, let's tootle on up to the house now, if you like, and I'll see if I can lay my hands on it.'

While Celia was looking for her husband's poem, I rang William at Greta's, *Uncle Vanya* in my hand.

'How's Greta?'

'Not good. She's gone to pieces.'

'I suppose it's suddenly hit home – she's alone now. All those things left unsaid.'

'No, it's got nothing to do with that. It's just that the cat's been missing ever since that afternoon, no sign of him anywhere, and we thought he must've, you know, got the vibes and skedaddled. But when we got back, I started clearing away the broken pot and, well, found the cat squashed underneath it. He killed the cat. She's inconsolable.'

It didn't seem like the right time to tell him about my idea for *Uncle Vanya*. It was a brilliant idea, and I had the feeling he'd take to it like a flash.

'I'll call you tomorrow. Love to Greta.' Replacing the receiver, I glanced down and saw a bedraggled terrier sitting at my feet, black eyes locked wistfully onto mine. 'Hullo, Terpsi,' I said, kneeling to give her a pat. She swished her tail on the tiles, hoping for an intimate moment, but Celia was already advancing on me from the library, waving a small sheaf of typed pages in triumph. '*Beyond time and space, in some everlasting Now, Through the Gateway of the Sun . . .*'

'Perhaps I could take it with me, Celia?' It was entitled, I noticed, 'The Divine Dovetailing'.

'Absolutely. You need peace and quiet to drink it in.'

In the event, I left it in the taxi – I was in a hurry to get inside and divinely dovetail with *Uncle Vanya*. There was that feeling again, the feeling I'd had on the first morning in Kester's house: the white wax coating the writing-tablet, smooth, newly virginal, on my knees, and my stylus, needle-sharp, poised just above it, ready to write.

— PART THREE —

You said: 'I'll go to another country, go to another shore,
find another city better than this one.
Whatever I try to do is fated to turn out wrong
and my heart lies buried as though it were something dead.
How long can I let my mind moulder in this place?
Wherever I turn, wherever I look,
I see the black ruins of my life, here,
where I've spent so many years, wasted them, destroyed them totally.'

You won't find a new country, won't find another shore.
This city will always pursue you.
You'll walk the same streets, grow old
in the same neighbourhoods, turn grey in these same houses.
You'll always end up in this city. Don't hope for things elsewhere:
there's no ship for you, there's no road.
Now that you've wasted your life here, in this small corner,
you've destroyed it everywhere in the world.

C.P. Cavafy, 'The City'

1

'Why do we do it?' It was one of those late night questions – not even a question. Scooping up another handful of sunflower seeds from the saucer on the grass, William lay back, hands under his head, and began to munch thoughtfully in the darkness. Snatches of Gershwin wafted round the corner from the kitchen where Greta was on the telephone to somebody or other. Bursts of laughter, whole sentences in throaty Greek. A tiny owl streaked out of the myrtles, bent on murder.

It had been an exhausting evening – the first run-through of the whole play without a script, a dog's breakfast of a performance, with everyone getting very snappish. 'Why we did it', however, I knew perfectly well. I'd known since I was eleven or twelve.

One summer in the early 1960s, down the side of our house in Largs Bay, under the magnolia-tree by the fence, my father took it into his head to put up a car-port. In those days everyone was doing it: alongside gracious old sandstone bungalows all over Adelaide – those showily prim but faintly sinister houses that bring to mind fine china, vicars and arcane perversions – men started erecting car-ports, often with a little shed at the back. They looked hideous, like gumboots on a debutante, but my brother and I were ecstatic. It meant we were modern. And having just been to a matinée performance of *The Pirates of Penzance*, I knew instantly what our car-port's higher purpose was: a backyard theatre.

It's all in the curtain. Everything else – writing the play, the raids for props and costumes, the daily betrayals and clashes with puffed-up egos – is tumultuous fun, but it is that final moment, when the neighbours are sitting on cushions and chairs on one side of the curtain and we are poised with cardboard swords and a trunk of pebbles wrapped in silver foil on the other, that is alchemical. This is the moment, as my brother jerks the bed-sheets apart, when the mystery descends, and in the blink of an eye we are both ourselves (our tiny, backyard, childish selves) and not ourselves (miraculously beautiful, even good). The parting curtain has wrought a miracle, a collision of worlds, and this miracle is witnessed with rapt attention. Everything now matters – every trivial word, every crooked finger, every raised eyebrow – *everything*.

Kester Berwick, as he'd told William, signalled this transfiguring moment with 'a sweet gong', at least in the early days at his studio performances in Adelaide when a curtain would have struck him as too bourgeois (as well as too expensive). Darkness and a gong did the trick for Kester with much more power.

When my brother yanked the curtain closed on the final scene of mass slaughter that first Saturday afternoon (every child in the street lying stone dead amongst the grease-spots), I knew what wonder was. Needless to say, it wasn't the kind of thing I could ever explain to my father, who in any case had spent the afternoon at the cricket.

'We do it,' I said to William now, 'because it's our way of making up for the utter ordinariness of our lives.' It didn't sound particularly pompous, because the impossible final words of *Uncle Vanya* were still ringing in our ears ('*We shall hear angels, we shall see all the heavens ablaze in diamonds, we shall see all earthly evil, and all our suffering, drowned in mercy which will flood the whole world*' . . . only the vicar had seemed unembarrassed by this gush of turgid claptrap).

William said nothing. At this moment – lying at midnight on a lawn in the hills behind Corfu Town, his mind half in Russia and his whole young life a choppy sea of surprises – he probably wondered what on earth I meant.

Who'd have thought that *Uncle Vanya* could 'make up' for anything? Of all plays, this gloomy little clutch of 'scenes from country life' might seem the least likely to make our everyday lives glow with significance, echo with meanings. Our little rounds of tea-drinking, crossword-solving, pruning, banal infatuations and visits to the hairdresser were surely beyond redemption. They hardly justified getting up in the morning. What light could Chekhov's cast of whining mopers throw on any of it?

~

'Frankly, I think we should do a Coward or *An Ideal Husband* – something uplifting,' Greta had said at our first meeting, once I'd explained what *Uncle Vanya* was all about. 'This sounds about as interesting as cleaning the silver.' Arthur's Chilean friend, Alberto, who'd been a member of some university drama club in Santiago, thought we should 'jazz it up a bit', call it *Vanya on Corfu* and turn it into a series of satirical sketches on the lives of the island's ex-patriate community. 'It'd be a hit. You could even have a TV on in the corner showing Greek soaps – not too loud, of course, just as a sort of symbol.' Yes, but of what? The vicar, to my dismay, thought this a splendid idea – he was thrilled by anything that was relevant to the community. Even William, who was stage manager as well as designer this time, seemed infected. 'And instead of typhoid fever,' he said, 'it could be AIDS, say, that's killing the peasants off like flies and in the end the professor could go off to London instead of Kharkov.' And get himself a little flat in Putney? I began to droop.

But this is the mystery of it: as this rag-bag collection of amateurs listened day after day to what Chekhov had written, and their lives seeped into Chekhov and Chekhov washed back over their lives, all talk of Greek soaps, bouzouki music and Noël Coward faded. It's hard to explain it in words that don't sound sentimental . . . but they *made friends* with their characters: Prue (she told me) waited all day for the moment to arrive when we would gather on Greta's terrace and she could slip through the looking-glass into her Helen self, that languid, simmering, brooding, fretful self – a cat, not a woman, that eats and sleeps and stretches in the sun, drawing every man to stroke her . . . only to cuff him, claws at the ready. Even Bernie, I sensed, tearing over to Greta's when her bookshop closed at six, dumpy Bernie, alive (it seemed to me sometimes) to nothing but migrating woodsnipe, was hungry every afternoon to be Sonya–Bernie – good, ugly Sonya–Bernie, pointlessly in love with Dr Astrov (Arthur's Chilean), who in his turn is pointlessly in love with Helen–Prue, who loves no one and nothing except her own beauty, least of all her squeezed lemon of an academic husband (played by the vicar with devastating truthfulness). The excitement for Bernie was being allowed to stand up every evening in front of her friends and neighbours and say without blushing, 'I am ugly', 'I slave every day for nothing' and 'there is no reward for my goodness – except, of course, in heaven'. It desperately needed to be said – Bernie knows she's just a frog in a puddle nobody even knows is there, but who could she ever say it to without losing every last shred of self-respect?

Even Arthur's glossy Alberto, I have to say, who spent Monday to Friday behind a desk in one of the consulates down in the town centre, seemed to enjoy paying hopeless court to Prue, hitting the bottle and complaining out loud to Vanya that they were the only two decent, cultivated men in the district, although they too had been 'dragged down' by the narrow-minded, philistine life around them and become as petty and vulgar as everybody else. There was a passion in his voice – in his whole body – when he talked about his failed hopes to stem the tide of ecological degradation in the district, or to find anything at all to do that wasn't ultimately meaningless and a waste of time. It was the kind of passion that rarely animated the clerk from the consulate, although you could guess at it sometimes when he talked about Chile during his student days.

It's not the pointlessness of these provincial lives which makes the play dark, though, I've decided. In truth, they're no more pointless, or petty and vulgar, than ours are. After all, most of the men and women in Greta's living-room fill their days with sweeping the steps, filling the cat's saucer, working to make others rich and aimlessly narrating the loose ends of their lives to people who can hardly wait for them to finish their sentence before launching into tales of their own. No, Chekhov's characters don't strike me as especially vulgar or shallow. What they are, surely, is utterly unremarkable, worn thin by the unrelieved ordinariness of their lives. Any fool, as Chekhov himself said somewhere, can deal with a crisis – it's day-to-day living that wears us out.

What makes this play seem so much darker, so much more stifling, than *Three Sisters* or *The Cherry Orchard* (almost a gay romp by comparison) is the complete failure of eros to light a spark of meaning in the gloom. Unable to conceive of any other kind of transfiguring experience (except, dimly, by God's mercy, in the afterlife), eros is these characters' only hope. They call it 'love', naturally, as they would, but in *Uncle Vanya* what else does 'love' mean but eros? There's barely a glimmer of any other kind of affection, as far as I can see, from the first line to the last.

Erotically, these characters' lives come across as an empty plate. And Dr Astrov knows why. He could almost have been an ancient Greek!

Living here on Corfu at the moment, how could I have any doubt that eros strikes us first through the eyes? We look – and are harpooned by beauty. (It would be fascinating to know how it works for the blind, but for the rest of us the eyes do their work first.) Watching Helen idling on the swing and drifting like a sleep-walker through the house, Vanya and Dr Astrov lose their breath at her sheer beauty.

Having looked, we then open our mouths and start spouting the most abject nonsense – about films we've seen, the weather, all the things clogging our souls and our minds. We join yoga classes and listen for hours to old Bob Dylan records with the object of our desire; we talk, we stroll, we go for drives, convincing ourselves that this beauty we wish to possess (and penetrate to its quick) is also lovable, brimming over with kindness, say, or wit or sensitivity. This is the playground love and desire tussle in – for a season. It quickly empties, as we all know, once grim-faced marriage marches in – especially in Chekhov.

Dr Astrov has Helen's measure, however. 'Everything *about a person should be beautiful,*' he tells Sonya (herself half-crazed for love of him). '*The face, the clothes, the soul, the mind. Helen is beautiful, there's no argument about that, but . . . all she ever does is eat, sleep, wander about and bewitch us all with her beauty – she doesn't do anything else. There's nothing she has to do, others do all the work for her . . . isn't that so? And an idle life is already a blemished one.*' Beautiful, but too obviously empty. Beautiful, but inwardly lifeless. Eros has nothing here to play with, and Eros (just a boy, let's remember, according to the Greeks, and mischievous) likes to play. Alberto, with his own particular kind of knowing beauty, carries this scene off brilliantly.

Sonya and her uncle, Vanya, are so unprepossessing that Eros hardly bothers to slide an arrow from his quiver. Their longings are pathetically unrequited. In desperation, poor Vanya claims to have leapt right over the top of eros and landed straight in the lap of friendship. '*She's my friend,*' he says to Dr Astrov, his rival for Helen's affections. '*What? Has it come to that* already?' Astrov sneers.

When Helen and the professor finally gallop off to

Kharkov and Dr Astrov goes back to his country surgery, leaving Vanya and Sonya to rattle their abacus over their accounts in the half-dark, the greatest failure is not to have made no sense of their hum-drum, home-spun, woebegone lives, but to have seen beauty, wanted it and then found it lifeless, just a corpse.

Needless to say, there's a failure of the imagination in *Uncle Vanya*, as there usually is in Chekhov's plays: nobody seems able to think beyond the family – or at least a mock-up of a family: two lovers or two loving friends. When this sort of set-up proves impossible, they all just fold their tents and vanish into the darkness.

Is the darkness in *Uncle Vanya* unrelieved? Well, no it's not, surely. Like our own lives, the play never reaches the purifying heights of tragedy. Nor, like our own lives, does it quite descend into soap opera or farce. It hovers irritatingly in between. We all know the feeling. What we *can* hold onto in it, however, is Chekhov's astonishing ability to make small things greater and big things . . . not smaller exactly, but big for smaller, more human reasons. Drinking tea, loving a woman, saving the forests, playing the guitar, a botched operation, a thunderstorm, the pointlessness of everything . . . somehow or other (it's a mystery to me, I can't fathom it) all these things make space for each other, allow each other their own particular value, refuse to shout each other down. In life things may not work out like this, but they do in the play. Life, so to speak, may not be beautiful, but its translation can be.

I tried to work some of these ideas into our discussions of the play, but I don't think they made much impression. Alberto in particular was adamant that some things in life are utterly trivial and some things worth dying for, especially in Chile, and the vicar, for completely different reasons, agreed with him. In the end, my players came most alive when they were playing their version of *Vanya in Corfu*, with only the names sounding Russian, like a courtesy to protect the guilty.

2

I'm getting to the bottom of it (sort of) bit by bit. To the bottom of Kester Berwick, I mean. And therefore (and this is mystifying) to the bottom of something else.

As soon as the sun hits the tiny terrace in front of Kester's front door, I've taken to setting myself up there in a comfortable chair to skim through some of Kester's manuscripts and cuttings. Up on the hill in front of me, half hidden by the cypresses, I can see that monument to failure, Sisi's palace, while to my left the road winds down into the somnolent, white-washed village. Occasionally I fancy I can smell fresh bread on the breeze.

Leafing, for instance, through the bound manu-script of yet another of his novels set on Lesbos, *Harps in the Wind*, I've found myself strangely drawn into his tale of a young Australian's arrival in Molyvos and the upheaval it causes over the year that follows. (This is one of those manuscripts he's pro-duced by '*tap-tap-tapping* away', as Arthur put it, 'page after dreary page'.) He arrives in Molyvos on a whim, but not unheralded – half the village receives a letter from an admirer of his in London, urging a warm welcome for him: 'I am sure that you will find him . . . unusually charming . . . Although an Australian, he . . . has various cultural interests (a little gauche perhaps, but so good-looking!).' (This from a minor British diplomat whose 'cultural interests' extend little beyond collecting Regency candlesticks.) To tell the truth, although absolutely nothing happens from the first page to the last – our hero comes, creates havoc and goes, he's really a mockery of a hero – I feel more drawn in by this book than *Head of Orpheus Singing.*

Some things do happen – a year can't go by in a Greek village without *something* happening – but nothing that happens matters very much. There are in point of fact two murders, a suicide in imitation of Sappho's, thefts, adultery, sundry disappearances, one stroke, several spells in prisons (both Greek and Turkish) and a spate of final farewells. (As usual in Kester Berwick's books, everyone either leaves or dies. Quite Chekhovian in that regard.) It's just that, related as it is in that rather prim, parson's voice that seems to come naturally to my landlord, it's all much of a muchness – rape, rheumatism, backgammon in Nick's taverna, the rounds of the rubbish collector with his donkey cart, a saucer of syrupy jam and a cup of coffee with a neighbour, film night in the old mosque, stealing icons, hopeless love, madness, the priest's frantic crocheting of cyclamen-pink doyleys – it all just goes into the mix. Nobody learns anything. Nobody changes. This Australian drifter whose beauty transfixes the village and then shatters it, just bobs along like a bottle on the tide, feckless, rootless, unanswerable for the commotion he's caused in women's hearts (and one or two men's, too, with names like Julian and Mat) or for the little rents he's opened up in the fabric of village life. Eventually he just heads off back to Australia to marry a shadowy figure called Rosemary whose only role in the novel up to this point has been to send him a packet of preserved apricots. Nice boy, no doubt about it — and quite an eyeful, according to the locals, when he sunbakes in the raw — but, like Helen in *Uncle Vanya*, lacking something a good life grows out of.

What is so seductive about this chronicle of a year in Molyvos — especially for a reader sitting out in the sun, as I was, on a bend in the road in Gastouri, just the odd cat stirring, old Spiros with his walking-cane grunting a greeting as he hobbles past — is that it dawns on you as you read why whiling away your life in an insignificant Greek village is so life-enhancing for many foreigners — at least at first: here, magically, *everything* matters all of a sudden — a broken flowerpot, the priest's wife's gossip, your neighbour's sprained ankle, the beauty of the mountains against the molten evening sky, a funeral, a drowning, fried sardines with friends down by the water . . . and also doesn't matter. What matters most now, in a way that's almost impossible in our great metropolises, is the quality of your relationship with others — your 'friendships', in other words, those moments you have every day in villages like Molyvos or Gastouri which are filled with affection, longing, kinship, good-humoured care and conversation. It's time-travel, really. It can't exist at home, where your failure to live a significant life is advertised on the side of every passing bus. And no one in the little circle of foreigners in Molyvos will give it up without a fight.

There's sex, too, naturally. Foreigners, with their marvellous lack of serious family ties or obligations to anyone in the village, live in an enchanted space as far as the local fishermen and their sons are concerned. Sex with no consequences is miraculously just there for the asking. Indeed, one of the characters in Kester's novel, Belinda (a married woman, but her husband is understanding) doesn't even ask – she just snaffles it up: soldiers, fisher boys, the town crier – it's immaterial to Belinda. She comes to a sticky end.

Why is at first unclear. Why does Berwick punish Belinda so brutally? (She's raped and drowned. No salacious details, no dramatic consequences – she's just put a stop to.) After all, there's no secret about it now – Kester Berwick, despite his penchant for psychic experiences and tidy marriages at the end of his books to women called Claire and Rosemary, obviously enjoys a romp with any muscled baker's boy who happens to be passing as much as his Belinda did. What is his point?

Little by little, delving into his stories and diaries (all shame has fled), I think I'm getting the picture.

'Intimacy' is a word I find my mind homing in on more and more often when I think about Kester Berwick. And I think he's onto something. His point, I believe, is intimacy.

In those three great loves of his, which Leila seemed to know so much about, as well as in the stories he's spun and his chance erotic encounters – all those Theos and Georges in his diaries, all those bare-chested sailors in his stack of snapshots – it seems to me more and more that what he's been seeking is utter intimacy. It's not a matter of the flesh or the spirit, as I see it now, or of moving between a night-time and a daytime self – not for Kester – it's a matter of striving for intimacy where he is, and as he is, now, even as a rather scrawny old man in his eighties.

I sense it, for instance, in the way his heroes stand apart from the crowd. It's never people they shun, but the tribe. What they yearn for is a sudden blaze of recognition between two people (something the herd, as we know, instinctively distrusts). On several occasions in Molyvos, I now recalled, men who'd known Kester in his early years in Greece had remarked on how he himself had shied away from joining the gaggle of bright young things in the taverna down by the water of an evening to argue about the colonels' coup or the latest issues of the *Partisan Review*. And just one bar of Theodorakis, who was strictly banned, of course, after the coup, 'and he was out the door and scuttling back up the hill to his room like a frightened rabbit,' according to an American painter I met out on the breakwater one blustery morning. 'Tucked himself up in bed with Madame Blavatsky, I guess,' he snorted. 'Or a soldier boy from the barracks.' He sneered into the wind. 'Or both.' Well, possibly – did it matter? In any case, I doubted that he'd fled up the hill to his room below the castle simply because somebody had played a few bars of Theodorakis.

Intimacy is more, though, than just a burst of loving recognition between two people. I know it is. But what is it? Is it perhaps the experience we have sometimes – rarely, but we do have it – of growing transparent, softly penetrated to every corner by another's knowing gaze? And of his or her being pierced and known in turn by our inner eye? (Yet we start with the outer). You can't even think about intimacy without starting to muse on rawness, a kind of loving wounding of each other. So invulnerability (such as Belinda's, in this manuscript I've been reading) is a sin.

The narrator in Kester's writing is so transparent he's hardly there at all. He's like a translucent membrane, filtering for our delectation others' thoughts and actions. And as for Kester Berwick himself – well, in the diaries I've found stacked in cardboard boxes upstairs, he to all intents and purposes simply fails to exist. 'Notis, 8 p.m.' might be one entry. 'Went to Cos.' 'Maxwell arrived.' 'Posted letter to JT.' 'Severe earthquake around midnight.' 'Krishna-murti died this day.' It's almost uncanny.

'There's no such thing as friends,' one rather sour, although witty, French writer once declared, 'there are only moments of friendship.' I can now imagine Kester, after a thoughtful pause, nodding in reluctant agreement. The way he writes his stories and the way he seems to have lived his life both remind me of a deep-sea diver, stabbing at the enveloping darkness with his searchlight, marvelling at what he sees, drawing closer, striving to make sense of some freakish eel or squid, and then moving on. There is no great scheme of things (except, in Kester's case, for a moment or two at a Theosophical Society lecture), just a roving illumination. The rest is darkness, and it doesn't matter.

Kester dreams of something more lasting than this – of 'friends', in other words, not just 'moments of friendship' – of course he does. So do his characters: this one dreams of a life in Sweden with a visiting Swedish yachtsman (and drifts off-stage, northwards), this one of marriage to a wispy, apricot-chewing figure called Rosemary half a world away, this one of going 'home' to the bosom of the family. But these dramatic twists are no more believable than Ranyevskaya's lover in Paris or Vera's monastery – they're plot solutions, not the stuff of life.

After a scratch lunch, my mind will slowly start to fill with Helen–Prue, Alberto–Astrov, Bernie–Sonya, the vicar's professor and all the others. As the sun inches westwards towards Italy, and the time for our rehearsal looms, Molyvos and Gastouri, with the barest of kaleidoscopic shakes, will merge into a mouldering estate in Russia, a weirdly Freudless, Jungless, Marxless world – with Einstein not even on the horizon. Yet word for word it's this world now. By what sleight of hand? I begin to smell tea and thunderstorms, and my head is already echoing with smatterings of conversation, the vapid, meandering monitorings of undramatically failed lives. It's a bog, not a play. I feel a *rage* to get to Greta's and plunge into it. At any moment, I know, I'll hear the putt-putt of Greta's Volkswagen winding up the hill from the village to fetch me. Will it be Greta at the wheel or William? Given the events of a few nights ago, quite possibly William.

3

The vicar didn't care for Maxwell Coop and (let's be frank) Maxwell openly loathed the vicar. This gave a certain useful edge to our rehearsals.

One sultry evening soon after Greta's husband's funeral, William and I had been walking up the hill from a restaurant down by the docks towards the stretch of cafés by the park where I'd once sat writing him that postcard featuring Achilles' buttocks. Through the muggy drizzle you could just make out occasional yellowish shudders of lightning over Albania – you get a sweeping view across the straits deep into its menacing blackness as you trudge up that hill – and William and I were pretending to be talking about *Uncle Vanya*. In reality, of course, we were locked in battle – nothing rowdy, not a free-for-all – just a kind of scrimmage over love, over what was possible and what wasn't. It's exhilarating, this sort of sparring, a wonderful mixture of fierce sentiment and hostility, great gusts of recognition and jabs of pain. You love the way he talks to the waiter, eats his soup and uses words, you hate the way he's never heard of Nietzsche and isn't bored to death by cricket.

All of a sudden, the woman walking up the hill ahead of us stumbled and fell sprawling face down on the pavement. Portly, and dressed in a not altogether suitable floral print, she was flapping feebly by the time we got to her, trying to hoist herself into a sitting position. Eventually we managed to prop her against the wall, murmuring the usual comforting things in English – 'Are you alright?' 'How can we help?' After a moment or two of silent heaving, she lifted a lightly powdered hand to her nose, felt the blood and groaned. Then, patting gingerly at her hair – a towering tangle of auburn curls, which looked strangely lopsided in the streetlight – she opened one heavily made-up eye, squinted at us, then said in a throaty baritone: 'I'll sue the sodding council if I've broken anything. This footpath's a bloody disgrace!' She winced and shifted onto her other hip. 'How do you do?' she went on, opening the other eye and offering us a limp hand. 'I'm Maxwell Coop.'

Maxwell, as it happened, lived just a few doors along the street in a lovely old four-storeyed house with blotched façade and green shutters looking out across the water to Albania. We each took an elbow and, staggering slightly, slowly walked the limping Maxwell to his door. William carried his handbag, which had a brilliantly coloured silk scarf wound around the strap. Two youths on a motor-bike jeered as they flew by.

'Won't you come in for moment?' Maxwell turned

to us with a smeared smile. For all the world you'd have thought we'd just driven an elderly fellow parishioner home from a coffee morning at our local church. 'I'm sure I can rustle something up.' A large brandy, probably, or a strong port.

In fact it was Earl Grey tea with a slice of lemon and a little pile of Scottish shortbreads. 'I'm just back from Tunisia, you see,' he said, tossing his wig onto the dining-room table, where it sat glaring at us like a dishevelled cat, 'and, needless to say, you can't get decent English tea anywhere in Tunisia for love or money – and, believe me, I've tried both. Wherever you go over there it's the same mint muck, don't know how they get it down their throats.'

Tunisia, it transpired, was where Maxwell Coop spent most of his time nowadays. 'Used to work at the BBC, you know,' he said over his shoulder, easing a gemstone necklace up over his head (short back and sides now) while he boiled the kettle in the kitchen at the back. 'Radio drama, mostly. God knows who was listening – just the terminally ill, I should think, or pensioners who hadn't the strength to reach over and turn it off.'

'How did you end up in Corfu?' I asked, more polite than curious.

'One visits, one makes friends, fits in, comes again, and then suddenly one belongs. These days I prefer Tunisia, I must say – one has certain freedoms in Tunisia, so to speak, that are disappearing here in Corfu – too many damned foreigners here these days, might as well be living in Berlin – but I still feel a great attachment to Corfu. Or at least to certain people here.'

'Your friends.'

'Well, what else is there for someone like me to feel attached to?'

I wondered briefly about the bazaars of Tunis and the sorts of jellaba-clad satisfactions they might provide from time to time, but looking at him as he turned, tray in hand, a stocky, middle-aged man in crushed frock and torn stockings, I could see what he meant.

'One has one's music, of course, and one's books, and I'm learning Arabic, and I write a little from time to time . . . just doodling, really . . . Have a biscuit, Fortnum and Mason's, got them at Heathrow yesterday with the tea. Subtle in a way the Greeks would never understand.'

While we took our first sips of tea, Maxwell went upstairs to change. Not out of any obvious embarrassment, I should make clear, but more out of a sense that tea with two gentlemen callers required attire of a more understated kind. When he reappeared, now limping only very slightly but still casting aspersions on the Greek cuisine, he was transformed. Into the expensively upholstered armchair opposite us sank an utterly ordinary man in slacks and ironed shirt – not even portly, to tell the truth, just . . . a man like any other. I hardly recognized him. Neither fat nor thin, nor old nor young, just a square-jawed man with a sore-looking nose and a friendly, non-committal smile.

'So tell me about you,' he said, abruptly dropping the subject of stuffed calamari and swivelling, ever so slightly, to study William.

'We're really just passing through,' William said. But when he mentioned staying with Greta, Maxwell guffawed.

'So Greta's clutched you to her bosom, has she? How's that husband of hers, by the way? He's had one foot in the grave for years, of course – drinks like a fish, I expect you've noticed. Does he still toss the bottles out the window onto the lawn?'

'He died, actually. You've just missed the funeral.' I tried to sound respectful.

'Really? Not a moment before time. Crabby old bugger, mind half shot, don't know why Greta didn't throw him out years ago. They didn't speak, you know. Haven't spoken since the day Thatcher became Prime Minister.' He seemed to drift off for a moment, remembering. 'Gorgeous weather that day, I remember, the day the news came through. May, I think it was – early summer, anyway – what was it? Seventy-eight? Seventy-nine? I rang and said how about a little excursion over to Paleokastritsa – it's divine over there in May, hardly a bloody German in sight. They were still squabbling about Margaret Thatcher when they got in the car. You could've cut the air with a knife. It wasn't the Thatcher business that triggered it, though. I said: "Which way do you want to go? Overland or round the coast road?" He said overland and she said round the coast. In two seconds flat it was a screaming match – you could've heard them all the way to Albania. Everything was dragged in – some barmaid down in Benitses, the cat, the whisky, things she said to him before they were married – and then they just stopped talking. Lunch was an appalling strain. And not another word has passed between them since, as far as I know. He moved upstairs and she stayed downstairs. Marriage is a peculiar thing, don't you think?'

I was on the point of wittily quoting Oscar Wilde on the subject (the bit about the widow whose 'hair turns quite gold from grief') when Maxwell suddenly looked up and asked how Greta's husband had died.

'He fell from an upstairs window,' I said.

'Fell?'

'Or jumped. It's not clear.'

'Toppled, I dare say. He wouldn't have had the guts to jump.'

Feeling uncomfortable about the turn our conversation had taken – however you looked at it, the man had died a wretched death – I started to ask about other friends we might have in common.

'The widow Berwick?' he said to William. 'Of course I know him. Bit of a windbag, and completely potty, but you can't help being fond of him. Australian, of course, but surprisingly well-read and informed.'

'We're Australian, too, actually,' William said, with warmth in his voice.

'You don't say!' Maxwell said, brushing a few crumbs of shortbread onto the carpet. 'Well, you've both polished up very nicely.'

As we were leaving – in the twinkling of an eye Maxwell had grown tired and twitchy – Maxwell leant towards me and, emboldened no doubt by what he'd imbibed earlier in the evening, asked me directly: 'And so are you two boys . . . you know . . . ?'

'No,' I said, 'not really.'

'Just good friends, then?' Maxwell was swaying slightly and steadied himself against the door-jamb.

'No,' said William, with a grin I found a little unsettling, 'not yet.'

'Fascinating!' Maxwell said, with the touch of a finger to his purpling nose. 'I do hope you'll find the time one day to tell me more about it.'

∽

'Do you know what I'm wondering?' I said to William, while we were ambling along one of those medieval Venetian *calli* up near the bus-station. 'I'm wondering if we might have found our Vanya.'

'You'd have to talk to him when he was sober, first. What struck you about him?'

'His capacity for unhappiness, I suppose,' I said, thinking aloud.

'He didn't seem all that unhappy to me,' William said.

I ignored him. 'And that marvellous voice.'

'Yes,' said William, 'I noticed the voice.'

A strong but bruised voice, I thought. And that's what I wanted for Vanya. (In the event, when I rang next day, Maxwell, as he put it himself, couldn't have been more tickled to be asked. He didn't at that stage know about the vicar.)

Empty and silent by the time we got there, the bus-station was just an expanse of greasy puddles. Nothing moved. A man lit a cigarette in the blackness of the bus-sheds across the tarmac.

'It looks as if it will have to be a taxi,' I said. And that's how it happened.

To tell the truth, I'm still not sure precisely what did happen. On the surface what happened is that the taxi, without any discussion between us, took us both to Gastouri, where we both got out, paid off the driver and climbed up the outside staircase to the bedroom at the top.

At another level, though, I must admit I'd known there were no buses to the hills at that late hour even while we'd been zigzagging through the maze of the old town towards the bus-station – and William must have known, too. Yet it was William who told the driver to take us to Gastouri, without any mention of going on to Greta's, and William who got out of the taxi in front of my house and shut the door, although it was I who had paid the driver without asking if William were staying. Nothing was said in the taxi about what we were doing – just a few *non-sequiturs* about the man we'd just met and a bar

William had heard about in one of the ramshackled seaside resorts north of Corfu Town called the Hopping Kangaroo.

Perhaps it was just time. Time to close the gap. Time to see what sort of intimacy might be possible. Time to shock ourselves out of just endlessly playing games.

4

Who doesn't remember Tolstoy's description of the aftermath of Anna's first adulterous coupling with Vronsky? The first time I read it, aged eighteen – and it *was* the sixties – I was dumbfounded: I thought I'd never read such a load of old Christian drivel in my life. 'What for nearly a year had been the single thing Vronsky desired in life . . . ; what for Anna had been an impossible, terrible, yet all the more bewitching dream of happiness – now this desire had been satisfied.' (At this point much sobbing, guilt-ridden appeals to God and the lowering of shame-stricken heads.) But then came the puzzling part: gazing at the woman he has just had sex with, Vronsky 'felt what a murderer must feel when he looks at the body he has robbed of life'. Murderer? At eighteen I couldn't for the life of me see why that which for at least four years had been the one absorbing desire of my life should be called murder. 'The body he had robbed of life was their love, the first stage of their love . . . And, just as the murderer throws himself with fury on the body, as if with passion, dragging and hacking at it, so he covered her face and shoulders with kisses. She held his hand and did not move.' Extraordinary.

Now, all these years (and many an unchurched coupling) later, I've begun to see what Tolstoy might have
meant. Still, a child of my times, I'd put it differently:
I can see now that in knowing beauty – seizing it, I
mean, and knowing it with a fierceness that leaves
you unconscious of whether you've been ravishing
beauty or been ravished by it – you must entertain
bereavement. A poem, an orchid, a sky, a Daphnis, a
Chloe – it doesn't matter what or whom you seize, for
the instant you stretch out your hand to touch it, you
hear the whisper: *This will die.* Not the poem or
orchid, not the beloved – not this Daphnis or this
Chloe – but this *particular* moment of enchantment,
this *particular* experience of the orchid's or Chloe's
beauty. We fear that the beauty that is making us feel
so alive might prove to be nothing but what it seems.
Where there was a living body, so to speak (to echo
Tolstoy's perception), we fear we might soon wake to
find a corpse. And so, in a frenzy, as if with passion,
we try to breathe new life into it – you'll be a wife, we
say, you'll be a friend, a cherished being, a beautiful
memory . . . *but you will live.* An illusion, naturally –
and we know it. Beauty – an embarrassing word, but
I can't find a vaguer one – and mourning go hand in
hand. Tolstoy got it exactly right.

Climbing that iron staircase to the bedroom that
night, however, with William's light, firm step
behind me (the touch of a drumstick on the rim of a
drum), it wasn't Tolstoy and his corpses I was thinking about. It's so life-quickening, that moment,

when Eros takes the last arrow from his quiver and, smirking, stretches his bow, that it's easy to leave all thought behind and just drown in feelings. All the same, I knew when the door clicked shut behind us and we felt no need to say another word that, whatever happened next, something was about to die and what might spring to life I couldn't name. It's a moment shot through with exquisite terror.

Some kinds of beauty, especially in men and women, excite us to know – to know utterly, body and soul, to take into ourselves – what we can never be. Then the disrobing, the inch-by-inch undressing, is an unbearably arousing prelude (or so we imagine) to a timeless reliving of our bliss. After unexpected mergings of this kind it can be off-putting next morning when time is real again to find the beloved sitting up, bright as a button, waiting for coffee and toast, for example, or wanting to help you paint the house. Sweet in prospect, sour when it happens.

Other kinds of beauty, however, seem to excite us to do the opposite: not to know what is strange so much as to know ourselves – or at least to amplify, each time we meet, our sense of who we are in the world. A 'special friend', I suppose I mean, a 'soulmate', the sort of friend Montaigne loved four hundred years ago (his name was La Boétie) and loved for no other reason than 'it was he and it was I'. Here the body is of little account – even when the love is almost frenzied – because your own is of such little erotic account to you, there being too little space between you and it. (All the same, some standards may apply: bus-stop legs, say, or halitosis may stop friendship in its tracks.) Real time is now of the essence: you fill it lovingly together, talking, walking, probing, arguing, sitting, having breakfast and painting the house. The moments you have together are all you have.

Is there a middle course here, where these two kinds of love might stay intertwined? For a while, perhaps, early in a marriage. And possibly in France, where they have a special term for this sort of intertwining (*amitié amoureuse*), but not, generally speaking, in Adelaide. Or London or Corfu or Toronto. Not really. Not nowadays.

'Beautiful enemies' had been my little stab at translating *amitié amoureuse*. Emerson, I'd thought, with this quirky phrase of his, might magically have shown me a middle way: the loved rival, as it were, whom you fight in order to embrace.

⌒

What William actually said, by the way, when we awoke next morning was simply: 'How did you sleep?' He grinned and lay back against the pillows, arms behind his head, scratched his scalp and said: 'Let's have a coffee, then I'd better be off.' No rabbiting on about Montaigne or *amitié amoureuse*, the nature of friendship or murdering love. But then, at that point, that's why I was in bed with him – he wouldn't.

He bit me on the neck, threw off the sheet and, naked, went over to the window to stretch in the shaft of sunlight slicing between the half-closed shutters. Downstairs the clock struck nine.

5

Maxwell, as I've mentioned, made it quite clear from the start that he found the vicar insufferable, and the vicar who'd been all tea-and-scones with the rest of the cast, froze the instant Maxwell came into the room the following evening. 'Silly stuffed toad,' Maxwell muttered a few moments into the first rehearsal when the vicar started in on one of his little homilies apropos of something Vanya had said about fidelity. '*There's no logic to it,*' Vanya cries in frustration at Helen's faithfulness to her 'dried-up old haddock of a husband'. '*Deceiving an old husband you can't stand is immoral, while trying to stifle your wretched youth and vitality is not immoral!*'

What the vicar had to say about marriage and fidelity was predictable, but hardly offensive (not that I took much of it in, my mind being a bit all over the place after what had happened the night before). It was the sort of thing we take in with our mother's milk: sexual intimacy, unredeemed by committed love, is wrong. (As one of Vanya's companions points out to him: once you start betraying your wife or husband, the next thing you know you'll be betraying your country.) No one believes it, naturally, possibly not even the vicar, which is why there was a lot of stroking of Greta's new kitten and chit-chat about who did and didn't take sugar in their coffee while the vicar held forth. Still, as even Vanya should have understood, fidelity in marriage is a useful ground-rule for other people.

'What's going on between the vicar and Maxwell?' I whispered to Greta between Acts II and III. She was slicing up an orange tea-cake on the kitchen bench, trying not to step on the new kitten. Everyone else was taking a breather on the lawn outside.

'There was an unpleasantness, dear,' she said. 'I'm surprised you didn't know.'

'What sort of unpleasantness?'

'A storm in a tea-cup, really. Are you sure you need to know? It was at last year's Christmas party up at the Big House. Maxwell was over from Tunisia as usual – Christmas is a bit of a wash-out in Tunisia, apparently – and around midnight Martha – you remember Martha, silly as a goose, but they won't get rid of her . . .'

'Yes, I remember Martha.'

'Well, around midnight she went round to the old stables to light a candle to the Virgin behind the boiler where she had her vision – did I tell you about her vision?'

'Yes.'

'Well, when she struck the match, she had another vision, but not of the Virgin Mary this time. My

Greek isn't good enough to have caught *everything* she said – screaming like a banshee, she was, setting the dogs off, and George was roaring like a bull, the priest was crossing himself – but I gather she'd stumbled across Maxwell and the vicar's son, Ashley, *in flagrante delicto*. Do be a sweetheart and take this cake out onto the lawn, would you?'

'Was there trouble?'

'Oh, a bit of a stink for a while, but, to tell you the truth, it was the most interesting thing that happened all day. Nice boy, Ashley, goes to one of those schools boys like Ashley go to in England . . . can't think of the name, not Roedean, that's for girls, isn't it, but somewhere like that down in Surrey. Just comes here for his holidays. I think the vicar's hoping he'll read Classics at Cambridge.'

When I got out onto the lawn with the cake, the vicar took me aside. He's a gentle, slender man – it's actually Maxwell who is the more toad-like, oddly enough, an intriguing cross in middle-age of Noël Coward and a rugby coach – but he took me firmly by the elbow and edged me over to a spot behind the terrace wall.

'Look,' he said with a vehemence I hadn't noticed in him before, 'I'm sorry, but I'm not at all sure I can take part in this production of yours if Maxwell Coop's involved.'

'Why not? You're doing a terrific job. I think you're bringing to the role of the professor something —'

'I can't go into details, not here, but relations

between Maxwell Coop and me are, to say the least, extremely strained.' He was sounding more and more like the professor every second.

'I'd hate to lose you at this stage. I think we should just try to be professional about this.'

'But we're not professionals. It's an amateur production.'

'All the more reason,' I said, with a persuasive lack of logic. The vicar was momentarily stumped. 'Let's go back in, read through the last two acts and see what happens.'

Act III (the crisis act, as usual in Chekhov) fizzed and rumbled then went off like a land-mine, thanks largely to the undertow of hostility between the vicar and Maxwell. When the professor (conceited old fraud of a man) has finished trying to swindle Vanya and Sonya out of their inheritance, and Vanya, half-crazed with hatred for this has-been who has enslaved him, rushes out to get his revolver to shoot him, I wondered for a moment if we might see a repeat of that scandalous performance in the Ukraine a few years ago when Vanya really did shoot the professor over some messy off-stage affair with his wife. In this Ukrainian version, Vanya even failed to fail – he's supposed to shoot twice and miss – and so vaudeville turned into farce. Or tragedy, depending on one's point of view.

But no. After Act III the air cleared nicely. The final after-the-storm scene, in which everyone recovers their mediocrity, was deeply moving. I was quite proud of my little band of enthusiasts that night – they hardly seemed to be acting at all. As far as they were concerned, Chekhov had already written *Vanya in Corfu*. Every syllable was perfect.

6

If you set out due west from Adelaide – directly to the west, following the sun at the equinox – you won't hit land again until you get to Uruguay. You'll miss Africa altogether. It's true that you'll first have to skirt a flat, yellowish prong of land not far off-shore, shaped a bit like a miniature Italy, but it's of no account. In principle there's nothing but water all the way to South America. You're at the bottom of the world.

Standing on the jetty at Largs Bay as a child, staring westwards, with nobody for company in the late afternoon except for a couple of seagulls, I would think about that watery emptiness, that light-blue blankness on the map. It was there, not far from where I stood, that my great-great-grandfather, or perhaps great-great-great-grandfather (I'm vague about family trees) must have been rowed ashore from the creaking sailing ship he'd crossed that vastness in over many months. He'd then have either walked or been pulled in a dray across the sandhills and through the scrub to the settlement some miles inland on the banks of the Torrens. What must he have thought, stepping down from the dray, of this yellow, fly-blown jumble of huts and limestone buildings he'd crossed oceans to come to rest in? Perhaps he wept, or perhaps my great-great-grandmother did, if he had a wife with him. The air would have been alive with the piercing squawks of parrots and cockatoos, and at night (so they say) the hills to the east would have lit up with menace – the fires in the native encampments.

Or perhaps it wasn't like that at all. Perhaps my ancestors moved straight into a turreted villa on South Terrace, living much as they had back in Richmond or Chelsea, with picnics in the shady parklands after church on Sundays, an organ concert in the evening and in the week that followed, before it was time to go to church again, a pleasant round of dinner-parties to go to. Around fine oak tables polished by maids, the news from England would have been discussed, copper mines would have been bought and sold, children married off and plans for profitable vineyards in the hills pored over. This is the Adelaide Anthony Trollope so admired in the 1860s. He particularly liked the new post office.

What I do know is that in the early years of the century little Frankie Perkins – and that was the name the wraith beside my chair on the terrace was born with – wandered along the same jetty alone as a small boy, wearing smoked glasses to calm his nerves, thinking much the same thoughts about oceans, ancestors and emptiness at the bottom of the world. And the reason I know is that it's one of the things he tells me in his notes. (As he gets older, sculpting his queer, muddled life into an interesting shape seems to be growing into an obsession.)

Every morning straight after breakfast I draw another sheaf of carefully typed sheets from the piles of papers on his shelves – manuscripts he's failed to publish, old radio talks, drafts for his still unwritten memoirs, articles he's sent off to provincial newspapers, pages torn from ancient exercise books, even a letter or two, never sent – and go out into the sun with it. For an hour or two I sink deliciously into this life which isn't mine, yet is in some ways the perfect counterweight to mine, so that I sit reading in a kind of equipoise. When old Spiros or Agape, or any of the villagers, walk by and call out *Yássou!* or *Kaliméra!* I sometimes hardly dare call back for fear of upsetting the balance.

When I was growing up in the 1950s, the broad, silent streets leading down to the sea in Largs Bay were lined with sandstone bungalows, each with its wind-blasted garden, a pine or two, a few date-palms and the odd straggly melaleuca. Fifty years earlier, however, when Frankie Perkins in his smoked spectacles wandered these same streets – he had a whole year of 'running wild', his nerves were in such a state from having to go to school with other children – the streets can't have been much more than furrows in the sand-dunes, dotted about with boxthorns and rushes. The city was a long train-ride from a station far off across empty paddocks to the east.

Since his elder brother was a sailor on a windjammer, he used to wander down to the jetty almost every day (as he now remembers it) to gaze westwards across the water towards Uruguay, read books too old for him, legs dangling over the water, and talk to himself in strange voices nobody had ever taught him. And not only to himself, but also to 'various odd characters' he found 'hanging about' on the jetty and around the wharves at Port Adelaide not far up the beach. I wish I'd done that. I can just imagine the look on my mother's face if I'd told her that's how I'd spent the morning.

Children like Frank Perkins know surprisingly early (I'm sure he already knew while loitering on the jetty) that something isn't quite right. In my day not only conversations in the school-yard, but the newspapers, the cinema, the radio and then the television told me that something wasn't quite right. All the other boys were little cubes (that's how I thought about it), sturdy little building-blocks with stable futures, while I'd turned out shaped like a pyramid, a cuttlefish, a party balloon – anything, but not a cube.

How Frank Perkins knew something wasn't right is hard to say at this distance – there was no radio when he was a boy and he'd have been well into his twenties before he started his weekly dose of Ramon Navarro, Maurice Chevalier and Marlene Dietrich at the talkies at the Hoyts Regent. But he'd have known, I'm sure of it. What little boys like Frank Perkins know is that they will never be building-blocks, they will only ever be decoration. They will be the scrolls and spangles, the arabesques and curlicues on life's plain edifice – hardly a manly function in Adelaide in 1910. And the tools of their trade, it's clear from an early age, will be their bodies and their clever tongues.

By the time he was a twenty-five-year-old reporter on a local newspaper of no consequence, I gather Frank was dressing with a certain flair (striped cambric shirts and wide silk ties), moving with a grace learnt on the dance floor and talking rather too well for someone of his class – his voice a touch plummy for Largs Bay, like those announcers on the radio everyone was, by then, listening to with wonder. But their voices really came from 'over there'. And that's the other thing that little boys like Frank Perkins drop to almost as soon as they can walk and talk, especially if there's a jetty nearby to moon about on, staring out to sea: full lives are only possible 'over there', beyond the horizon. One day, whatever it takes, however much you have to slave to save the money for the fare, however painful it might be to make the break, you'll clamber aboard an ocean liner and sail off to the old world where decoration is appreciated, indeed sought-after, and people shaped like pyramids or party balloons can live a civilized life. It's never quite true, but we all believe it. I flew, but I was a late starter.

Another thing that wasn't quite right when Frank Perkins was young was Mrs Perkins' Theosophy. There's no sign, it's true, that young Frank was actually embarrassed by his mother's enthusiasm for spiritual shenanigans (Himalayan Masters of the World, reincarnation and shonky seances), but it must have deepened his sense of being oddly shaped. All the other little boys in Largs Bay trudged along to Sunday School at the Methodist or Anglican Church to learn about sin and the true meaning of Christmas, while he and his mother took the train into the city of a Sunday evening to hear lectures by ladies in fawn frocks on 'Remembering Past Lives' and 'The Threefold Cord of Fate'. Part of the appeal for Frank may have been the 'nutmeg Hindu with the buck's eyes', Krishnamurti, whose portrait hung enticingly in the Society's entrance foyer, promising things far more exciting to Frank than fate's threefold cord or fantasies of past lives. I wonder if, like so many young Theosophist boys at the time, he also took to parting his hair down the middle.

For Frank – it seems to me, as I write – once he'd reached his mid-twenties, the Theosophical Society was more a stage on which to practise his entrances and exits than a fount of wisdom. (All the same, a glance at his bookshelves here in Gastouri shows a lasting theosophical bent: books on spiritual masters from Meister Eckhart to Gurdjieff and Bhagwan alongside pamphlets on 'The Awakened Ones' and True Paths to this and that.) He seems to have been in charge of the 'stage arrangements' at various Society functions, for instance, mounting uplifting playlets (such as 'The Veil', a soul-searing piece about a woman with a hideous birth defect) and accompanying visiting contraltos on the piano. These provincial divas, I notice, had a predilection for vocal items with titles like '*Un ange est venu*' and '*J'ai soif de ton âme*'.

At the same time he was taking part in the amateur theatrical scene, acting in skits and 'jests' with a small troupe he'd linked up with – performers such as 'Adelaide's phenomenal whistling genius', Miss Edith Marshal, who, according to the press-cutting I found floating amongst Kester's papers, 'charmed her audience with her remarkable talent, rendering well-known songs with surprising ease'. 'Remarkable' must have gratified Edith, but she probably didn't want to think too deeply about the rest of the notice.

In short, this queer little boy from the sandhills on Adelaide's fringe, not particularly well-educated (just a smattering of Latin and French, a bit of arithmetic) and burdened with outlandish beliefs, had decided to play with the cards in his hand – and play well. I have to admire that. There was just one card he swapped for another: his name. Frank Perkins came back from a brief sojourn in Sydney calling himself Kester Baruch. Perhaps he'd had a transformative experience in Sydney which demanded a brand new sobriquet, something more singular than Frank Perkins. But why Baruch? Why a Jewish prophet's name? A decade later in Austria, when the Nazis marched in, it proved an unwise choice, so he changed it to Berwick. I doubt the desire to be a prophet has faded, though, if that's why he lit upon Baruch. I have the feeling that this desire is still simmering away there somewhere deep in his soul. Needless to say, it will never come to anything.

One Sunday evening in 1930, when Kester was twenty-seven years old, for want of anything better to do – well, there was nothing at all to do in Adelaide on a Sunday evening in 1930 – he went with his friend Helge Hergstrom to the regular seven o'clock lecture at the Society's rooms in King William Street. It was the usual crowd – middle-aged women in smart frocks, one or two with a husband, several with fox-furs round their shoulders because the evenings were turning chilly – and they settled down, Kester and Helge, minds wandering, at the back of the small hall to peer through the sea of hats at the serge-suited figure on the rostrum clearing his throat to address them. He was rather overwhelmed by the gigantic floral display Violet de Mole had arranged in an urn by his left elbow – indeed, it was actually quite difficult in the face of this eruption of chrysanthemums and roses to focus on anything otherworldly at all – but bit by bit the audience sank into thoughtful consideration of the speaker's comforting message – something about the soul's psychic journey before rebirth, according to Kester's diary.

Then suddenly Helge nudged him sharply in the ribs. 'Who can those two be, down near the front, do you think?' he whispered to Kester, mind clearly on the here-and-now. Surprisingly, sticking up amongst the hats and careful perms were two unhatted, unpermed heads – young men's heads, one fair, one glossily dark.

In the foyer after the lecture Kester pounced.

Who needed psychic wanderings between past lives? Here and now, right in the middle of King William Street, Kester was already launched on a psychic journey of his own, littered with signs and portents. Theosophy, the theatre, music, painting – Kester and these two young men turned out to have so much in common, it was almost as if they'd been biding their time until this instant in order to slot into their preordained roles in life.

After a few minutes, Helge drifted over to talk to a group of young women he knew by the staircase. Four had become three.

Kester liked two, so he felt a tiny spurt of excitement when the dark-haired young man was seized on by Violet de Mole and dragged off to meet the speaker. Two was much better.

There was a minute pause as Kester and the fair-haired stranger looked at each other, grinned and registered that the colouring of their conversation would now be different. Then Kester began slowly to draw him out.

His name, he told Kester, was Alan Harkness. Kester was instantly smitten.

Both members of a Shakespearean touring company from Melbourne, Alan and his companion were a bit at a loose end in Adelaide during the day. Even then Kester felt drawn to anyone who was adrift – not so much to the merely homeless or desperate, of whom there were masses roaming Adelaide's streets in 1930, some on the point of starvation, but to the rootless and the spiritually rudderless. The hunger on the streets was for others to feed – the women's guilds, the Salvation Army, the various relief funds, perhaps even the politicians – whereas Kester's skill was in feeding a deeper, more abiding kind of hunger no women's guild or politician could hope to assuage: the hunger for a good life in a more profound, more subtle sense. Something was gnawing at this young actor with the lank, fair hair and plain, boyish features, and Kester felt a delicious impulse to find out what it was. They agreed to meet for lunch the next day for a little tête-à-tête.

'A really interesting fellow, didn't you think?' Kester said to Helge as they walked off up King William Street together towards the station.

Helge looked at Kester and smiled. 'Hardly spoke to him, really. But yes, *très gamin*.' Helge's French was annoyingly good, although he refused to accompany Kester to the meetings of the Alliance Française – he said the Alliance crowd was too 'la-di-da', and anyway, Russian was the language of the future.

In point of fact, as he told Kester the next day over sandwiches by the river, Alan Harkness was also facing hunger of the more everyday kind. It seemed that the touring company was on its last legs – people had money for the latest romantic trash from Hollywood, but not for *Romeo and Juliet*. Once back in Melbourne, it looked likely that the company would fold.

Kester found the prospect of this further uprooting almost thrilling. In his commotion he threw the rest of his sandwiches to the ducks.

A few weeks later in Melbourne the company did fail – and Kester was at its final performance.

Adrift there himself, he tried vainly to be an anchor. For some reason or other, though, Alan kept bobbing off. Perhaps it was the brilliance of the circle he mixed in – painters, dancers, actors, writers (Vance and Nettie Palmer were close friends of his, for example), bohemians like Justus Jorgensen . . . Alan was forever floating away from Kester on a tide of conviviality, witty conversation and easy intimacy – arms thrown around shoulders, sprawling with friends on cushions on the floor, that kind of thing. Kester would watch him from the sidelines, only half-listening to the young would-be actress pinning him to the wall with her earnest insights into Stanislavsky. How could he, Kester, a boy from Adelaide who gave private French lessons for a living, played the hind part of a donkey in Christmas pageants and still lived at home with his mother compete with this scintillating crowd? Kester took the train back to Adelaide earlier than he'd intended, feeling slightly miserable. But determined.

They wrote. Even when Alan went to New Zealand with a handful of other actors from the company to see if they might have more success there (they failed), they kept writing. Even now, it seems, judging by his recently typed notes, Kester remembers with extraordinary vividness the bittersweet mixture of anguish and delight he felt as he dropped letter after letter into the box outside the station on his way into the city. Nobody nowadays remembers what that long silence after a letter disappeared into the slot felt like. Nowadays nobody has to wait for anything.

One day when the weather was warming up again, Kester wrote a different letter from the sort he usually wrote. 'My dear Alan,' it began – even at twenty-seven there was a tinge of the elderly in Kester's phrasing. (I'll leave out the inconsequential bits – the items of news, the advice on what books to read, the coy theosophical jokes and so forth.)

I've had an idea. Unless you have something better in view, why don't you come over and join me in Adelaide? We wouldn't starve – Mother would see to that, she'd always spare us something – and what I've been thinking is that we might even start something together – a small experimental theatre, say. What do you think? I don't know much about such things, but you do. The acting side of things would necessarily be in your hands, but I'd help you as much as I could if you explained to me what you wanted. I could take charge of the lighting, for instance, make properties and scenery and handle the organisational side. Please think about it very carefully. It could be wonderful for both of us.

I dare say nobody words their letters like that any more, not even clergymen's daughters. What Kester meant, obviously, was 'do *not* think about it very carefully – just for God's sake do it! I'm going mad.'

When I look up of a morning here in Corfu at the brown and yellow self-portrait of Alan Harkness on the wall beside the window, I can now imagine all too well Alan's train pulling into the station in Adelaide exactly three weeks later, the surge of joy in Kester's heart as Alan stepped down onto the platform, struggling with his suitcases, their restrained, manly greetings, the silly chatter, the averted eyes, the uncertainty mixed with knowing. This morning my mind drifted a little farther with them to wonder whether they then took a taxi (unlikely in the Depression) or, more probably, another train, and, if so, where to, and did they finally spend the night together? 'So there we were at last two close friends,' is all Kester will allow himself to say in his notes. (Punctuation, Kester! Is a comma too much to ask for?) 'This marked a great turning point in our affairs.'

Onto the peeling door of an empty building on North Terrace some days later Kester and Alan nailed a freshly painted sign in green and gold: THE AB-INTRA STUDIO. With his usual genius for awkward titles, Kester had come up with a name that called to mind the medical term for an obscure internal organ. It meant 'from within', encapsulating his belief that the theatre existed to give expression to movements and patterns in the soul, not as a setting for acting out novels and short stories. Talking, according to Kester and Alan, was for the talkies.

The premises had not been hard to find – the city streets in the 1930s were lined with papered-over shopfronts and abandoned offices plastered with TO LET and FOR SALE signs. For just a few shillings a week in 1930 you could rent a whole building in the heart of the city. Inside it was a shambles – not a stick of furniture, no gas or electricity, just a rabbit-warren of dank-smelling rooms laced with cobwebs. Undeterred by the shabbiness – even quickened by it, I suspect – Kester and Alan, together with a small band of supporters, swept the floors, lit kerosene lamps, boiled the kettle and, sitting about on sacks stuffed with seaweed, set the first small fuse under Adelaide's theatrical establishment. It was Japanese and called, intriguingly, *The Demon's Mask*.

7

'Have you ever thought of going home, Greta?' We were getting supper ready together in the kitchen, William had just taken a plate of her quince crumble out onto the lawn where the actors were lying about exhausted, swatting at insects, and we were alone. The question just popped out.

'To Australia, you mean? Not really, dear.' Greta was pouring coffee into mugs on a tray. 'It's too late for that. This is home. Why do you ask?'

This is home. I could see that. It was here that Greta mattered. Not vastly, not like Pablo Picasso or Mao Tse-Tung, but that was surely the point: here in the hills behind Corfu Town, and in the streets down by the water, it was all the little rituals of her daily life that fitted into a pattern with a meaning of sorts – in the bakery, at the garage, at the golf club, here in the kitchen with us. Greta wasn't journeying homewards, there was no Ithaca over the horizon she was sailing slowly back towards. Instead, she was floating along asking the greengrocer about his grandchildren, meeting Prue for coffee and chatting with Bernie in her second-hand bookshop as she chose another Margaret Drabble or P.D. James – but was this enough? Wasn't there something shallow about mattering in that way?

'Do you believe in roots?' I asked, instead of answering her question (to which the answer, in any case, was obvious).

'Roots?' Someone's cigarette had ashed itself in the sugar bowl, so there was a pause while she scooped it out. 'You didn't see that, did you . . . Roots. No, I don't give much thought to my roots any more. I'm a snail, not a daisy – I carry everything with me. Which are you?'

I shrugged. I didn't know what to say.

Greta put the tray down on the bench. 'Are you wondering if it's time to go home? This island is full of people wondering if it's time to go home. They had small lives at home, so they came here. Now they have small lives here, so they dream of going home. Carry on about it all the time. And Kester's the worst of them. Every time I see him he brings it up. "Do you think I should move back, Greta? Do you think I'd be better off back home? Things have changed, you know, I might be quite happy there." It drives me mad. I've told him I don't want to hear another word about it. "You know where the airline office is, Kester," I said to him. "If you want to go home, go and buy yourself a ticket. Otherwise for God's sake shut up about it." If you're small, you're small – Adelaide, Abu Dhabi, Timbuktu – it makes no difference.' Picking up the tray again, she sailed off through the french windows onto the terrace.

'So what's wrong with small?' I called after her, but she was already serving the vicar. 'You're a treasure, Greta,' I heard him murmur, helping himself to two large spoonfuls of sugar, 'and your quince crumble is a miracle.'

I can see what you mean, Greta, I thought to myself, but it's not the whole story. The words are wrong – 'small' and 'big' somehow miss the mark. Yet the right ones kept hovering just out of reach.

⌒

Yesterday morning, since it was drizzling and I didn't feel like sitting in my bedroom talking to ghosts, I took the bus into town and bought myself a ticket on the ferry for Brindisi. Since everything's been decided at last – the dates for our two performances and where we'll stage them – there's no reason to put off my departure any longer. I'll leave at midnight straight after our second performance. The following afternoon I'll be in Rome. A day or two later, if that's what I want to do when the moment arrives, I could be home.

Actually, not quite everything has been decided. I've only booked one ticket to Brindisi. William doesn't know I've booked it yet. I was going to tell him last night, but somehow or other the moment was never right – Bernie burst into tears because I was sharp with her, Maxwell couldn't walk because his left leg was gouty, Greta was all atwitter because

Kostas, her *síndrofos,* was arriving on the late flight from Athens, Act IV was a mawkish mess . . .

I'll tell him I've booked when he comes to pick me up this afternoon. My ticket in its blue and white cardboard jacket is already lying prominently on the kitchen table. If William wants to come with me, he can go into town and book his own.

⌒⌒

'So, did Kostas eventually arrive?' I asked William, when I opened the door to him about three. He ducked inside quickly out of the shower, spiky hair glistening with raindrops, grinning broadly. Behind him the sky was a brilliant buttercup yellow after the lunchtime storm. Everything glowed. The roadway in front of the house was a trail of mirror shards, jagged little pools of gold.

'Eventually, yes,' he said, shaking himself like a puppy. 'Well after midnight.'

'So Greta's purring?'

'It's weird – Greta of all people. As soon as he walked in the door, she turned into a kitten. Incredible. But he's great, I really like him.'

'What's he like?'

'Well, not young, must be in his seventies, white-haired, but quite wiry, not your usual pot-bellied —'

'No, I mean, what's he like . . . you know, is he friendly? What does he talk about?'

'He talks about everything,' he said, sprawling in a

chair at the kitchen table. 'Never stops talking. And he's got a wicked sense of humour – makes us both laugh. Asked us about *Uncle Vanya* – he loves everything Russian. He's terribly well-read, Dostoevsky and all that. Made me feel a bit of an idiot.' He was looking idly around the kitchen as he spoke, but didn't seem to notice the ferry ticket. In his hands he had a book.

'What's the book?'

'It's for you. Greta asked me to give it to you. She said you might find it interesting, after the conversation you had the other night.' He put the book on the table next to the ticket. As he read 'Strintzis Lines: Passenger Ticket', I read '*C.P. Cavafy: Selected Poems*'.

Not Cavafy again, I thought, with a surge of irritation. A couple of my older London friends could hardly finish a sentence without mentioning Cavafy. What was this cult of a versifying Egyptian civil servant all about? On the cover, smeared with raindrops, was a pen sketch of two lumpish young men, one lying back on a couch with one arm behind his head, the other, wearing a tie, standing hand in pocket behind him. This insipid cover more or less summed up my impression of Cavafy. I flicked.

A skin as though of jasmine . . .
that August evening – was it August? –
I can still just recall the eyes: blue, I think
    they were . . .
Ah yes, blue: a sapphire blue.

Faded memories of an effete lust. August, blue, September, green — what does it matter?

> The ageing of my body and my beauty
> is a wound from a merciless knife.
> I'm not resigned to it at all.

Well, the rest of us resign ourselves to it without much fuss. If anyone delivered himself of a line like that in real life, we'd all just think *drama queen* and roll our eyes. I snapped Cavafy shut and dropped him back on the table. William was studying my ticket.

'You didn't tell me you'd booked to go home?'

'I was going to today. It was a spur of the moment thing. Tea?'

William was silent while I stood at the stove, boiling the kettle. 'Perhaps I should come,' he said. 'Would you like me to?'

'You know I would, William, but it's for you to decide. Are you ready to go home? Are you ready to go home with *me*?' With my back to him, I kept my eyes on the tea-pot I was filling.

The hesitation was momentary but it was there. 'I'd like to give it a try, yes,' he said, then stood up, hands in pockets, and went to the window. 'I'm not blind, you know. I can see you're worried that it's not going to work.' He chuckled and turned to look at me. 'I can tell . . . in the morning sometimes, from your eyes, from the way you don't want to talk about what's happening, the way you want to talk about the play or Kester or the weather or anything, just not about what's happening.' He came over to the table and picked up his mug of tea. 'Well, maybe it's *not* going to work – who knows? But maybe *something* will work, something we haven't thought of yet. What do you think?' He took a sip of tea, watching me over the brim of his mug. Marvellous arched eyebrows. Poised for flight.

What did I think? A thousand things, in tumbling drifts. I thought, for instance, of what it must be like to have a friend whose mere existence in the world, each time you contemplated it, was a kind of joyful homecoming. And I thought in tingling gusts, as we drank our tea, of what it must be like to want somebody's beauty so much your whole body strained to lay hold of it, bear it aloft and fly into the future with it in your arms. And I looked at William, as I turned out the light and locked the door, and thought: I certainly like you very much.

'Don't you think, for instance,' he said a few minutes later as we putt-putted past Sisi's palace in Greta's Volkswagen, 'that we could start something in Adelaide – I don't know, something on the fringe, something . . .'

'Experimental?'

'Why not? Something different, something with a bit of pzazz. What have we got to lose? It'd do us both good to spread our wings a bit. There'd be an audience, I'm sure of it, even in Adelaide.' I wasn't so sure, but I smiled back when he shot me a glance and grinned. He drove with a new zest.

We dropped by the travel agent's office in town on the way to Greta's and William bought his ticket for the ferry to Brindisi.

Although it was not August, his eyes were certainly blue this afternoon, as blue as opals, no doubt about it. In London they'd always struck me as sky-grey.

8

'Ravishing!' was Violet de Mole's first word to Kester
at the close of the first performance of *The Demon's
Mask*. Then, grasping Alan's hand, she said it again.
Or perhaps she said '*Ravissant!*' (which is not quite
the same thing, but Kester could never quite recall
which she'd said) because they were, after all, at the
Alliance Française and the whole thing had been
done in French. Not that it mattered what language
they'd used: it was a Japanese *noh* play, written by
two Australians, Kester and Alan, and the few words
spoken in it were simply not of the essence. *Noh*, as
the French would understand, being foreign, was all
about stylized movement, poetic utterances, mime,
song and dance. ('Dance' was perhaps to put too fine
a point on it. 'Rhythmic movement', to which
kimonos were so kind, was perhaps a more accurate
description.) *Noh* was a visual, rather than intellec-
tual, experience. Adelaide, however, unlike Violet de
Mole, was simply nonplussed.

Nothing daunted, in a flurry of mask-making and
hessian-dyeing, Kester and Alan began working
towards another season of scenes from Old Japan: a
short farce or two followed by several Japanese

poems set to music and, with the aid of subdued lighting from jam-tin reflectors, 'interpreted' by Kester and Alan in masks and flowing robes.

> I hear you call,
> Pine-tree –
> I hear you call upon the Hill
> By the silent pond where the Lotus-flowers bloom;
> I hear you call,
> Pine-tree –
> What is it you call,
> Pine-tree –
> When the wind blows,
> When the rain falls . . .

Very affecting, I imagine, in the original Japanese, but, even with Kester and Alan waving about in yards of green chiffon as they intoned these lines, it's easy to understand the audience's puzzlement. Older patrons regularly walked out, tripping and stumbling as they picked their way amongst the bodies huddled on cushions on the floor.

However, despite the mockery of the press – 'a display of St Vitus' dance', 'the audience froze with boredom', 'the average pugilist could give them points in footwork' – the Ab-Intra boys and their clutch of followers seem to have struck a chord with what the Adelaide *Truth* called 'the arty set'. It was dazzled by the sensuousness of each jewel-like scene, the revelling in sheer visual beauty. Each low-lit cameo for them was like an incantation, and they thirsted to be inducted into the panoply of rites.

For the next few years (as far as I can make out from the press-cuttings Kester has pasted in no particular order into albums) Adelaide regularly woke up to read in its morning newspapers about some new sensation at the Ab-Intra Studio. If it wasn't something avant-garde by Pirandello or Thornton Wilder, it was Joan Joske with one of her terrifying (and untutored) 'plastic interpretations' of de Falla's *Ritual Fire Dance.* After interval – and Ab-Intra intervals were famous for the hobnobbing over coffee in a fug of Russian cigarettes – there might be a Persian offering, such as *The Poetasters of Isfahan*, a swirl of orange silks and green organdie, or some of Kester's poems recited by a half-naked man (Alan) swathed in cyclamen velvet. In the old draper's shop on King William Street which was Ab-Intra's new home, girls in close-fitting tunics danced spontaneously to Debussy; obscure French and Russian plays, full of tearless sobs and furtive glances, stunned the audience into respectful silence; on one occasion, since anything Russian seemed so thrilling, they had a wild success with a 'Russian' play by a certain Alex Svetloff which Kester and Alan had actually written themselves; they even held a bridge night interspersed with scenes from *Macbeth.* All this was heady stuff in Adelaide in the early 1930s, so the notices preserved in Kester's albums are as often outraged as they are admiring. Humbly, he's kept them

all, good and bad. They sit yellowing side by side, in
happy disagreement with each other, in this record of
a promising youth.

～

    Young man, Prot., 'refined', wants furnished
    room with fireplace close to city.

This, I imagine, is the kind of advertisement Alan
Harkness must have placed in the newspaper once
he'd had time to find his feet in Adelaide – once the
awkwardness of finding himself *à deux* with the
intense, strong-jawed young Theosophist he hardly
knew had passed. I have to imagine it because,
although I've stuck my nose into every notebook,
diary and cache of letters I can find, I've come across
no mention anywhere of how Alan and Kester lived
during those first years. Not at Mrs Perkins', clearly,
although she'd no doubt have been pleased to have
her son's nice new friend from Melbourne stay for a
few days when he first arrived – feed him up a bit
(he was painfully thin), arrange a tennis afternoon
with a couple of delightful girls from the Society . . .
not that her son ever seemed to make much headway
with any of them, but still, this Alan did seem to be
a rather superior sort of young man . . . very well-
connected in Melbourne, Frankie said, and he also
painted, knew the theatre inside out –
    But how would I know what Mrs Perkins thought?

How, for that matter, would I know what Kester thought? He will not tell me.

What I do now know is that, whatever Kester's feelings were for Alan – and I'm sure he saw him as *slender*, not as *thin*; a tender sapling, not a stick – he'd have thought of their twosome as the intertwining of two 'special' natures, a many-sided love affair with beauty, not as some sordid Oscar and Bosie affair, just lust for another man propped up with highbrow theatrical escapades. When Kester first read the small item in the newspaper about the bank messenger 'charged with having committed an unnatural offence' (it's tucked away at the bottom of the page he's cut out for the review of Ab-Intra's Christmas pageant), I doubt he'd even have felt any connection with the hapless youth.

I try to find a word for what I imagine this twosome was, but none of the usual words seems to fit. Scenes from their life together, on the other hand, are easy to conjure up: pouring sodden paper into clay moulds to make their fantastic masks; slurping ice-creams down at the beach in a heatwave, both oiled up for a 'nigger brown tan', as it was called then, watching the youngsters toss their rubber beach-balls on the sand, one ear out for the lifesavers' shark-gong; lounging in a deck-chair in the dark at an open-air cinema, eyes fixed on Greta Garbo or Clark Gable in some romantic melodrama; Sunday lunch *en famille* around the solid oak dining-table at Mrs Perkins', perhaps, before setting off for the city to attend the evening's lecture at the Society . . . the everyday round is easy to picture. It's the right word for the kind of love they had that I find hard to come up with. Strangely, the word that keeps buzzing around in my brain is 'romance'. Such an old-fashioned, syrupy word, so rosy-cheeked, so wafting, courtly, seemly, smiling at you like Ginger Rogers, two rows of perfect, gleaming teeth . . . And yet . . .

Under all the painted perfection of romance lies buried a sense that I like of a spiralling story. It's a double helix: desire coiling around adoration. And so, at a loss for another word to describe it, what Kester and Alan had, I suppose, was a Great Romance. It's rare. And doomed, naturally. To ordinariness. The wonder vanishes – as it does from any long-winded tale in prose, however rollicking. So does the desire. But at the beginning when, awash with pleasure, you stand amazed by what you've just seen, the spiralling tale is still all in your head. That's romance.

Tonight is our big night at the Big House. No old draper's shop for us. Bernie offered her bookshop, but it would have been awfully cramped; Maxwell thought one of the rooms at the old Reading Club would be perfect, but its gloominess depressed me – the smell of dead flowers and furniture wax was overpowering; the vicar offered his church hall, but

I'm fed up with echoing church halls, however you spruce them up they feel sad. And then Greta said: 'Why don't I give George a ring and ask him about the Big House?' So tonight we're all trooping out there for a run-through. I think it's going to work.

9

It's definitely going to work.

When we came in the door out of the heat, George was sitting up at the table facing us in the half-dark, like a king waiting for the barbarians. Other cars were driving up outside and we could hear the scrunch of footsteps on the gravel outside.

'This is a crazy idea,' George barked across the room at us. 'You're mad. A Russian play. Who wants to see a Russian play? Is he a Communist, this Chekhov of yours?' Silhouetted against the evening sky filling the doorway, his face was just a black mask. A whiff of dog-pee pinched my nostrils.

'How *are* you, George?' Greta said brightly. 'So sweet of you to let us come! Martha, dear! *Kalispéra!*' Martha had come wandering in from the kitchen with a dog or two, smiling broadly and wiping her hands on her apron.

'Well, what do you think?' I murmured to William, who was still standing by the front door, looking around the room, wide-eyed. After the late afternoon glare outside, it was hard at first to make anything out, but I could see him starting to take in the flaking, blotchy walls, the dark oak table and sideboard and the mournful countess high above the piano to our right. He nodded slowly. 'It's great,' he said, still peering about him. 'We can do something with this.'

Then Maxwell came in the front door with Alberto. George leapt to his feet as if stung by a wasp. Banging the table, he roared: 'Get out! Get that man out!'

'Now, George . . .' Greta began, putting a hand on his arm.

'Get him out of my house! I won't have that man in my house!' And he thumped the table again with his fist, loosening one of the legs. The table tilted. A vase of purple irises toppled and rolled onto the floor.

'*Tha párete tsai?*' Martha asked. 'Some tea?'

Nobody spoke.

'*Ena ouzáki?* Some ouzo?' Martha was beaming. She loved seeing the house fill up with visitors and obviously hadn't the faintest idea in the half-light who Maxwell was. The dogs were lapping at the water trickling from the vase.

Then Prue and Bernie came in, followed by the vicar. George swore loudly in Greek (something unspeakable involving all our mothers), kicked a dog out of the way and strode out onto the balcony at the back. There was a slight pause, then Martha's wavering voice scratched at the silence.

'*Tha párete tsai?*'

'No, thank you, Martha,' Maxwell said, flinging the strange straw hat he was wearing onto a chair, 'it'll taste like dog's piss. Coffee would be splendid.'

'*Kafé?*'

'Yes, thank you, dear,' Greta said. 'Let me help you. Why don't the rest of you go and take a quick look at the garden before the light goes?'

'Good idea,' I said, and everyone nodded and began talking at once. We had to explore the garden because, when I'd told William about the orange orchard and rows of cumquat trees, the old chapel and paved courtyard behind the house, he'd said why not stage Act I out there and move inside for the last three acts? It would be perfect. Unless there were a storm like yesterday's. You never knew on Corfu. Something always seemed to be brewing in the Albanian mountains across the strait.

As we turned the corner of the house, I heard Alberto say to William with that faint, but annoying, American accent of his: 'Have you thought any more about that idea of mine?' They were just a few paces ahead of me, but I couldn't catch what William said in reply. 'Really?' Alberto said, brushing the hair out of his eyes with long fingers. 'Well, if you change your mind . . .' Dawdling for a moment, he reached out one tanned arm and plucked an orange from the tree beside the steps. Following in silence, I stepped around the curls of orange-peel on the path, trying to keep my thoughts on *Uncle Vanya*.

In the event we had a merry evening. Behind the boiler around in the stables William and Alberto found a plank and some rope, so we even rigged up a swing for Prue to sit drinking her tea on, and then back in the house, with a little rearranging of the furniture, we found the main salon ideal for the three interior scenes, the kitchen and balcony doors in just the right place, the atmosphere quite claustrophobic with the blinds drawn, as it should be for the gradual shrinking inwards of the final scenes. Celia turned up at last, too, with Kester's bedraggled dog under one arm, to play the nanny. After days of indecision, waffling on interminably about the superb productions she'd seen at the Old Vic in Bristol and the RSC – Gielgud (a close friend of her late husband's) had brought tears to her eyes, Sheila Hancock had been 'magnificent, heartbreaking' – she'd agreed to do it. Clearly the whole notion of mucking in with the vicar, a Chilean and two Australians was beneath her, but she rose to the occasion with grace and surprising competence. Having few lines, she was word-perfect straight away, and even brought along some knitting, as called for by the part. Even more astonishingly, when the rehearsal was over and everyone was tucking into Greta's cold chicken and rice, it was Celia of all people who sat down at the piano beneath the countess and struck up something from *Oklahoma!*. Everyone gathered round 'for a bit of a warble', as the vicar put it, except for William and Alberto who had gone off together to scour the house for extra props. We were all swept up in a wave of lightness, a sudden desire to joke and clown about, which was an elixir after the bleakness of Act IV.

It didn't last long, though. After a few minutes, right in the middle of 'Surrey with a Fringe On Top' (the Queen's favourite song, according to Celia), Martha came down the stairs to ask us to stop. George had a blinding headache and the singing was driving him mad. By the time William and Alberto came back in (Alberto's hair laced with cobwebs), we were packing up to leave.

~

I dreamt last night of empty, cobwebbed paths strewn with orange-peel. At the end of the trail of white-and-orange coils, William was lolling on a swing amongst the trees, drinking tea. '*Tha párete tsai?*' he called across to me, but by the time I got to the swing, he'd vanished. It didn't matter: my eye had been caught by a bandstand strung with fairy-lights not far away through the trees. In the middle of the bandstand stood the Queen, singing bits and pieces from *South Pacific*. 'Do have an orange,' she said when she'd finished. 'I've already eaten six.' I can't remember what happened next, but when I woke up this morning I was in an unaccountably excellent frame of mind. Even the thought of dipping into Cavafy seemed quite appealing all of a sudden, so I dropped him onto my breakfast tray and took him out onto the terrace with me into the sun.

10

Those two young men lounging on the cover of the Cavafy give the wrong impression. I can see that now. In the first place, it turns out to be a David Hockney print. Hence the whiff of gay coupledom in Maida Vale. Cavafy's Alexandria – the one he recollects when no longer young: the seedy, sensual turn-of-the-century city of furtive loitering and voices choking with desire – is not even a ghost in the Hockney pair's nondescript, suburban living-room. All they're thinking about is who it might be amusing to invite back for supper after the ballet on Saturday night. They've never courted doom, as Cavafy did. Moreover, in the second place, this recollected Alexandria of corruptible, pale faces glimpsed in darkening streets and exquisite, naked bodies given to debauchery without bounds, is hardly the most engrossing thing about his poetry any more, not at the century's end. I'm sure the two young men in the Hockney print would find Cavafy's pinpricks of memory inconsequential, sad, embarrassing – poems about handsome young men with black and perfumed hair vanishing into the shadows of arcades, barely glimpsed (decades before) in their godlike beauty as they passed in front of lighted shop-windows . . . Who hankers after this sort of thing nowadays?

The act of recollection is engrossing, though – that's what I missed when I snapped the book shut the other day on that poem about an August evening ('was it August?') and blue eyes ('I think they were . . . Ah yes, blue: a sapphire blue'). It's not the month or colour of the eyes that's interesting – perhaps it's not even the poem that's interesting (it's just one tile in the mosaic): it's watching the delicate creation of the mosaic that is so entrancing – not these fingers straying to this sculpted chest, not these grey eyes or this rumpled bed, but the taking shape, the *moving towards*, that some kinds of poetry (and some great paintings – paradoxically, in an instant) can embody.

I wish, by the way, that Kester Berwick felt freer to recollect with Cavafy's honesty.

None of this was of much interest to me this morning, however. What took my attention on the terrace this morning, especially given that I was using my ferry ticket as a bookmark, were two early poems, both written in the same year, 1894, which seemed to contradict each other in quite a startling way – and on a subject I urgently need to get straight in my mind: going home.

In the first of the two, 'Ithaca', there's a lightly borne wisdom that's hard to credit in a thirty-year-old clerk in the Irrigation Service with the scrappiest of educations and still living with his mother. Almost everyone has heard the opening lines:

> As you set out for Ithaca
> hope your road is a long one,
> full of adventure, full of discovery.

Nothing too earth-shattering here – it's the sort of thing you might find inscribed on a tasteful greetings card, or the kind of improving message an aunt might think of sending a nephew about to set out on a trip to India, not realizing that Ithaca is actually home. Cavafy is talking about going home.

As I read on, though, the poem gathered force. It looked me in the eye and spoke to me. After racing through it once, I went back and began to read it again, this time out aloud. Agape, who'd come round with some artichokes in an onion and carrot sauce she thought I might enjoy – and to snoop, of course, although she's never found anything remotely scandalous in the house – caught me at it and I flushed. When she wandered off, however, I did it again, very slowly.

> Laestrygonians, Cyclops,
> angry Poseidon – don't be afraid of them:
> you'll never find things like that on your way
> as long as you keep your thoughts raised high,
> as long as a rare sensation
> touches your spirit and your body.

Laestrygonians, Cyclops,
wild Poseidon – you won't encounter them
unless you bring them along inside your soul,
unless your soul sets them up in front of you.

My Ithaca, needless to say, furnished my soul with few sea-gods, one-eyed monsters or giant cannibals to carry with me – indeed, my years away may have been more life-quickening if it had. Nor, to be honest, did it leave my spirit and body as vulnerable to 'rare sensation' as Cavafy's apparently were (at thirty). When I was young in Adelaide, 'rare sensation' was something you bought in bottles, or in small twists of paper on the back verandah around midnight at somebody's party. Is my journeying doomed, then, to be a waste of time? Might I just as well have stayed at home?

In the second poem, 'The City', written seven months later, Cavafy's answer seems cruelly categorical: yes.

You'll always end up in this city. Don't hope
for things elsewhere:
there's no ship for you, there's no road.
Now that you've wasted your life here, in this
small corner,
you've destroyed it everywhere in the world.

Who knows why his vision soured? He wrote those lines in August, 1894. At some point that summer, had one of his taut-bodied young men, handsome as a discus-thrower on an ancient coin, abandoned him? Married, perhaps, or moved to Athens?

In 'Ithaca', by way of contrast, while you can never completely escape your home city – nor should want to – voyaging (does he really mean 'living'?) need not be pointless even if your life has been 'a black ruin'. Not if you keep your eyes and ears – and nose and mind – open:

> May there be many summer mornings when,
> with what pleasure, what joy,
> you enter harbours you're seeing for the first
>   time;
> may you stop at Phoenician trading stations
> to buy fine things,
> mother of pearl and coral, amber and ebony,
> sensual perfume of every kind –
> as many sensual perfumes as you can;
> and may you visit many Egyptian cities
> to learn and go on learning from those who
>   know.

Summer mornings, harbours and cities there have been aplenty, but I know I haven't looked and listened, marvelled and sniffed the air as often as I should have. Cavafy is an Alexandrian – his twin gods are pleasure and learning. I'm not from Alexandria. Too often on this journey I've looked out on the world through the template I was given and so, as he warned, I've seen my Ithaca everywhere.

Yet I must not blame Ithaca, according to Cavafy, or cast it from me. On the contrary, he writes:

Keep Ithaca always in your mind.
Arriving there is what you're destined for.
But don't hurry the journey at all.
Better if it lasts for years,
so you're old by the time you reach the
    island,
wealthy with all you've gained on the way,
not expecting Ithaca to make you rich.

Wealthy? Hardly. But no poorer, I suppose. And I don't expect Adelaide to make me rich. That's not why this ticket is in my hand. Why go back at all, though, if at root I never left and all I can take back with me are a few 'fine things' from Phoenician trading stations, a bottle of perfume and a couple of lessons learnt in 'Egypt'? Why bother?

It's true, of course, as Cavafy goes on to say, that

Ithaca gave you the marvellous journey.
Without her you wouldn't have set out.

He means, I suppose, that she made me whatever it is that I have been on this journey and I should acknowledge that – think through what it means, not be ashamed of it or let it go. That's fair. But then he says (and it's an arrow in the heart):

She has nothing left to give you now.
And if you find her poor, Ithaca won't have
    fooled you.
Wise as you will have become, so full of
    experience,
you'll have understood by then what these
    Ithacas mean.

End of poem. I'm lost again. What *do* these Ithacas mean, these Ithacas which have nothing left to give us now?

It took me half an hour and a plate of basted artichokes to see: I must go back to find out. And these years of journeying, since I am Ithacan, won't make sense until I do. Unless I go back, it won't have been *my* journey – or my life – at all. All the mother-of-pearl and coral, new harbours and Alexandrian sages in the world won't make these years part of the epic (however dun-coloured) my life could be (to me, at least). The old beginning must be made new. Otherwise my life will be like one of those shapeless conversations you have in trains with complete strangers – interesting enough at the time, but in the end little more than random noises.

I was not unmindful, as I read and reread these lines about fullness and emptiness, shape and shapelessness, that for Odysseus, home, when he reached it, was no haven – landing on Ithaca was in some ways the most dangerous step he ever took. 'Whose land have I lit on now?' he cries in anguish, looking around him, heart racing. 'What *are* they here – violent, savage, lawless? or friendly to strangers, god-fearing men?' I was aware, too, of Sisi's palace, ablaze in the summer sun behind the cypresses and holm-oaks on the hill in front of me. Every time I lifted my eyes from the page, there it was, a stone's throw away, vulgar monument to a traveller who did not 'keep Ithaca always in her mind' and therefore ended up not a traveller, but merely adrift. She died on that quay in Geneva with no new beginning in sight.

~

There was time, before William came to pick me up, for a quick walk up to the palace and back. The view from the garden across the city and the straits was, as it was bound to be, spectacular on such an afternoon.

In the event, I didn't stay long, though, because it was too vast for my mood. Too many cloud-shrouded mountains and shimmering coves, too many islands, villages and towns, all too far away. The sweep knocked the breath out of me, my mind went blank.

Walking back down to my house in the hollow, I came to life again with thoughts of more intimate landscapes – the darkening drawing-room in *Uncle Vanya*, the balcony Cavafy stood on year after year watching the street below (watching Alexandria become a memory), the smell of fish in the sun on the jetty at Largs Bay (they smelt of Uruguay) – things that were small, but by no means empty.

11

For years afterwards, what everyone first recollected about the Ab-Intra boys' farewell performance at St Corantyn, on the eve of taking ship for Europe, was the extraordinary scene on the mansion's lawn after the final curtain had fallen. It wasn't the play they remembered, nor the flamboyant floral display (brass bowls of zinnias, asters and hollyhocks in every corner), nor Mrs Lavington Bonython's sensationally strapless black matelassé gown, but the sight of a dozen lithe young actors in nothing but loin cloths and a dusting of bronze glitter, cavorting in the moonlight at St Corantyn with the cream of Adelaide society. Glasses of claret glinted and clinked, cigarettes glowed like fireflies amongst the trees, and Mrs Prosser even threw off her fox-fur stole and danced with a man in a purple coat. Nobody had understood what on earth the play was about (although everyone agreed that 'intriguing' was a useful word to bandy about), but the party afterwards was a Roman orgy on a scale not seen before in polite society in Adelaide. Kester left early.

It had been a coup, having Mrs Lavington Bonython offer St Corantyn for their farewell performance. As soon as she heard that the boys would only have thirty pounds left in the kitty between them, once their fare to Genoa had been paid, she put out a hand, gold bangles jangling, to touch Kester's arm. 'I think I can give you my word that when you get off that ship in Genoa you'll have a lot more than thirty pounds in your pocket, Mr Berwick. Just leave it to me. I'll think of something very special.' At the very apex of the Adelaide social scene, Mrs Bonython, whatever might be said about her taste in clothes, was indefatigably committed to good works. Her clothing appeal during the Depression was legendary, as were her working bees for destitute mothers and the campaign she'd led for years against cruelty to animals. These two plucky, talented boys deserved to be sent on their way in style. A slap-up do at St Corantyn would be ideal, something dazzling that would loosen people's purses. With its chandeliers, its spacious white ballroom and gracious gardens, St Corantyn would be the perfect setting for Ab-Intra's final performance – something really out of the box this time. A curio stall in the drawing-room, say, might raise a few pounds, too (an eye-catching display of red lacquer trays, some pottery coffee pots, a few sketches by the Heysen girls, if they could be talked around). In fact, she wondered if Hans Heysen himself might be persuaded to donate a painting or two to be auctioned. All Kester and Alan would have to do would be to put on a play.

'What do you say? It could be tremendous fun.' Mrs Bonython loved a mission. In her mind's eye she could already see the parade, up and down the grand staircase in the entrance hall, of deliciously modish young women and excitingly disreputable young men. As the boys stammered their thanks, she drew on her gloves, patted her orange pork-pie hat (a bit of a mistake, but with the stiff green quill in front it was certainly striking) and picked her way amongst the cushions on the floor towards the door. 'It's a deal, then,' she said, turning in the doorway to seal the arrangement with a smile. 'Now you'd better get busy and write something that will really bowl us over. *Au revoir!*'

The trouble was that what Kester and Alan wrote bowled nobody over. Indeed, bowling people over was not what they excelled at. As one reviewer put it (admittedly in the social pages), *Archway Motif* was 'no doubt much more amusing for the actors to stage than for the audience to watch'. In the words of another reviewer, one half of the audience was 'frankly puzzled', while the other half was 'desperately anxious to appear *au fait*' with something they could make neither head nor tail of.

As far as I can make out, relying on scraps in old newspapers, Kester's notes and fragments of the playscript, *Archway Motif* was a play about how good and evil (love and hate, folly and wisdom, and so on) – and this sounds numbingly Theosophical – when seen as part of a whole rather than as opposites, can, like the two sides of an archway, create a structure of 'poised majesty and still splendour'. Where the gambolling, bronze-dusted fauns came in, whether they represented good or evil, I cannot say. There was also a Snow Queen in a frozen, northern ice-palace, a heroine with 'eyes twin pools of dew', a hero with 'hair like honey', and a fair bit of lute-thrumming, although to what end is now a mystery.

Just before the 'slow final curtain', a ghostly choir intoned:

There is a state
beyond joy and sorrow.
There is a state
beyond tears and laughter.
There is a state
beyond the opposites:
riches
poverty
wisdom
folly
good
evil.
Just as opposites
form an archway,
so they resolve –
all of them –
into some great thing,
comprising them,
yet surpassing them.
Behold! Here a pathway opens,
a pathway forward,

more endless and shining
than the stars . . .

It's hardly surprising, after an evening of this kind
of tosh, that the audience headed for the claret on
the back lawn. Nobody wants to be taught anything
on a hot Saturday night, particularly by art.

It doesn't surprise me, either, that after one shandy
and a bit of ritual mingling with the crowd, Kester
walked out into the darkness and made his way
home. Mass jollity never appealed to him, and he
must also have had some sense of an ending that
night – to an experiment, to being young, to standing out from the herd in his home town. The ticket
to Genoa waiting at home on the side-board would
have been a comfort, but his mood that night, I
would guess, once he'd left the torch-lit gardens,
would have been melancholy. It can't be true, as one
particularly snaky gossip columnist suggested, that
Alan also left early and in the company of a young
actress from Melbourne 'in a frock like an old Greek
kirtle in that divinely heavy crêpe that never crushes
and looks so expensively simple'. This is just venom,
surely. On that last night at St Corantyn . . . well, I
just don't believe it.

12

When Bernie came to deliver the very last lines in the play – ludicrous, tragic lines; I've heard famous actresses fail to carry them off – the audience in the salon at the Big House seemed almost to stop breathing. It's the ultimate anticlimax – not a death or marriage in sight, just the prospect of endless drudgery, unrelieved by even the hint of a higher purpose. The mood is one of cold hysteria. In the light of a single candle, while their old friend Waffles quietly strums his guitar in the shadows, Sonya kneels at Vanya's feet, lets him cradle her head in his arms, and says with a kind of bitter meekness, crushed by the unending futility of their lives:

'What can we do? We must go on living . . . We'll live through a long, long succession of days and long drawn-out evenings; we'll patiently bear the trials that fate sends us; we'll work hard for others both now and in our old age, knowing no rest, and when our hour comes we shall meekly die . . . and God will take pity on us, and you and I, Uncle, dearest Uncle, shall glimpse a life which is full of light, beauty and grace, we shall rejoice and look back on our present misfortunes with tenderness, with a smile – and we shall find rest. I believe in

this, Uncle. I believe in it fervently, passionately . . . We shall find rest! . . . You've known no joy in your life, but just wait a little, Uncle Vanya, wait . . . We shall find rest. We shall find rest! We shall find rest!'

And the silence in the room was so brittle – nobody clapped, nobody stirred – that I thought the walls might fall in if anyone so much as sneezed. Not one of us believed her – not for an instant, not even the vicar's wife in the front row with Ashley – yet she made us yearn to. Every single person in the room – the consul and his wife, holidaymakers from Benitses, Arthur, Greta, the owners of the Hopping Kangaroo, even George – every last one of them seemed to be stretched to breaking point between wanting to shout *Yes! a ruined life can be redeemed* and bursting into mocking laughter at the mere thought of such an illusion.

Then they began to clap, softly at first and then with growing exultation. Thousands of miles from Russia, separated from Chekhov's blathering non-entities by a whole century of tumult, the audience was swept with a kind of jubilation (there's no other word) simply because they'd heard voiced things they'd felt but had never dared say to each other about their own deeply unremarkable, unrewarded lives. When Bernie came into the kitchen where I was watching and waiting, I whispered: 'You're a genius! You did it!' and, befuddled with relief and pleasure, we hugged each other (briefly). Then, with the applause continuing – there were even a few bravos from the back, mostly from Kostas, Greta's jovial paramour – the actors all trooped back out into the salon, beaming, to take another bow.

While the crowd was ambling around to the back of the house to the trestle tables on which Greta had set out the refreshments, I stole off alone up the drive towards the gates. There were still two hours until the second and final performance at seven, the afternoon, although still sunny, had turned pleasantly cool high up on the hillside, and all I wanted to do was to walk with my own thoughts amongst the olive-trees and broom, and rest. For a short while the sound of excited chatter and peals of laughter still reached me in muted gusts through the trees, but then, once beyond the old stone gates, all I could hear was the occasional chirruping of some invisible bird in the olive-grove beside the road. I knew I should be back in the courtyard, chatting with our guests, praising the actors and saying goodbye to people I'd grown quite fond of – after all, we'd be leaving for the ferry-wharf straight after the next performance. My suitcase was under the table in the kitchen. I was ready to vanish into thin air as soon as the clapping died away.

Suddenly, through the gnarled tree-trunks, I caught sight of William walking quickly along the roadway in the sunlight, peering about him as if he were looking for someone. I called out, and he stopped and stared into the grey-green shadows beneath the foliage. Then he waved and began to make his way towards me, stumbling slightly amongst the stones and fallen branches.

'What are you doing out here? Everyone's looking for you,' he said when he got close. No peck on the cheek.

'I suppose that's why I'm out here!' I said, trying to make a joke of it. 'Well, we did it, they loved it, it was fantastic. Are you pleased?'

'Yes,' he said, but he didn't look elated. He stared at the ground briefly and then, running his fingers through his hair, said: 'Let's sit down for a moment – there must be a log or something we can sit on.' I followed him deeper into the grove. A mosquito bit me on the neck.

'Look, I don't know quite how to say this,' he began, still looking at the ground, once we'd perched ourselves rather awkwardly on a rotting log. I didn't try to break the pause that followed – why bother? I just let it stretch and stretch. When someone says a sentence like that, while looking at the ground, no more words are needed. You know what will be said. And he knows you know.

'You're not coming tonight,' I said eventually, my eyes on the tip of his boots which were scrabbling in the dust.

'No,' he said. 'Had you guessed?'

'No, I hadn't. How could I have? I'm not a mind-reader.' My voice sounded dull, I knew, there was no fire in it, as there should have been. The bird chirruped again, brightly. Out on the sunlit road the vicar trundled past in his battered old Vauxhall, ferrying Ashley home, away from scandal and temptation. 'Well, are you going to tell me why you've changed your mind so suddenly? Is this something you and Alberto have . . . cooked up between you?'

'Alberto? No. Why Alberto?' He looked genuinely puzzled.

'Well, I just thought . . .'

'No, it's got nothing to do with Alberto. He's said I can move in with him if I want to – have you seen his flat? It's enormous, views right across to the mainland – but no, it's nothing to do with him.'

'What is it then?' This time something inside me was going dead. This time I didn't want to play.

'I'm just not ready to go home. That's all it is. I haven't finished . . . oh, I don't know . . . I haven't finished . . .' But he couldn't think of what it was he hadn't finished doing. *Entering harbours he was seeing for the first time, stopping at Phoenician trading stations to buy fine things, visiting Egyptian cities . . .* I knew what it was he hadn't finished doing. He felt no need yet of a new beginning.

'And, to tell you the truth, Kester's coming back any day now – he knows you're leaving today, he's been in touch with Greta – and I'd really like to see him again. It's been a couple of years.'

I stood up to go, feeling very weary all of a sudden. 'It's probably not for long,' he was saying, as I looked away from him, down towards the nunnery at the bottom of the hill. 'Not for long at all. I'll come, but first I'd just like to spend a bit more time here. Alberto —'

'Alberto?'

'Alberto says he's sure he can fix me up with some work in a hotel down at Benitses. Just for the summer.' I winced despite myself. William in a hotel at Benitses over the summer would never sleep. I could hear the music in the night, see the oiled and suntanned bodies strolling, sprawling, lounging on the sea-wall, conjure up strange lips and fingers on my Horus-eye. 'Then I'll be ready, I'm sure.'

'To come?'

'Yes, to come.' He stood up himself now, unfolding his long legs in the gangling, slightly coltish way he always did, but this time nothing melted inside me. 'I did mean what I said to you that day, you know. About being together.'

'I'm sure you did, William,' I said, looking at him now. But he was drifting away on some tide he'd just miraculously caught. He couldn't believe his luck. Perhaps he'd been fearing I'd start pleading with him, or arguing, even violently. Maybe he thought I'd threaten to drag him to the ferry-wharf by force.

'I'll come, I promise you I'll come,' he said, grinning now, relieved. 'Going back to the house? Come on, let's go.'

'No, I think I'll just walk for a while, I'd quite like to be by myself. Just down to the nunnery and back. See you in a little while.'

He shrugged, gave me a quick smile and turned back towards the road. Through the tree-trunks, I watched him emerge into the sunlight, a moving, glowing patch of blue and russet reds, and then, in ever smaller scraps of colour, disappear. And that, without a doubt, is the last I'll see of William.

13

Nose pressed against the glass to watch Albania glide past, I know I should be engrossed in the sinister drama of the searchlights, clawing at the darkness from the cliffs to starboard. Although its rocky shore is so close I could swim to it in five minutes if I jumped overboard, I might as well be looking at Jupiter through a telescope. Instead, my mind keeps floating back to the quay in Corfu. What happened there an hour or two ago — it seems like moments — gave me quite a jolt. To make it seem like seconds, all I have to do is look around: spangles of yellow light draped around the bays, the hills, the castle . . . the town has hardly moved at all in half an hour, perhaps Corfu is coming with me, perhaps Corfu is going to tag along behind me like a naughty fairy all the way to Italy, casting spells.

Speaking of mischief, I didn't go 'just down to the nunnery and back'. Even as the words came out of my mouth, I knew they were nothing more than random syllables. 'Nunnery' is just a particularly delicious word. Nor did I have the slightest intention of seeing anyone 'in a little while'. I'd gone. I'd set sail the instant the words 'I don't quite know how to say this' reached my ears. Aware, meandering about in the olive-grove, of birds' wings whooshing, the humming clouds of gnats, dogs yapping in the valley far below – alert, in other words, to how the emptiness surrounding me was full of life – I also had the strange sensation of soaring off into space at the speed of light, away from the Big House (just a speck now on the smudge of hills on Corfu), away from *Uncle Vanya*, Chekhov, Greta, Bernie, Prue, Alberto, William, even Kester, far, far away from foolish Austrian empresses, dogs with colic, boiler-rooms, hotels in Benitses where the music would thump and thump deep into the night . . . and there in a far-away Nowhere my mind (Cavafy would say my 'soul') turned gentle somersaults, not even knowing it was waiting.

When the last cars had chugged up the drive to the house for the second performance, and everything was still again – not a trickle of sound from the house, no slamming doors, no squawks of laughter, no hum of a crowd – I knew Act I must be under way in the courtyard. The house would be empty. And indeed I was in luck: there was nobody in the salon and nobody in the kitchen, not even Martha. I was just bending down to slide my suitcase out from under the table when I heard a woman's footsteps behind me. It was Greta, an empty wine-glass in her hand.

'So there you are! Where have you been? Is something wrong?' Her smile faded when she saw the suitcase in my hand.

'I'm going to leave, Greta. Now, before everyone comes back inside. I'll call a taxi.'

For a moment I thought she was going to tell me not to be so silly, how bad it would look, how hurtful to the actors and my friends. But she didn't. I'm sure it was on the tip of her tongue to snap, How dare you just sneak off like that! How rude! How spineless! – But instead she took her wine-glass to the sink, rinsed it, stood it upside down to drain, and then, turning to me, said:

'Alright, I'll drive you. Let's go quickly, I haven't got much time.'

She knew.

When you've already left inside, waiting for your body to catch up, as it were, is nerve-wracking. You want to whip time like a horse, make it fly to where you're already waiting for it further down the road. So I was hardly conscious of the meadows and houses we were driving past, hardly had the patience to say all the things I should have said as we threaded our way through the outskirts of the town towards the wharves. I forgot to say goodbye to the Venetian fort, the arcades by the cricket-ground where I'd so often sat drinking coffee, the spot where we'd lifted a dazed Maxwell to his feet – I even forgot, in a sense, to say goodbye to Greta.

'You'll come back one day, I'm sure,' she said, kissing me lightly on both cheeks on the pavement outside the ferry-terminal. 'And nothing will have changed – we'll all still be here, bickering with each

other as usual and talking vaguely about going home
− at least for Christmas!' She laughed. 'But you're
right to go now. I think we've probably given you all
we can.' With a wave, she slammed the door and
lurched off into the traffic. It was a very strange last
line.

With hours to spare − it wasn't even dark yet − I
sat in a grubby café across the road for a while, wrote
a note to William, tore it up, wrote another,
scrunched it up and jammed it into my empty coffee cup. Out on the twilit street the crowds were
thickening, horns were blasting, music was pouring
from tavernas and radios, and the smell of roasting
meats and sweat and car-fumes was seeping into my
clothes and up my nostrils.

Sea-monster-like, the ferry from Brindisi suddenly loomed up out of the darkness, out of
nowhere, ablaze with lights, and all those wonderful wharf noises started up like an orchestra −
bangs, clanks, whistles, raucous shouts. I felt as I'd
often felt before, waiting at a bus-stop for the bus
home after I'd left the theatre. Make-up wiped off,
the theatre empty, my stage self (lover, husband,
pirate) long since cast off, hung up back in the
dressing-room with my stage clothes, I would stand
at the bus-stop, nobody for a while, just watching
dogs saunter by or lights going out in upstairs windows. Then slowly I would begin to recover, with
delight, my own ordinariness.

What broke my reverie at the wharf, however, was

not a bus. Walking up to the glass doors into the terminal, I saw Kester Berwick standing facing me on the other side of the glass.

Like me he was wearing a crumpled mackintosh and holding a small, brown suitcase in his right hand. Neither of us moved. I looked at him, filled with a kind of wonder that I knew this man I didn't know at all so utterly, so presently, that no words were needed any more. And, strange to relate, he looked at me a little quizzically as if to say: *Which one are you, now?* And then the door slid open and we moved past each other, each back into his own world. Just as it's enough sometimes, when a dearly loved friend rides by in a bus, simply to see the face, not even to wave, just to know that somewhere in the world today he is being himself, and all is well just as it is, so I didn't even turn around to watch him vanish.

Now, as I write these lines in an exercise book on my lap, Corfu is just a faint smudge of gold in the blackness far behind us. We're beginning to toss a bit and heave.

Tomorrow Brindisi. I wonder what time the first train leaves for Rome?

— EPILOGUE —

'Farewell, my friend! And when you are at home,
home in your own land, remember me at times.
Mainly to me you owe the gift of life.'

(Nausicaa to Odysseus)

Adelaide, June, 1999

Five years to the day after that momentary crossing of our paths at the ferry-wharf, Kester Berwick died. At the bottom of Greta's Christmas card that year, there was a brief postscript. 'PS: Kester Berwick died in June,' she scribbled. 'A shame you never met him.'

Not so long ago, on my way back from a trip to Albania, where I'd been exploring Roman ruins on a bay just across from Princess Margaret's helipad near Kassiopi, I took a room at the Hotel Cavalieri for a few days, thinking I might look up one or two old friends. Nothing had changed at the Hotel Cavalieri since that first Easter visit so many years before. There was even a vase of asphodels by the telephone at the front desk. In fact, after the surreal chaos of Albania, Corfu felt a trifle dull.

Under the arcades on the Listón, where I went to have a coffee for old times' sake, I remembered the first time I'd sat there, trying to write that postcard to William – the one of the dying Achilles with the amazing buttocks. Since that moment in the olive-grove at the Big House, when he'd disappeared piece by blue-and-russet piece amongst the tree-trunks, there had been no sign of his existence. Not even two lines on a Christmas card from London or (a city plucked out of the air at random) Santiago. Sometimes, when I recalled that moment, it seemed as if the tree-trunks had dismembered him before my eyes. To scatter my thoughts I tried to read the newspaper someone had left lying on my table, but it was in Dutch.

I went back to my room and rang Greta.

⌒

'Tell you what,' she said when she came to pick me up the next morning, looking as chic as ever, although a little stiffer in the joints. 'I'll whizz you up to the British cemetery on the way out to Gastouri – you can pay your respects at Kester's grave.' I loathe cemeteries, never setting foot in one if I can help it, but Greta seemed so pleased to see me when she came through the doors of the hotel, so eager to make the morning special, that I hadn't the heart to say I'd just as soon go straight to Gastouri.

It's an almost gay profusion of tangled wildflowers and shady, deep-green copses, the British cemetery. It's a delight to stroll in, bending in the strong summer light to read the terse reports of failure to make it safely home. Sailors killed in a naval accident, whole merchant families carried off in epidemics, diplomats, eccentric exiles, children's nannies, and

children, too, with names like Fanny and Hilda –
hundreds upon hundreds of graves of Britons, going
back almost two hundred years, who did not in the
end take ship for home.

We scraped purple pansies back to read one grave-
stone (EDITH HESTER SMYTHE 1866–1924 BELOVED WIFE
AND FRIEND) and then trampled through freesias and
nasturtiums to peer at another (Maxwell's, quite by
chance – I hadn't even known he'd died).

'I'm sure I told you in a letter,' Greta said, looking
around for somewhere to sit with our thermos of tea
and shortbread biscuits. 'We all thought he'd gone
back to Tunisia, you see, so nobody really noticed for
weeks. It was Ashley, the vicar's son (do you remember?), who found him in the end – terribly unpleasant
business, the whole thing, what with the heatwave
we'd been having and the awkward question of why
Ashley had a key to the house. Awfully distressing for
everyone concerned, especially Ashley. Sent home to
England on the next plane, naturally.' We sat back on
our park bench in the shade, relishing the tea and but-
tery shortbreads. 'Left him everything, though, so that
was some compensation.'

'Maxwell left Ashley everything?'

'House, paintings, money – the lot.' It was clear
from the way she drank her tea that Greta thought
this a rather civilized arrangement.

We talked for a while, as you do in cemeteries,
about other people who had died or gone back to
England in recent years – Martha, for example, not

unexpectedly, during Christmas dinner up at the Big House, and Celia, quietly in her sleep not long after Kester. We moved on, as one does, from death to malaise of a more general kind – serious illness, divorce and financial ruin (the consul's wife's attempted suicide, Prue's breakdown – she'd taken to walking the streets in her silk pyjamas – and George's brush with bankruptcy) – and then, although both aware that something was being left unsaid (something shaped like a Horus-eye in my mind), we set off towards the back of the cemetery to look for Kester's grave.

We found it eventually in a small clearing amongst the towering cypresses and holm-oaks near the back fence. On a mound overgrown with wild geraniums and a sprinkling of purple honesty stood a frail white wooden cross, barely knee-high. Painted on the cross in crooked black lettering was KESTER BERWICK 3.10.1903–29.6.92. No marble headstone, no gravel grave, just a small, green mound and a crooked cross. However, if, theosophically, his shade has taken note of his body's last resting place, I don't imagine it's deeply offended. A little more dignity for his mortal remains would not have gone astray, obviously, but in life Kester Berwick made so little fuss over arrangements for the body that I can't believe he's much exercised now over the décor for his corpse. After death a Theosophist, particularly one with a Buddhist bent, has much more interesting things to be getting on with.

'Do you think he had a happy life, Greta?' I asked. It was a mindless thing to say but, after all, we were in a cemetery and at a bit of a loss for something to say.

'No, I don't think so,' Greta said after a pause. 'But I do think he had a very good one.' We both stood quietly for a moment in the grey-blue shadows, thinking our own graveside thoughts, then set off without another word through the trees towards the gate.

In Gastouri everything had been freshly white-washed for Easter, the black-clad old men were still sitting smoking on the street outside the general store, the smell of fresh bread still wafted on the air, and my house still stood in its unkempt garden at the bend of the road, empty-looking and a little gloomy, staring back up the hill at Sisi's palace. We didn't linger.

Kester's third house, the one in which he actually died (at least, according to Agape, who lives opposite), is lost in a maze of old laneways behind the abandoned chapel. Brilliantly striped rugs were hanging out to sun on all the balconies along the street. The house itself, ramshackled and drowning in a sea of wildflowers and scraggly fruit-trees, looked just as melancholy as mine did. On the wall upstairs we could just make out where someone had painted over the words *Om mani padme hum*. Here, Greta told me, Kester had spent his last years, practically a hermit. Like old monks everywhere, he fastened onto rituals to get him through his days: the BBC news at nine, a stroll to the shop for some lentils or fruit before lunch on the dot of one, a short siesta, and then an hour or two of tinkering with the klavichord he'd built for himself out of old guitar strings and stray bottle tops. Late afternoon was reserved for conversation, while in the evening he might sit reading for a while with his cat (Celia had had Terpsi put down for him) or fiddle with his manuscripts, adding an adverb here in ink, pasting in a new paragraph there. Where was this life on paper now, I wondered? In a cardboard box at the back of somebody's cupboard? Burnt?

'*Er ist in meinen Armen gestorben,*' Agape whispered hoarsely, as she handed me a tiny saucer of fig *glikó*. She'd seen Greta and me wandering around the abandoned house and hobbled across the laneway to ask us in for a glass of water and a taste of jam. Died in her arms? Really? Yes, she said, at lunchtime on a Monday. She'd gone over with a loaf of fresh bread for his lunch, found him lying on his divan, paper-white, he'd smiled at her, looked heavenwards – or at least towards the ceiling – and, as she bent to touch him, simply failed to be still there. She'd felt his spirit, she said, brush past her, '*wie ein leichter Wind*'.

'Well, that's one version, anyway,' Greta said as we walked back down the hill to the car, stepping around thin dogs blissfully stretched out in the sunshine.

'There are others?'

'Several. People see what they want to see, don't

they. An actor friend of Kester's from Sydney told me he'd died in his arms in the hospital in town. Tied into his bed with strips of bed-sheet, smelling of urine and . . . well, it can be a smelly business, can't it. The whole house smelt of pee for years, to tell you the truth,' she said, offering me a little bag of dried apricots. 'That's partly why I never fancied, at any given moment, going to see him. Dreadful, isn't it? Such a small thing, but so off-putting.'

After a couple of days in the hospital, Kester had made it clear to his friend that he saw no point in waiting around any longer, sighed twice, said 'How beautiful!' with the precision he'd been known for all his life and 'went'.

'He said it was a "warm death", I remember,' Greta said as we got into the car again. 'I'm not sure exactly what he meant by that, but hearing him say it was a comfort.'

At the memorial service the vicar arranged some days later – rather bland because the vicar was not about to bring Madame Blavatsky or Gautama Buddha into the proceedings – several people spoke of vivid dreams of Kester the night he died. 'Like Father Christmas,' Greta said, as we bumped along the back roads through the hills towards her house, 'he seems to have been busy for the first few hours popping down people's chimneys all over Corfu to say goodbye.

'And not only on Corfu, either. One old friend of his I met at the service, an old lover, I suspect –

someone he'd been very close to, anyway – had been sitting up in a train in Italy, somewhere between Milan and Bologna. All of a sudden, at the exact moment Kester died, he looked around and, instead of the usual stuffy railway compartment full of cigarette smoke and snoring Italians, he was inside a vast dome, he said, covered in sumptuous images of God and His angels, and *whoosh!* right past his nose, Kester was sucked up out of nowhere straight through a hole in the middle.'

'Did you believe him?'

'Why not? Compared to the sort of thing the vicar rabbits on about every Sunday, getting sucked up through a dome outside Bologna seems quite unremarkable.'

We swept into her driveway. Ahead I glimpsed the dappled pink walls of her house through the oaks and myrtles. And the lush lawn, dotted once more with anemones. And the walled terrace. As empty, and as full of ghosts, as the stage of a seaside theatre between seasons.

'Let's have a spot of lunch,' Greta said, throwing open the french windows, 'and you can tell me all about Albania.'

'Grey of body and grey of soul.' That's what an Englishman I met that time in Molyvos said when I mentioned Kester's name to him. I've never forgot-

ten it. He'd known Kester years before in Molyvos
while researching a book on magic in the ancient
world. It was a cruel, dismissive thing to say, but I
was already growing accustomed by then to a certain
male distaste for Kester Berwick. The more I think
about this man I never knew, the more convinced I
am that men like that Englishman are looking at
Kester through the wrong lens.

Tacked to the wall of our bedroom in North Adelaide, for instance, right beside the window with its
peaceful, unspectacular view over limestone cottages
and the cathedral spires to the hills beyond, is a
black-and-white photograph of a double-bass riding
a bicycle. It's quite famous, I think – at least, I'm sure
I'd already come across it somewhere before I found
it in an album in a second-hand shop. I bought the
album just for this picture. It's one of Henri Cartier-
Bresson's, taken in Serbia in 1965. In the middle of
a bare landscape (just a scruffy tree or two, some
dusty bushes and a few unremarkable hills in the distance) a comically enormous double-bass, slewed
across the back of a man in a suit, is riding off down
an empty, stony track away from the camera. It's all
in subtle shades of grey, but it always strikes me,
when I first open my eyes and see it there on the wall
each morning, like an abrupt burst of laughter at a
funeral. The crafted beauty of this instrument sus-
pended against a desolate background, the reasoned
rigour of this erotic shape in that bleak wilderness,
the dandyism of this lone man in a suit on a plain

country road, the clownishness in an unsmiling landscape, the gentleness against the stones, the tottering ride into oblivion, the triviality made unforgettable . . . in a word: a delicate instrument in a stony place. Yet on that dusty road in Serbia that day in 1965 nothing was actually happening. Now there's an eye! What wizardry!

Up goes the blind beside the double-bass each morning – *snap!* – and, blinking in the glare, I lean out across the geraniums to see what I might see.